Desecrate the Darkness

Small Town Secrets Book 1
A.K. Hughey

Raven's Call Publishing

Contents

To everyone who has tried so hard to help uplift other people (often to their own detriment), and who had to climb out of the fallout from doing so: You are enough, you are worthy, and you are deserving of the same love and goodness that you pour so freely pour into others.

Chapter 1

Monday, August 27th

"I t's a card read error, sir. Try again." Lucia maintained her composure despite the customer's growing frustration. Rush hour was just beginning, and the line behind him was growing.

Beep-beep-beep! The reader chirped its error warning again.

"I wish you all would stop changing these stupid systems," the man griped, inserting his card into the chip reader too early–again.

Beep-beep-beep!

"What is wrong with this thing, Lu-see-ah?" he asked, squinting at her nametag as his heavy tongue bludgeoned each syllable.

"Lu-sha," she corrected, speaking slowly and skirting the edge of a condescending tone. "Like the island, St. Lucia."

Her hours–and therefore benefits–had already been cut, so she figured the least she deserved from the more impatient, childish, and rude customers was a correct pronunciation of her name.

"Whatever. I don't care. Just make this damn thing work."

She allowed one eyebrow to rise, gritting her teeth as he cussed under his breath. "May I?"

"Here!" He tossed his card on the counter, and it slid toward her.

I do not get paid enough for this crap, she thought grimly, shaking her head as she reset the transaction. She picked up his card and held it against the screen of the card reader. The machine emitted a happy ding, indicating a successful payment.

"Wait 'til it gives you the total and asks for payment, then hold your card against the screen until it makes that bell sound." It was probably the twentieth time that day she'd explained this. She passed the card and receipt back to him.

The man snatched them from her, grabbed his energy drink and donuts, and stormed out.

Lucia sighed and greeted her next customer—a young woman around her own age with clumpy mascara and blotchy eyeliner that did nothing to conceal her exhaustion. A cute toddler with slumped shoulders and flushed cheeks clung to his mother's legs.

The woman placed a bottle of orange juice and children's ibuprofen on the counter, then smiled up at Lucia. "Don't worry. I know how to use the reader."

Lucia returned the smile. "Is that everything? Twelve dollars and seventy-five cents."

The woman rested her card against the screen.

The *beep-beep-beep* rang out again, nails on a chalkboard to Lucia's ears. She glanced at her POS screen, and it read: DECLINED.

"I'm sorry," the woman said before Lucia could say anything. "Let me try this one."

The people behind her glared and muttered even as Lucia's coworker, Kristi, opened a second register farther down the counter.

As the woman waited for the reader to reset, her flush deepened. She tapped the screen again with a different card.

Beep-beep-beep!

Her eyes brimmed with tears as she tried the second card again with the same result. "I'm so sorry–"

"Here," Lucia said, holding out one hand to take the woman's card while inconspicuously sliding her own card from her purse hidden just beneath the counter. "Let me try."

She closed her fist around the woman's card and rested it on the counter while she tapped her own card to the reader.

Ding!

"There we go. It's working now. Let me bag this up for you."

The woman stared, slack-jawed, as Lucia placed the juice and medicine in a plastic bag.

As Lucia leaned down to nonchalantly put her card back in her purse, her fingers brushed the edge of a bill. There wasn't much money left in her account, and that twenty would be her last until payday. She only hesitated for a second before she slipped her card back into its pocket and pulled out the bill, folding it into a small rectangle with her fingers. After clasping it against the woman's card, she slid it across the counter to her with the plastic bag.

Hesitant at first, the woman picked up the card and the money and placed them inside her purse. She hefted her son onto her hip with one arm, then grabbed the plastic bag with her free hand. A tear slipped down her cheek, and she mouthed 'thank you' before heading for the doors.

Lucia gave her one more sympathetic smile before she turned her gaze to the next customer.

She relaxed when she recognized Tammy, a regular who stopped in each day for cheap menthol cigarettes and watery bargain beer.

Tammy grinned at Lucia as she set a bottle of ginger pop, a six-pack of beer, a travel magazine, and a bag of salt and vinegar chips on the counter. "Busy day?"

Lucia shrugged. "Same old, same old."

She scanned each of the items and then glanced through the magazine while Tammy deliberated over adding a candy bar from the countertop display. "Planning a trip?"

"Nah, I'm just dreaming," Tammy said with a laugh, her voice husky and deep from decades of smoking.

"Me too." Flipping through, Lucia studied pictures of turquoise water, white sandy beaches, shaded lounges with little tables holding colorful margaritas, and smiling models showing off the dreamy, all-inclusive beachside resorts. Her heart hurt as she studied the bright images. She wondered if her life could ever look like that.

She let her gaze linger over the image of a happy couple enjoying drinks in a hot tub, a vast sunset-painted ocean stretching out behind them. A tightening warmth grew in her chest as she thought of a certain sexy cop with a body like a Greek god who—by some incredible stroke of luck—was currently her boyfriend. She wished she could be sitting oceanside with him right now. At twenty-five years old, she was ashamed to admit she had never traveled outside of the Midwest. She'd never even seen the ocean.

Tammy tossed a chocolate bar on the counter, disrupting Lucia's daydreams.

"Anything else?"

"Yeah, gimme those menthols."

"These?"

"Nah, to your right. Yeah, those right there. Don't play, girl. You know which ones!" Tammy tapped playfully on the counter with her long, painted nails.

Though she couldn't have been over sixty years old, she had the skin of someone fifteen years older. She always dressed her best but reeked of stale smoke. The last thing the older woman's worn little body needed was another round of smokes and beer, but giving advice wasn't Lucia's job. No, she raked in a whopping eleven dollars per hour to keep her mouth shut and run the register at a thirty-year-old gas station on the big highway that ran through her dismally tiny town.

Each time she came in for her shift, she contemplated driving right past and riding the highway to freedom. In her imagination, it led to a promised land, a place of rest and easy money. In reality, the road led to Saginaw, then to Flint, Pontiac, and finally Detroit. She couldn't imagine those cities truly offered anything of the sort to a woman like her.

The realization of worse places and situations kept her tied to the register, where she sold discounted cigarettes, cold beer, and two-for-two-dollar pops and candy bars.

"Ya know," the older woman said, digging through her oversized purse for her wallet. Her expression was thoughtful and serious. They'd often chatted when the store was slow and had become quite close over the past year. Tammy never held her tongue when she had advice to share. "There's a point where you gotta decide what you want from your life, Lucia. What are you–"

The sound of a revving engine cut off any wisdom she'd intended to impart. Light flashed from just outside the giant glass windows, and everyone turned toward the entrance. The bright yellow glow of headlights raced closer. Too close. Too fast.

The vehicle hit a concrete wheel stop, launched upward, and exploded through the giant windows, sending shards of glass flying in every direction as people dove for cover. Lucia dropped behind the counter and covered her head. Screams, the crunch of metal, and the deafening roar of a car's engine filled her ears. Debris rained down on her until a final horrifying crash reverberated through the building.

Ears ringing, body trembling, Lucia opened her eyes. Bits of glass fell from her clothes with a tinkling sound that barely registered in her aching eardrums. She pushed herself off the floor and rose, heart pounding in her chest, breathing ragged.

Shocked tears welled in her eyes and blurred her vision. The sedan had hit the sturdy brick wall next to the beer cave, its hood smashed into the windshield and the front tire splayed out from its axle.

Mangled bodies lay among the wreckage of the shredded car, wrecked shelving, and destroyed merchandise. Some of the injured groaned or cried, while others lay still and quiet. Other customers, coughing from the smoke and exhaust that burned their eyes, began rising to their feet as Lucia had.

Anger flared in Lucia, her fists clenching as she returned her gaze to the vehicle that had done so much damage. Recognition hit her like a slap to the face. The peeling blue paint, the rusty quarter panels. The fake bullet strike stickers along the trunk lid.

She knew this car. It was her ex-boyfriend's.

Bright, blood-red spray paint covered the roof, but a low, hoarse groan commanded Lucia's attention before she could examine it. She leaned over the counter and searched until she spotted Tammy's body. Blood covered her jacket and seeped through the legs of her blue jeans. Lucia rummaged frantically for her purse and the first aid kit that had been next to it. With shaking hands, she dialed 911 on her cellphone, then vaulted over the counter and rushed to Tammy's side.

Events began to blur. Her first aid training kicked in, and she worked to stop the bleeding from a deep gash in Tammy's leg. All the while, she offered comfort and reassurance with whatever words her frazzled brain could muster—words she couldn't remember later for the life of her. The older woman's eyes locked on the ceiling, her eyelids fluttering as she fought to stay conscious.

Chapter 2

In less than five minutes, emergency responders arrived on the scene. Strong, steady hands pulled Lucia away so paramedics could take over and stabilize Tammy. Firefighters arrived next and began dislodging the debris that had trapped several people. As uniformed officers made their rounds to gather witness reports, one interviewed Lucia until one of the medics pulled her toward the back of an ambulance to examine her.

A female paramedic with a gentle touch was wrapping a cut on Lucia's arm when a familiar voice rose above all the muddled noise.

"Lucia?"

She met his eyes and blinked back tears.

"Sam!" She jumped up and threw her arms around his neck.

"Are you okay?" His gentle voice instantly comforted her. He'd always made her feel safe.

She pulled back and stared up at him, searching his face for the truth. "Is it... Is Rich in there?"

"Yeah." He squeezed her hand. "He's dead, Luce. And he took three others with him."

She choked back a sob and dropped her face against his chest. Sam rubbed her back with one hand. "I can't take part in the investigation. Dan's got the lead on this. Can you talk to him?"

Lucia pulled herself upright and nodded, wiping away tears but unable to force any words from her trembling lips. Dan was Sam's friend and a fellow officer, but over the past ten months, he had become Lucia's friend, too. He walked up to them as Sam comforted her.

"Hey, Luce." Dan sat next to her on the back of the ambulance. Sam walked away to give them privacy. "We found this spray-painted on the roof of his car."

Dan showed her a page in his notebook.

UR FAULT

A nauseating stillness overcame her, permeating her senses with dread.

"Considering it was your ex-boyfriend in the car, this message may have been intended for you. I need you to tell me everything you can about Rich's behavior and your last interactions with him." He clicked his pen.

"I..." She swallowed hard, unable to believe he was really dead. In the moment, she had followed her instinct to help Tammy and hadn't even thought to look inside the car. Her composure broke, and tears began streaming down her face again.

"It's okay." Dan placed a hand on her shoulder. "Do you know why he would have wanted to hurt you and take his own life?"

The thought made Lucia hesitate. She bit down on her lip to keep it from quaking. "Do you really think it was suicide? He was a lot of things, but he'd never actually..." She tried to swallow the lump in her throat. "He would never kill himself."

"At this point, we have to consider all possibilities. The more you tell us, the faster we can figure out the truth."

Lucia shook her head, dismayed they were even considering it. Yet, there was a growing seed of doubt in her mind. She hadn't spoken with him since they'd broken up, so maybe he had changed more than she wanted to believe.

"We haven't talked in over a year," she said, accepting a tissue when Dan offered it. "He kept texting me and emailing, but I never answered." She raised her hand to her mouth as the realization hit her. "He did once... When we first broke up, he threatened to kill himself if I didn't come back."

"Can you grab Frost for me?" Dan asked a nearby officer, referring to Sam, then returned his calm gaze to Lucia. "You can't think for a second that this is your fault."

Sam arrived, seemingly out of nowhere, and sat down beside Lucia before wrapping an arm around her.

"He said he was gonna get clean, get a real job, grow up." She fought against her trembling voice and the dizziness threatening to overtake her. "He swore he'd stop dealing and using so he could get me back. Even though we didn't talk, I heard he's been to mass at St. Joe's every Sunday all spring." She didn't try to control her quietly spilling tears anymore. Her thoughts were too entangled in the idea that he might have saved him from an early death if she'd stayed with him.

"We don't know exactly what happened yet, Luce, but we'll figure it out." Dan rose, and Sam helped Lucia to her feet. "If he was trying to get out, then that's when he was in the most danger. They start to get clean, start making promises to their families. And that's when some people like him disappear. These guys who got him doing this, they don't just let people go."

Her heart ached as she realized that the man she had spent three years of her life with was gone now. His once lithe, slender body was now cold and still. She wasn't convinced he'd killed himself. No, someone had stolen his life from him just as he was trying to fix it and make something of himself. Her stomach rolled with nausea, and she squeezed her eyes shut.

"Okay, Luce. Sam is driving you home. Get some rest, and just send me a text or give me a call when you're ready to talk again." Dan patted her shoulder before walking away.

As soon as they were in Sam's car and on the road, he reached across the center console and squeezed her hand. His touch was enough to help her feel centered again, to calm her shaking body.

His phone vibrated, and he let go of her hand to answer it.

"Sam. Yeah, that figures... Oh? No, she never mentioned it... Wait, what? No, I'll call you back." Sam turned to her after he hung up the phone. "Luce..."

"What?" she asked softly, steeling herself for more bad news.

"Dan got into Rich's phone already and started going through his messages. He owed a lot of money to his boss. But all the texts suggest things were going okay, and he was paying it back. With substantial interest, of course." Sam hesitated, meeting her eyes briefly before returning his gaze to the road.

"Did you know about a woman named Cassie Henkel?"

Lucia clenched her jaw. "Yeah. Rich always complained 'cause I refused to use with him, so whenever he wanted a girl to party with, he'd call her. And I know they knocked boots even though we were together. I think I heard that she took off down to Cave City, maybe a year and a half ago."

She studied the deceptively calm surface of the Pine River as they crossed the highway bridge that spanned it. Its gentle rapids reflected the red and orange sky as the sun fell to the horizon.

"Well, it appears she came back when she found out you dumped Rich. They found that in his recent messages with her, he professed his love for you." Sam rolled his eyes. She knew he'd never veil his disdain for her ex. "So she flipped out. She threatened to kill him, his dad, and even you. It sounds like she's buckets of crazy, but she told Rich that if you were dead, then she was sure he'd finally love her again."

The hair on Lucia's arms prickled, and she knew in her gut that Rich hadn't killed himself. It simply wasn't something he would do. Maybe

Cassie had snapped when he refused to take her back. Maybe she killed him, and what happened today was only the beginning.

Sam turned the cruiser into Lucia's driveway. "Listen, my next shift doesn't start until seven tomorrow. I'd feel a whole lot better if I could keep you company tonight."

Her eyes stung as she leaned across the console and grabbed his right hand from the steering wheel. "I would love that." She smiled through the pain.

She trudged up the walk to the house and unlocked the side door. For a moment, she dared to think that maybe things were going to be okay. She had broken up with Rich so long ago, after so much pain between them, so why should his death affect her this much now?

And Cassie... Well, she wasn't too bright. Lucia could hardly imagine the woman was capable of murder. Perhaps the message on the car wasn't actually meant for Lucia. She scoffed at the idea as she pushed the door open.

They entered through the mudroom and stepped into the living room. Before they went any farther, she turned and hugged Sam tightly. Being close to the one person who made her feel safe was the only thing that kept her on her feet.

"Could you start some tea, please?"

He kissed her before responding. "What kind?"

"I don't really care." She leaned her head against his shoulder, then hung up her jacket and slipped off her shoes.

"No problem." He headed for the kitchen and she turned down the hall toward the bathroom.

She dragged her fingernails against the daffodil-yellow paint on the walls, hoping the sensation would ground her to the earth and settle her dizziness. The drywall and paint were imperfect, the uneven surface bumpy beneath her fingertips. She loved this battered old home despite its obvious structural and cosmetic issues.

Sitting on a little side road just off Main Street, Lucia's rented home was originally built in 1905. The owners had updated the place enough to bring it up to code, making it rentable. As soon as Lucia laid eyes on it, she'd fallen in love. Before she found this house, she and Rich had lived on his father's farm outside of the rural agricultural community of Pine River, named for the swift-running, deep body of water that flowed through the middle of it.

Although she had loved living on his dad's farm, she came to realize she was too deeply entrenched in Rich's emotional problems. She had to admit, she couldn't counsel, couldn't fix, couldn't be the one to save him. For so long, he had struggled to gain his father's approval, and that factored into his turning to drugs and alcohol to cope with what he perceived as his failures as a son. Her original plan had been to get him a job in town, off the farm, and into a place of their own. She hoped he would see how good life could be without constantly trying to prove himself.

His father, Liam, had warned her against trying to fix Rich, but she'd seen a light in him. So much potential for goodness, for greatness. When he was drunk enough, she caught a glimpse of the confused, tortured human behind the facade. He told her that he wanted to be good, like his father, but he just didn't know how.

Living away from the farm for the first time should have helped him finally grow up. Instead, it sent him further down the spiral into a deep, dark, and lonely abyss of self-destruction.

"I think they're clean."

Sam's voice startled Lucia back to the present, and she realized she'd been scrubbing her hands and rinsing them repeatedly while she dredged through her memories and regrets.

Her throat tightened, and she found she couldn't face herself in the mirror.

"I'm sorry," she replied out of habit, then turned off the faucet.

He put an arm around her shoulders and pulled her close. She was truly safe now, and the past was behind her. He kissed her on the head and led her back to the living room.

They sat on her worn beige sofa, and Sam put on a movie. As tired as she was, she was also afraid to fall asleep. Afraid she would see Rich. Terrified that his piercing gray eyes might be waiting for her when she dozed off into unconsciousness.

"I don't want to sleep," Lucia said aloud.

Although she wasn't in the mood to talk, Sam was happy to discuss the latest edition of National Geographic at length. His low, gentle voice was comforting and helped her keep from diving too deeply into her memories of the day's events. Tammy's mangled body covered in debris. People scattered, some moaning, some screaming for help. Some silent.

She hadn't seen Rich's body in the car. Although the thought made her sick, Lucia wished she had seen it so she would know for sure it was him. That he was really gone.

"What will happen next?" she interrupted Sam as he excitedly described a newly discovered ancient shipwreck. "Will they ask me to identify him?"

"No," Sam replied softly. "His next of kin will do that."

"It's morbid and completely mental, but I wish I'd seen... him."

"That's a perfectly normal reaction," he said, rubbing her hand.

"Would it be easier if I had seen him? If I saw his... body?"

"There's no right answer. It hurts like nothing else to see someone you know after they've died. To know for certain you'll never hear their voice again."

As much as she wanted to, she couldn't hate Rich even after all he had put her through.

"Hey?" Sam's voice broke through again, and Lucia gazed up into his deep green eyes. He pulled her close and kissed her lips gently. The tick of the old cherrywood clock on the wall was all she could hear as they sat together in the quiet.

She needed a break from thinking of Rich. Everything that had happened between them, everything they had been through together, was like a trainwreck that her mind loved to watch over and over again. Now, it was all fresh once again, and a new wound had been added. There wasn't any time left to reconcile with him, to come to some amicability, to see him get on his feet and have a good life.

Sam, on the other hand, had been nothing short of a godsend. Each new day with him felt easier than the last. Well, except for worrying about him when he was on duty as a state trooper. Other than that, there was a distinct absence of drama, tension, or fear.

Lucia couldn't believe Sam had stayed with her, even after learning about her dubious connections and her dark past with a drug-dealing, addict ex-boyfriend who had a well-known criminal record. Sam had offered her the chance to be more than her history, and even though he wasn't perfect, he was damn close.

She couldn't imagine going through all of this without him. He was the one person giving her hope that a "good life" could exist. Even though they'd shied away from the L-word, life with Sam was comfortable and easy-going. Still, Lucia had a little inkling of fear ever on the edge of her mind. A little voice warned her that, one day, all the baggage that came with her history of bad decisions was going to be too much for Sam to accept. One day, he would be forced to cut his ties with her.

One day, the voice insisted, Sam would leave her.

Lucia batted the unwelcome whispers back into the farthest reaches of her mind. She was numb with pain, and exhaustion had settled in her bones. Finally, she lost the battle to stay awake and fell into a deep sleep against Sam's warm body.

Chapter 3

Tuesday, August 28th

Lucia woke in the morning to the side door creaking, the glass of its window rattling as the old wood was shoved back into its frame. Knowing it was Sam, she refused to open her heavy eyelids. Her throat was dry and tight from dehydration, and her tired limbs failed to cooperate with what little will she could exert. Instead, she burrowed farther into her pillow and pulled the covers tighter around her body. She vaguely remembered falling asleep on the couch and had no idea how she had gotten to bed.

The noise from the kitchen continued as her mind slowly rose to consciousness. Thinking of Sam, she smiled reflexively for a brief, warm moment. At least until she realized the memories of the previous day's events hadn't been a bad dream after all. It was a living nightmare that now breathed ice down her spine.

"Lucia." He sat on the edge of the bed. A strong but gentle hand rubbed her back. "Lucia?" She slowly opened one dark eye and peered up at him. "Can you join me for coffee and breakfast before I head out?"

"What time is it?"

"Quarter after six."

She groaned in response, but his smile remained.

"You don't have to. I thought I'd offer." He patted her shoulder. "Please let me treat you to breakfast." He stood and left the room.

Not wanting to disappoint him, she forced herself out of bed and quickly made her way to the kitchen. Sam handed her a glass of water and a bottle of ibuprofen with a kiss. As she took the pills, he set her cup of coffee and a plate of eggs and toast on the table.

"Look at you," she said, cocking an eyebrow at him. "All Suzie-homemaker and everything." Sam grinned mischievously as he finished making his own plate.

Sitting down beside her, he chewed his toast for a moment before speaking. "So, how do you feel?"

She stabbed at the eggs with her fork. "I feel like I was hit by a truck." Then she realized she *had* almost been hit by a car but decided against sharing that observation out loud.

"I need to see you eat something." He pointed at her food with his own fork.

"Seriously, I'm fine."

"Nope."

"Um, yes." Lucia's cheeks were suddenly hot, and her pulse began to race. "You're not my dad, and you're not my doctor." Her own anger and the words coming out of her own mouth shocked her.

Sam seemed unphased by her outburst and spoke between bites. "You're right. I'm not your dad, not your doc. But I care about you. And you need to eat." He sipped his coffee as if nothing had happened.

She reflected on her resentment in silence. Was she really upset with Sam just for caring? Lucia knew she couldn't forgive herself if she pushed him away. It was her stubbornness and pride that kept her from apologizing for snapping at him. Instead, she drank her coffee and scooped a forkful of eggs onto her toast, though the thought of food made her nauseous.

Sam, looking sharp and formidable in his dark blue Michigan State Police uniform, stopped eating and stared at her in silent insistence that she consume something. With a sigh, Lucia took a small bite of her eggs on toast. As soon as she swallowed, he resumed his own breakfast.

She glanced at him between bites, still wondering what the catch was with this guy. Lucia used to believe he was completely out of her league. He was a former soldier who had been to both Iraq and Afghanistan, complete with a stellar military record, no drug or alcohol abuse, no violence, and no severe psychological issues. Well, as far as she knew, anyway.

On top of being an accomplished soldier and a well-respected rookie trooper, he also had a four-year degree in criminal justice and volunteered every week to support a local church's efforts to feed and clothe impoverished families in the area. A man like him should be with an educated woman, an all-star, hell-on-heels model type.

Not a broke, dysfunctional college dropout who fell for broken men. There was something unexplainable that often attracted her to the ones so damaged they were sinking like the Titanic and taking everyone down with them.

Her self-deprecating thoughts were cut off by the handsome man in blue as he stood from the table. When he returned, Lucia rose and threw her arms around his neck. Standing on her tiptoes, she leaned in close and whispered, "I'm sorry."

Sam returned her embrace and rubbed her shoulder. "It's okay," he said before kissing her cheek softly. "I have to get to work, but if you need anything while I'm gone, call Dan."

She nodded, wishing he didn't have to go and understanding she couldn't bother him while he was on patrol. As he drew away, Lucia kissed him deeply, the action of a woman terrified of losing a small but special moment, and she knew he recognized it from the hesitant way he returned her kiss.

He pulled back, and she looked into his eyes without knowing what to say. Even though they were close, he held her away for a second, as if he were denying her everything she wanted impulsively. It made her knees shake and her heart pound beneath her ribs.

Her lips fell into a pout, and her bottom lip quivered with the weight of all the insecurities she was incapable of saying aloud. Sam relented and pulled her in for a gentle but passionate kiss. "I'll get my clothes after my shift ends and come straight back here if you want me to."

Tears left wet tracks down her cheeks before she realized she was crying. She nodded and leaned against him. "Please," she said, her voice barely above a whisper. He hugged her tightly once more before walking out the door.

Lucia sat down again at her tiny, rickety dining table and cradled her coffee cup in both hands as tears rolled down her face. She didn't bother wiping them away anymore, preferring instead to let them flow until the wells were dry.

The exhaustion of grief carried her to sleep, far from the living nightmare when she passed out on the couch later that morning.

Chapter 4

The Michigan State Police post in Pine River was a small, ordinary-looking two-story building with a basement. Its dark, red-brick exterior had faded beneath the relentless summer sun and a season with little rain. On the way to work, Sam's thoughts were consumed by Lucia and all the caution he had exercised around her.

Even though she hadn't yet finished college, she was bright and intelligent, qualities he saw demonstrated in her quick wit and careful consideration. Unlike most young women, she wasn't hasty to jump in the sack with a man, and he was glad there hadn't been any pressure to have sex at the beginning of their relationship.

Recently, a trooper new to the Pine River post created a scandal by almost simultaneously impregnating three local women, barely of legal age. Their rightly pissed-off families riled the community against the post. Only after the special early transfer of this promiscuous young officer did the community return to their usual attitude toward their locally-assigned State Police—holding them at arm's length but being grateful for having a police presence in a community increasingly plagued by the influences of drugs, sex-trafficking, and youth violence.

Although Sam had wanted Lucia badly at first, he'd held back and waited for the right time. It took three months, but they were both sober, so he figured it had been long enough to be sure it would be more than a one-night stand. This was the best way to avoid any chance of a scandal and to keep his record squeaky clean in this new career as a state trooper.

Sam had been excited to get assigned to a post this far north. Not only was he a rural-born man with a strong dislike for big cities, but most of his family lived in Cadillac, and his little sister was now in school at Ferris State University. Being posted in Pine River meant his parents were only an hour's drive away rather than three or four. It kept him close to home and family and out in the country where he could hunt, fish, and hike. Where he could easily find solitude.

"Sam," Dan called just as Sam had set his coffee thermos and gym bag on his desk. He turned and strode toward the detective's desk. In a post this small, there were only a handful of offices. Most everyone was on the main floor, sitting at desks placed in neat rows and columns.

"Can you check out something for me?" Dan had a clipboard in one hand and clicked a government-issued ballpoint pen in the other.

"Yeah, I've got a report to follow up on first, if that's okay."

"Sure." Dan handed him a piece of paper with a hastily scribbled address. "What is it?"

"The neighbor was driving by and said he heard screams. Like someone was dying or being tortured. That's how he described it, anyway. He didn't see anything, though. So really, there's not enough info to go barging in. I need eyes on it. It should be empty, but you never know."

"No problem."

Sam stared at an address he didn't recognize: *21195 Odom Road, Pine River*.

After leaving the post, Sam drove for twenty minutes along a maze of pothole-riddled country roads before reaching 21195 Odom Rd. This far outside of town, most homes were early 19th century farmhouses spread miles apart.

Occasionally, these old houses were accompanied by new dairy barns and crop silos, but most of the farmers here, whether raising livestock or crops, still worked with outdated structures that teetered on the edge of collapse. It might be dangerous to work in 100-year-old barns and other structures, but it was too expensive for most families to replace them, even if they had created a corporate brand under which they could receive increased government subsidies.

Sam turned his cruiser onto the dirt driveway, careful to avoid the crumbling edge that fell away into the ditch. The two-story house was clearly in disrepair. Beyond the fact that it probably hadn't been painted in at least a half-century, the once-gray shingles on the roof were covered in thick green algae that had crusted in the mostly dry summer weather. Considering the sagging points in the roof and the plastic tarps covering many of the windows, Sam thought the place should be condemned.

Despite the poor condition of the property, he caught sight of a newer Mercedes parked on the far side of the house. It was obscured from the road and parked beneath the shade of a towering weeping willow tree.

Although many people, out of the need for transportation in these rural reaches, had cars in much better shape than their homes, this was at least a forty-thousand dollar car. The state of the house didn't match the state of the vehicle.

Sam stepped out of the cruiser, his freshly shined duty shoes crunching on the gravel and kicking up fine dirt. The scent of clover in the grass drifted through the air, mingling with the earthy smell of the dust.

The area had been experiencing a relative drought, save for a few quick spurts of rain. It had been nearly a month without a proper rainstorm, which in turn put the massive field sprinklers into overdrive. An after-effect of the high use of those sprinklers was seeing the local creeks that fed into the Pine River drying out and watching the river level continue to sink.

Give me rain for my harvest. Sam mused on how all civilizations needed just the right amount of rain to avoid famine as he approached the eerie old house. If any of those haunted house companies wanted to get the perfect look for Halloween, they needed to visit this place for lessons. Before Sam reached the steps, a man suddenly pushed open the screen door on the main threshold and came striding out of the house.

"I don't give a rat's ass what he thinks, you tell that fuc–" The man with a cell phone pressed to his ear stopped mid-sentence, halting as soon as he caught sight of the trooper.

Sam was a model of what a state trooper should look like: fit, intimidating, and ready to pounce. It was important because life-changing decisions were made based on the way an officer looked in his line of work.

"I'll call you back." The stranger slipped his phone into his pocket and walked down the steps toward Sam.

He looked the stranger up and down, committing his image to memory. Thick black hair topped a pale face with icy blue eyes, sharp features, and thin peach-colored lips. It wasn't a face he was familiar with, and he had been in the area long enough to see most folks. Through his volunteer work, he'd met many people in the small community–including both the needy and those well-off.

"Can I help you, Officer?" The man shoved his hands in his front pockets.

For a moment, Sam studied the man's guarded body language.

"I hope you can, sir. We've had repeated reports of disturbances at this address." Sam kept his voice level but strong and studied the stranger's reactions carefully.

"Disturbances?"

"Yes. Officer Williams visited last week in response to a report of gunshots, and the week before, there were calls concerning noise. Sounded like someone screaming, the caller said."

The man grinned and looked around, gesturing at the vast distance across the fields. There wasn't another house in sight.

"Well, I don't know about that. Maybe it was from the next farm over. It's a dairy farm, I think. Take a right at the stop sign. It's the first one you see. I know they raise veal, so maybe it's those poor baby calves crying for their mothers." There was some hint of dark comedy in his voice, and it rankled Sam's nerves.

"Can I get your name, sir?"

"Phil McNamara. Yours?"

"Officer Frost."

Phil stifled a laugh. Sam kept his cold gaze steady on the man.

"Well, Officer Frost, those sounds weren't coming from here. What else can I help you with?"

"Are you the property owner?"

"Yes."

"Do you mind showing me around?"

Phil shifted his feet and crossed his arms in front of his chest, his smile faltering ever so slightly.

"I'm sorry, Officer, I really do mind right now. I just stopped up here to prepare a list so I can get bids from contractors to fix the place up, but I have to get back to Detroit for work." Phil paused, his blue eyes glinting back at Sam. "Do you have a warrant to search my property?"

Sam shook his head. "Do I need—"

"Could we just schedule this little chat for another time, officer?" Phil interrupted. "I swear, I'm not trying to be difficult, but I'm on a very tight schedule. I'm sure you understand."

Sam pulled a card from his pocket and held it out. Phil stepped forward to accept it.

"Call me," Sam said, keeping his tone even and unreadable. "Let me know when you'll be back in town."

"Sure." Phil's smile broadened, but it never reached his icy eyes. "And here's mine." He slowly pulled a flashy, silver business card from his pocket, keeping his eyes locked on Sam the entire time. "If you know any general contractors actually worth their cost, send them my way."

His smile turned to a toothy grin that made Sam bristle. He fought his raging instinct to pummel the man, instead offering an overly-polite smile of his own.

For a moment, the two men stood with their eyes locked, like wolves ready to fight to establish dominance. The feeling subsided as rationale and reason reminded Sam he was in uniform and it would be career-suicide. Besides, he vowed he would never be the cop who would lie or fudge the facts on a report. Starting an altercation now–especially with a rich kid from any well-equipped family in Detroit–without a proper cause other than the feeling in his gut could set him as the focal point in a law enforcement scandal primed for national news.

"Have a good day, Officer Frost."

"And you, Mr. McNamara."

As he drove away, Sam relaxed, but something still nagged at his brain. Legally, there wasn't much he could do right now without probable cause to get a search warrant, but something was off-kilter about the stranger and the property.

His jaw was sore. He hadn't realized he had been so tense. He shook it off, stretched his jaw, and headed back to the post to write up his report and update Dan.

Chapter 5

Phil watched as Officer Frost pulled out of the driveway, the gravel grinding beneath the cruiser's fresh tires. He unlocked his phone and scrolled through his contacts until he found the one he was looking for.

"Hello?" a man answered.

"Hey, Dylon. Heads up. I might need you up in Pine River."

"What's going on?"

"Just had a visit from a state trooper." He glanced at the card in his hand. "Officer Samuel Frost."

"Well, what do you have at that property?"

"My, uh, friends." Phil hated calling them that.

"You mean like your bros or your girlfriends?"

"Mostly girlfriends."

"You better get that shit under control."

"I told him I was here to fix the place up."

"Need me to send you some contractors?"

"Yeah, the usual guys." Phil thought of the small group of men who were happy to pretend they hadn't seen anything if they could make a few thousand dollars extra. They were good at their jobs, and they were discreet.

"Consider it done. I'll also draw up a complaint in case they want to snoop around again. Why were they there?"

"Apparently, the neighbors complained about the noise." Phil sighed.

"You better go make friends with the neighbors. Put on that rich-boy charm and win some hearts and minds."

"I could do that in my sleep."

"Good. Get on it, then. I'll start working on my end of things. Try to stay out of trouble, will ya?"

"You're my lawyer," Phil chided the man. "Not my father."

"Seriously. Don't make my job any harder, or we're both fucked."

"Bye." Phil ended the call and slid the phone into his back pocket. "What to do?" He rubbed his hands together before cracking his knuckles. Looking across the fields, he decided it was best to attend to business in the house first.

He crossed the threshold and entered, his black boots clunking over the worn wood floors. He stopped, closed his eyes, and inhaled deeply, enjoying the musty scent of a building that had been empty for more than a decade. There was something about old, abandoned places that he loved.

He knew that with the right man's touch, it could be beautiful again and serve its intended purpose of supporting life. It was the same with women. They were designed to support life. To enhance their husband's life and give him children.

Of course, not all were meant to be mothers, but even those women still had a use in his eyes. He fully believed, as his father had taught him, that some of them existed for the sole use of pleasing men.

Phil walked into the quiet living room and turned his gaze toward his fresh lot of lost girls. He loved lost girls. Some were runaways, some had been groomed and convinced to run, and others had seemed perfect and were taken by force. They were all like broken houses.

They just needed a strong man to fix them up. To restore their purpose.

All five of the young women looked terrified. Phil couldn't blame them as he eyed the way his two men towered over them. If Phil didn't own those men, he might be intimidated by them, too.

"Well, ladies, it's time to talk about how you're going to earn your keep. We, uh, need your help here."

Phil's sharp eyes caught sight of a glimmering tear rolling down a soft cheek. One, who looked to be the youngest, maybe thirteen years old, was crying. He thought she might be the smartest of this lot.

"Get up, girls." He motioned for them to stand, and, reluctantly, they did as he asked. Even the crying girl. "Come here," he said to her.

She failed to hold back an audible sob as she walked to him. He reached out and touched her arm, sliding his fingers down until he could interlace them with hers and pull her close to him. He made her face the rest of them.

"Why are you crying?" Phil raised his other hand, and she flinched. "And why are you frightened?"

"I just..." She let her words trail off, hesitant to finish.

"Go on." He nodded, smoothing her hair with one hand.

"I wanna go home," she sobbed, tears streaming down her cheeks.

"No," he said gently. "No, you don't. They can't take care of you. They don't want you there."

"I know my parents are looking for me."

"Don't you think that if they really missed you, they would have done something to find you by now?" he asked as he leaned in close. "I mean, they haven't even been on TV to ask for you to come home. Doesn't that bother you?"

Phil placed one finger beneath her soft chin and tilted her face so he could meet her gaze. The hurt he found in them confirmed he had successfully planted the seeds of doubt.

"They..."

He shook his head. "They aren't even looking for you."

The girl squeezed her eyes shut as the tears overcame her. He pulled her into an embrace and continued stroking her hair. "We got you," he whispered into her ear. "We're your family now. Matt?" He turned to one of his men.

The burly, red-headed giant was a softie, but he was smart too. He could take care of the girls without being dumb enough to let them escape. Plus, he would never hurt them, excepting Phil's direct order. The other, Sean, would absolutely hurt any that were left alone with him.

"Yeah, boss?"

"Take..." he paused. "What's your name, honey?"

"Beatrice," she responded, sniffling as she wiped away the tears.

"Take Bea upstairs. I think she needs her own room for a while. Would you like that?"

She nodded and put her hand in Matt's when he offered it.

"Good." Phil smiled, following them with his gaze until they were out of sight. He waited until he heard a door shut before he spoke again. "Now, as for the rest of you, it's time to get to work. Who's ready first?"

The women looked at him, then at each other, their eyes brimming with fear. None of them stepped forward.

"Come on." He winked at them. "I need a volunteer. Who is going to be my best girl?"

No one moved a muscle.

Phil sighed. "All right. You win. We'll do this your way, then. Follow me." He nodded at Sean, who grabbed one of the young women by the shoulder and firmly pushed her forward. Phil knew he would ensure the girls followed him like little ducks in a line following their mother. Except a mother duck would never lead her babies to the fate Phil was leading these young women to.

He led them through a door in the kitchen, down to the old basement. Someone had updated it in the seventies, so there was more space than what was typical in an older farmhouse like this.

The stairs creaked and clapped with each step of Phil's shoes. A muffled moaning sound erupted as he switched on the lights. It was dusty and full of cobwebs, but that wasn't what made the girls gasp.

He knew they would better understand their situation when they saw the man duct-taped to the chair and chained to a supporting beam. Phil examined the man as he led his new stock forward. The man's eyes pleaded with Phil, but his muffled words couldn't be understood through the duct tape covering his mouth. Dried blood covered his gray face and the thinning hair on top of his head.

The ring finger was missing from the man's left hand.

If his folks didn't pay his debts soon, there would be more than just a finger missing.

"Here's your new home." He gestured to the far wall where four single mattresses lay on the cement floor. "And you can either work for your meals the way I'd prefer or..." He nodded to Sean, who was grinning from ear to ear. "Or you can earn your meals the hard way. By the way, Sean loves to spend time down here. And he will train you. Most don't like his methods, but he's very effective. He's quite the ladies' man." Phil laughed, and Sean joined in. "When you're ready to work my way, you tell him, and he'll tell me."

He started to turn back toward the stairs, but a frightened voice stopped him.

"Wait!" a girl called to him. "I'm ready. I'll work. The way you want."

Phil chuckled and shook his head. In a flash, he backhanded the girl. She cried out as she fell to the floor.

He leaned down, grabbed her by the hair, and pulled her face to his. "It's too late for that! I told you to tell Sean," he growled, twisting her hair tighter in his fist. "Now there's a fuckin' chain of command here, girl! Got it?"

Her frenzied nod and the fear contorting her soft features convinced him he didn't need to escalate his reprimand. "Good."

Phil released her hair and pushed her head backward before rising to a stand. Looking at the girls, their hunched shoulders and horrified expressions warned him they were regretting their compliance this far. "Back up," he said, pointing to the wall the mattresses were set against. "Sean, you have their new bracelets, right?"

Sean grinned and reached his hands into each of the two back pockets on his baggy jeans and produced five sets of handcuffs. He put all but one set back into his pockets before moving toward the girls. They flinched backward as he approached the first and grabbed her arm. He handcuffed her right wrist to an old iron pipe bolted into the cement wall a foot above the floor.

At first, they held back their tears and disbelief, but as the third one was being cuffed, the last young woman tried to bolt. She had shoulder-length black hair and flawless, tawny brown skin. Although she tried to skirt Phil, he was too quick. With an eerie calmness, Phil reached his arm out and snatched a handful of her black hair. The force with which he grabbed her against the momentum in her sprint caused her head to snap backward, and she landed flat on her back.

The other girls cried out in shock, but the young woman on the floor could only gasp for air. The fall had knocked the wind out of her. Phil dragged her by the hair toward her spot on the wall.

"Your new name," he growled as he heaved her onto her mattress, "is Marion. You like to run so much, we'll give you a runner's name." She finally sobbed as she caught her breath, and tears poured down her cheeks.

Sean, having finished cuffing the third girl, snatched Marion's wrist and cuffed her to the pipe. "I got it from here, boss."

"Goodnight, girls." Phil flashed them one last shark-like grin before heading back upstairs and leaving them to Sean's "training."

Chapter 6

When Sam returned to the post, he found Dan wasn't in his office and guessed the man was probably at the gas station working his investigation. He began typing his report while he waited. It was difficult to find words that would convey his uneasy feeling about the house and McNamara in a logical, objective, and detached way.

He used the technical writing skills he learned as a staff sergeant in the U.S. Army's military police. He would focus only on empirical evidence, what did and did not occur, and his logic-based assessments. In that regard, there wasn't much to write, and he quickly finished proofreading the report before sending it off. Still, he committed to telling Dan exactly how he felt about the encounter with Phil. He hit send just as Dan walked into the post.

"Did you check out that address?" Dan asked as they strolled toward his office.

"Yes, but there wasn't anything I could see or hear that would offer probable cause. There was a man there, but he wouldn't give me permission to search."

"What do you mean? The place should be empty."

"It's not. There was a late-twenties Caucasian male there, Phil McNamara, who claimed he owns the property and was there to begin repairs."

Dan didn't respond until they were sitting in his office with the door closed.

"Frost." Dan often addressed his friend by his last name in and out of work. "Nobody has lived there for years."

Sam pulled McNamara's flashy silver card from his pocket and passed it across the wood-veneer desk. Dan examined the card for several seconds before returning his gaze to Sam.

"This is in your report?"

Sam nodded. "Maybe the house finally has a new owner."

"I've gotten a few reports lately, so I guess it would make sense. I did a few drive-bys at night, but it's always been dark, so it looked empty."

"It probably got sold. That's not too unusual, right? I mean, something about the guy is throwing up red flags, but there isn't any actual evidence to suggest a crime has been committed."

"Who knows. But if all the noise bothers people, then we have to check it out. We're closer than the county cops, so they asked us to keep tabs on it." Dan turned on his monitor and reviewed Sam's report.

Sam could see the hesitation on the other man's face. "What else? I know there's something you're not telling me."

"As soon as I figure it out, I'll let you know."

Sam concealed his annoyance as he stood from his chair.

Dan held up a hand and stopped him. "Did you know Lucia's ex had been reported missing by his father back in June?"

Sam shook his head.

"I thought not. I bet she didn't know it either. It's not a fun topic, but that knowledge might help her remember something that can help the investigation."

"I'll try to find the right time."

Dan nodded. "Last thing. She doesn't have a job anymore, and I suspect she's at risk of a breakdown after all that's happened. If you really love her, you might want to put in for a few days off as soon as you can."

While Sam enjoyed that so many of his colleagues liked Lucia, he despised that they felt compelled to tell him what to do in his relationship. Dan was harmless, but Sam didn't feel his friend had all the best answers or solutions—especially when it came to relationships. Dan always brought a different woman to all the official events and holiday celebrations.

"Hell, you know I love her. I'll do everything I can to see her through all this," he said as he crossed the threshold. "Check your email. I already submitted my request for time off."

Chapter 7

Lucia woke from her impromptu nap and surveyed the living room, wondering what she should do next. Since the gas station was sealed off for investigation and was unserviceable, her regional manager had informed everyone on the Pine River team that they were laid off for the time being. Everyone, including Lucia, had been reassured that as soon as the building was ready to be reopened, they would have their jobs back. She wasn't convinced, but it didn't change where she stood now.

Her mind was too deeply entrenched in the knowledge that her ex's dead body had been in the front seat of the car that killed three people. Lucia's hands shook as she made a fresh pot of coffee and wiped mindlessly at the clean countertops.

As an eerie sense of false normalcy fell upon the little bubble that was her home, Lucia distracted herself with paying bills. Rent was cheap because she had agreed to do her own household repairs and continue the updates, but it was due again soon. Without a job, she wouldn't be able to afford it. The accident happened on Monday, so she would be short five days of work for the second week of the pay cycle. She needed every penny from her regular check to make the rent.

She would also need to find another job. There was a small hardware store in town that wasn't hiring, a medium-size regional chain grocery store that always took applications but never seemed to hire anyone new, an independently owned restaurant, and three tiny dive bars.

Every blink-and-you'll-miss-it village on the major highway that split the state had at least two protestant churches and one thriving dive bar. In most of these small, agricultural towns, there was a strong emphasis on community even as the rest of the world went global. People still met each other at church on Sundays, still prayed together through hardship and tragedy, and still headed to the rundown but beloved town bars most weeknights.

Although she loved the romantic and gentlemanly gestures Sam made, such as paying for dinner, Lucia ultimately felt like she should do more to show she wasn't taking advantage of him. She often tried to take care of the tip or give him part of the bill, which would frustrate and confuse him.

She saw that it hurt him sometimes, as if she were rejecting his kindness and romance, and she would attempt to explain why she felt compelled to do it. Unfortunately, she was having a hard time learning that a good man didn't build a tab for his woman, something to use against her later, and she knew he couldn't understand her desperation for constant control of her situation.

The topic of her rent would be unavoidable, and it was a conversation she dreaded. He would, inevitably, offer to cover her rent. And she would be obliged to decline. And the cycle of guilt and frustration would continue.

Unsure of what else to do, Lucia set herself to meticulously cleaning the house. Once everything was neat and tidy, she looked around her little home and realized how close she was to losing it all. What would she do? Move back in with her parents? She shuddered at the thought and sat on the couch.

She opened the laptop she got four years ago when she had first started classes at Ferris State. At the time, her parents had saved and sprung for a top-of-the-line model that was still functional and powerful even after all these years. Thinking of the other tasks she'd been neglecting, she decided to clean out her email inbox.

She worked through the entirety of her inbox until every email was sorted into tidy little folders such as "Family," "Friends," "School," "Job Search," and more. Then she went through each folder to clear out and delete any item that wasn't important.

When she had finished combing through everything else, she decided it was finally time to purge her "Rich" folder. She left it for last, wary of the pain it might cause now that he was gone. Everything he'd sent since two days after their breakup was unread, totaling three full pages of emails she had never opened. Now that she was looking at them, she wondered why she had filed them off at all. Why hadn't she simply deleted them?

The truth was, she couldn't. The part of her that had loved Rich wouldn't let her.

To her surprise, she found that in the two weeks preceding Rich's disappearance, she had received eleven emails from him, and seven had attachments.

What the...

Opening the first email, Lucia scanned the text, instantly struck by the odd, repentant tone and cryptic sentences. She jumped up and rushed to dig through the drawers of her desk. She planted a lined notebook and a handful of pens on the coffee table before sitting back down to read the message over again, her fingers furiously scribbling notes.

"They're going to kill me," he had written in nearly every email. Sometimes he wrote it several times in the same message.

Am I crazy? Lucia's heart raced in her chest. Rich's messages were filled with fear and paranoia rather than pleas for her return. They were also thick with enigmas, strange phrases, and repetition.

Rich was the reason she'd come to this town in the first place, the only reason she had quit school and allowed herself to get trapped in a life she couldn't stand. Now he was gone, and she didn't have the faintest clue why he had tried to tell her he was in danger so long after they had split up.

He always said he'd kept her in the dark to protect her.

Why would he change that dynamic now by sending her potentially dangerous information?

When Lucia broke up with Rich, she believed it would give him the motivation to get clean. It would also provide her a chance to reevaluate what she wanted out of life. She thought that when he was healthy, she would take him back.

It was the first time in her adult life she had lived on her own. No parents, no family, no roommates, no boyfriend. Only herself and the quiet history of an old house.

Eventually, she realized her initial willingness to stay with Rich wasn't because they were in love. It was out of pity. She pitied the man more than she loved him and, at first, she thought she could help him.

When Rich had come to her doorstep later, clean and sober of both drugs and alcohol, she found the only torch she carried within her was one that burned with furious resentment. No matter what he did to show her that she'd saved him, nothing could undo the hurt he had caused her.

The buzzing of her phone on the coffee table broke her from the mire of her dark thoughts.

"Hello?"

"Hey, Luce." Sam's deep voice vibrated across the line. "How are you feeling?"

"Okay, I guess. I want to sleep, but I can't anymore."

"Well, don't stress about it. Put on a movie or read something." His tone was gentle and reassuring. She felt warmth return to her cheeks. "I'll make dinner tonight and clean things up."

"Seriously? You don't have to do that, hon. Besides, I've already cleaned to hell and back this morning." She got up and walked to the kitchen for a drink. "I'm not bedridden or anything. I hate sitting around and feeling useless."

"You don't have to be bedridden to accept help. Hell, even if you were bedridden, you'd probably still put up a fight." He paused briefly. "Can you just let me help you?"

Her cheeks hurt as she surrendered to a smile. "Okay, okay."

"I win!" He laughed. "I should be there by seven-thirty."

After exchanging goodbyes, Lucia returned to the couch and surfed through her movie library. At first, she couldn't find anything that wasn't rife with loss and destruction but finally settled for a classic comedy.

Laughter turned out to be excellent medicine, and she began feeling better within a few minutes of starting the movie. The lightness of the film helped to calm the spikes of grief, sorrow, and confusion that rose and fell like ocean waves. She even laughed hysterically when the hairy man burst from the water in a white bikini.

When it was over, Lucia felt refreshed. She opened her laptop again, no longer able to ignore the thing teasing the back of her mind.

Reading the emails a second time, she carefully analyzed each line, every minor detail of phrasing and spelling. She knew there was much more than met the eye when it came to these messages.

Are those code phrases? Rich had always loved spy movies and said if things had been different, he would have tried to get into the CIA or something. He was full of grand dreams, none of which ever materialized into goals that would require taking action.

Lucia reviewed her notes before carefully combing through each email once more. In the past two months, she found three peculiar phrases repeated in his emails.

You should see where I burned our names.
Back at our favorite place to grill out.

I stopped by the place where you planted the roses.

These phrases weren't just Rich reminiscing about their shared history. He wasn't that kind of guy. They stuck out like a sore thumb whenever he was talking about his progress, the family farm, venting about his new day job, or rambling in paranoia about people following him.

After a moment of indecision, Lucia committed to keeping these thoughts to herself until she figured out whether she was making something out of nothing.

Although she trusted Sam and Dan, she didn't want them to think she was crazy. She hardly felt sane anymore, and she didn't want to lose credibility with Sam and his fellow officers. He would be understanding, but he had a career to consider. She would never stand in the way of what he loved. As much as she wanted to tell him about the emails, she worried that every new thing might act as a wedge to drive them apart. Unfortunately for Lucia, she had no one else to turn to.

Chapter 8

Knocking on the door woke Lucia. She'd been curled up and sleeping under a soft, gray throw blanket. Her notebook and pen were on the floor beside the couch. She'd fallen asleep while running through her notes to decide whether there was truly anything to decipher or if Rich had only been trying to get her attention. Her head ached, and her eyes were fuzzy. She rubbed them as she rose.

"I'll be there... in a sec." A dry mouth and tight, sore throat kept her voice from rising above a whisper.

She walked to the door, her brain slow to catch up with consciousness. She just wanted the noise to stop. Without her usual care to first look through the side windows to see who was on her porch, Lucia unlocked the deadbolt, doorknob, and chain before opening it wide.

Sam stepped inside and hugged her. "Hey! Are you okay?" His voice was strained and his eyes wide as he pulled back for a moment to examine her.

"Yes. What's wrong?"

"It took you a little longer to open the door. I was starting to worry."

"I'm sorry. I must have been in a deep sleep." She squeezed him tight before returning to the far end of the couch and pulling the blanket over her shoulders. Her head was buzzing from being woken so quickly, and she could feel her heart racing. Orange-yellow light streamed past the curtains, hurting her eyes.

Instead of sitting down at the kitchen table like she preferred, Lucia watched as Sam placed a plate and a drinking glass on the coffee table. He moved her feet out of the way and sat down on the couch. There were only milliseconds of discontentment before the smell and sight of the food reversed her attitude.

"Pizza?!"

Sam grinned at her before taking a big bite. "Mmmm," he teased, rolling his eyes backward to exaggerate how much he was enjoying it.

Before she could get up from the couch, he handed her the second piece from his plate. She closed her eyes, savoring the first bite of her favorite comfort food, then devoured the rest of the slice.

Sam laughed at her. "Maybe you were hungry after all, huh?"

"I didn't realize it until I smelled that pizza, but I'm freaking starving!" Lucia jumped up to grab another slice.

"Well, I guess I got the right thing for dinner."

Lucia wiped her mouth with a napkin as she walked back toward the couch with two more pieces. She leaned over and kissed him on the cheek before sitting down and putting one on his plate.

"You did awesome, babe." She emphasized the last two words. She paused before starting on her second slice. "Thank you for coming."

He stopped chewing and looked at her. "I was really worried about you."

"I'm sorry," she said again.

Silence fell between them. Lucia put her plate aside and moved closer to Sam. She handed him a napkin with one hand while she took his plate with the other and set it on the table. When he had cleaned up and tossed his crumpled napkin onto the coffee table, she snuggled up close to him and laid her head on his chest.

Although she had long struggled with the fact that normal relationships didn't endure constant conflict, tension, and unspoken resentment, Lucia felt like she could finally relax. It was slow at first, but she was starting to get used to this. In the deepest part of her heart, she prayed she could keep him.

There weren't any spoken expectations about their relationship, and they hadn't pronounced any commitment beyond being "steady." Neither of them dated others simultaneously or had any interest in doing so, and he was the most laid-back guy she had ever been with. He took her out to eat and picked up the bill, didn't ogle the waitresses, and even opened doors for her. He was everything she never thought could be real.

Sam stroked her hair as Lucia ran her fingertips over his chiseled chest. Sometimes his job required long hours and since she had known him, she was terrified for him. Her breath caught in her throat every time she heard sirens.

It was probably ridiculous to worry in their small, usually quiet community, where nothing beyond wind storms and a rare F-1 twister shook things up. People didn't usually get shot and killed here. Cops here weren't at all like the ones on TV. They were part of the communities they lived and worked in. In reality, she knew she shouldn't worry, but not worrying a little was impossible.

"Wanna watch a movie?"

He turned his soft gaze toward her and offered a heart-melting smile. "If that's what you want."

She grabbed the remote to turn on another comedy. Before her afternoon nap stole her consciousness, Lucia had again considered telling Sam about the emails. Now that she was relaxing in his arms, she could only think about how lucky she was to be with him.

Yet, part of her believed that meeting him and his friends hadn't been merely luck or chance; it seemed meant to be. The timing had been perfect for her bruised and tender heart.

Just over ten months ago, she had received a birthday gift of a little cash from her parents and took herself out to dinner at the Tavern early one

Friday night. Sitting at the bar alone, she watched the World Series without much interest since the Tigers had missed the playoffs that season. Again.

She'd been wondering if they would ever make a comeback when a group of men claimed the stools to her right. She glanced over briefly, then returned her attention to the game when she decided they weren't familiar faces.

Being nosy, she listened in as they ordered food and drinks while chatting about work. The man closest to her had his raven black hair styled into a short, high and tight haircut. It stuck out as being a particularly military haircut, the same one her brother had when she visited him at Miramar Air Station near San Diego.

While Lucia enjoyed her dinner from the bar top, the men's conversation fell into a lull. The raven-haired man glanced around while drinking his beer just as she looked up. Their eyes met, and she quickly turned away, her cheeks growing hot. From her peripheral vision, she thought she saw him grin before returning his attention to his friends.

She tried to go back to her dinner, determined to make the most of the rare opportunity. Being stuck at minimum wage meant she normally ate little, much less have dinner out and enjoy a drink. Her steak and fries were the stuff of a poor girl's dreams, and she savored every bite. She was nearly finished with her meal when she noticed the raven-haired man get up and take the seat next to her, closing the space between them.

"The Tigers were awful this season, weren't they?" He took a sip of his beer and smiled as she turned to look at him, covering her mouth as she chewed her food.

"Yes," she said after wiping her mouth and setting her napkin aside. "They keep breaking my heart."

"Well, we certainly wouldn't want that." He winked at her, his emerald eyes full of light. "I'm Sam." He offered his hand.

"Lucia," she replied, smiling as she accepted it. His warm touch ignited a spark in her. Their chemistry was undeniable. The first touch alone was enough to send electricity racing down her spine, and he seemed to feel the same shock. When he asked to buy her a drink, she threw caution to the wind and agreed.

Dan—his best friend—was there with him, and one-by-one she was introduced to the rest of Sam's friends. Although most of them took off after they finished eating, Dan stayed, and the trio spent the rest of the night drinking and shouting at the TV as they watched the game. Occasionally, Dan would leave for several minutes, and she knew it was to give Sam a better chance to get to know her.

She thought this situation was how two types of movies started: romantic comedies and serial killer thrillers. It had been years since the last time she was approached by a man, so she wanted to let herself dream and enjoy the moment. The flirting, the fresh spark of new romance, a wonderful dinner, and a decent baseball game all rounded out an extraordinary night. The incredibly attractive, green-eyed, raven-haired man with a delightful personality and a contagious laugh made it even better. In a single night, he had relit the fire deep in her heart.

Now, after ten months together, she had—for some unexplainable reason—avoided taking the next step, despite every sign that it was time. Sleep claimed her while she imagined what life might look like if she jumped in feet first, moving in with him and staying for the long haul. She hoped it could be as full of love as she dared to dream.

Chapter 9

Sam carried Lucia's sleeping form to bed and tucked her in. After settling her, he got to work cleaning up their dinner mess. Thankfully, she was neat and kept her house in good order. Even his neurotic level of wannabe-OCD could be at home here.

They had been practically inseparable since they started seeing each other, going on dates to Grand Rapids to see concerts and the burlesque show, fishing and hiking together, and spending chill nights on the couch relaxing or playing cards. Even in that short time, he could see the fear in her eyes when he left for work and the relief when he came back to her.

As much as he didn't want to admit it, he didn't want it to end. After eight years in the rigid world of the Army's military police and multiple deployments in various combat support roles, he thought he would have to chase cougars to find a woman he could stand to be around.

Instead, he found Lucia sitting at a bar alone. His buddies teased him that you couldn't meet good women at bars, but this one had been having dinner, not partying. He was glad he took a chance on her.

Sam washed the dishes, then put them away. He had dried his hands and was looking around for anything else that could be done when he spotted a notebook and pens lying beside the couch.

As he carried the notebook to her desk and put the pens back in the center drawer, he caught sight of what was written on the open page.

Rich's old emails...
1. You should see where I burned our names.
2. Our favorite place to grill out.
3. I stopped by the place where you planted the roses.

The sting of jealousy twisted in Sam's stomach. He closed the notebook and left it neatly centered on her closed laptop. He paused to consider why he was jealous of a dead man. After all the time spent falling for Lucia, Sam suddenly felt like he was being duped. Did she still love Rich? Was there enough room in her heart for Sam?

He went back to the cupboards and poured himself a glass of cheap whiskey to help soothe his discouraging train of thoughts. Sam nursed his drink until midnight before deciding that maybe it was too early for her to be serious with him. Although they were entirely comfortable together, she often seemed reserved, like she was holding something back.

Washing the single glass reminded him that he too had baggage; he was a lonely ex-soldier looking for something to believe in again, something bigger than himself. Was it a family he was looking for?

Although his fellow LEOs offered a tight-knit community, he was still a bit of an outsider. In the Army, he and his men worked, played, lived, and died together. Here, he went to a house instead of the barracks. He was left with nothing but his memories when he wasn't with Lucia.

New Army rules mandated counseling for everyone who experienced combat and was close to someone who died. At first, any soldier could fake their way through the sessions, but eventually, the psychiatrists and cognitive-behavioral therapists would dig their claws in and rip open the soul, revealing the deepest, darkest parts of a person's mind.

Sam was told he suffered with survivor's guilt. After one of the other men in his platoon broke his silence during a smoke break, he revealed he'd been told the same thing. Eventually, they found everyone who had been on any mission that went bad on that tour to Iraq had survivor's guilt, among various other diagnoses.

Whenever one of their men was killed, each of those remaining wondered if they could have taken the dead man's spot. The single men wished they could have saved wives and children the pain of such a devastating loss, and the married ones lamented their inability to save the young men. None of them wished that tragedy on the spouses, children, or parents who lost their soldier to a war that no one seemed to believe in anymore.

Sam abandoned his dark thoughts for the night before making sure the door was locked and turning off the lights. He took a quick shower before climbing into bed with Lucia. He pulled her close, smelling the coconut conditioner in her soft dark hair.

"Sam," she mumbled. "How late did you stay up?"

"A little while."

"I woke up and waited for you, but I fell asleep again."

"It's okay. Sleep." He kissed her neck and hugged her tightly, wanting her so badly in that moment but still stinging from his earlier jealousy.

"Thank you for being here with me."

He squeezed her gently but said nothing more.

Chapter 10

Shelby hated her "new name." Although she'd run track in high school and knew exactly who Marion Jones was, all of her good feelings for the association had turned sour when that disgusting man had tried to rename her.

"Fuck you, Tom," she whispered, naming the man who had lured her to the farmhouse.

There was supposed to be a farmhand job paying cash under the table. Her first sign that something wasn't right came when she realized the barn was empty and the fences were in complete disrepair. It was a far cry from a working horse farm.

Now, as she struggled against the rigid handcuffs, her body aching from Sean's assault, she continued to curse the asshole who had set her up. Although she wasn't too young to get a job, she was hiding from an abusive stepfather and a mother who buried her head in the sand about it.

She'd worked crap jobs for over two years and still couldn't get approved for her own place. But there was no way in hell she could continue to live with her parents. When her best friend Lauren got accepted into Central Michigan University, she invited Shelby to come with her. Lauren's family paid for her to lease a roomy apartment off-campus, so Shelby was able to stay with her even though she wasn't attending the university.

The two friends had only been living together for a month when Shelby came across a job posting on the community board at the grocery store.

Cash, no experience needed, must love animals.

It sounded ideal when she ripped a tab from the paper and even better when she called and talked to a friendly man about interviewing for the position. Tom had a kind voice and only gently grilled her about why she was having trouble finding a job. That, she explained, was because she was living in a town with a glut of labor. Too many college students were willing to work, and there weren't enough positions for all of them.

Worse, Shelby didn't have her own car, so she couldn't apply for jobs out of walking distance. When Tom offered to pick her up for a paid trial day on the farm, it sounded almost too good to be true. The low pay kept it realistic, holding back the alarm bells from going off in her head. The minimum wage job wouldn't make her rich, but she wouldn't have to depend on her best friend so much, either.

By the time she realized something was wrong, it was too late. She was sitting on the couch waiting for her "trial day" to start while the other girls arrived, one by one. The man had asked her to leave her phone at home since there wasn't any signal on the farm, anyway. Besides, he had explained, they had problems with new workers not focusing on the job.

It had seemed reasonable and believable when he'd made the request, but there was a pinch in her stomach, and her senses perked up. Brushing the feeling aside, she had complied, desperate for the work. She should have trusted her gut and stayed home rather than leaving her phone at the apartment and getting in the car. Tom had insisted on taking her to breakfast before she started what he warned would be an exhausting workday. Intent on not leeching money from Lauren, Shelby had barely eaten since they arrived in town. So, she jumped at the offer of a meal.

Over pancakes, eggs, bacon, and coffee, Shelby had let her guard down and told him everything he needed to know: she was basically a runaway—even though she was legally an adult—and in hiding from her family.

Loose lips sink ships, she scolded herself as she twisted against the cuffs. That was the wisdom the Army recruiters had shared, anyway. Although she'd been offered the opportunity to enlist, Shelby never signed the contract. She'd been too scared to take the leap. Now, as she sat bruised and violated, cuffed to a rusty pipe in a dingy basement surrounded by crying teenagers, she wished more than anything she had shipped out to basic training in South Carolina the month after she graduated high school.

Shelby examined the man duct-taped to the chair. His hands and feet were blue, and his head hung forward. There was no rise and fall of his chest, no twitching muscles in his neck or shoulders. She didn't think he was alive anymore.

Sean had assaulted her as his boss had suggested, but she hadn't given him the pleasure of hearing her cry out, despite how hard he dug his dirty fingernails into her flesh or bit into her shoulder, drawing blood as he climaxed. She had groaned against the bite, gritting her teeth, but she would never scream for him.

She had been brutally assaulted before. Quite often, actually, by her stepfather.

For years.

He had beaten and raped her since she was a preteen, and she'd never had the courage to tell anyone. She had always prayed that someday her mother would step in and save her. But the woman was a weak-minded coward. She would rather deny the truth than rise against the man who had brainwashed her into believing he was her true love. Instead, Shelby endured the abuse and found passive ways to fight back. Her resistance would be all she had now and, hopefully, a surprise to these vile men.

This situation proved what she had already known, the things the "safe" world had often denied. Not all sex trafficking happened with willing girls and women, whether they were brainwashed or not. Some were tricked, captured, threatened, bound, and beaten.

Shelby was bound and beaten now, but she wouldn't be for long.

Before he left the basement, Sean had promised to break her. She had deliberately held his gaze, defying his attempt to instill fear in her. He was a whole lot of bark and only a little bite. Very little indeed.

The other young women seemed to be half-dozing despite their occasional sobs. They hadn't even been abused by him yet. They were simply afraid. Shelby flexed her hands, then clenched them, trying to get her blood flowing. She needed nimble fingers if she was going to free herself.

Dead or alive, she would find a way out.

If she played her cards right, maybe she could take down one or two of these assholes before she drew her last breath. As her mind worked through the possibilities, she gathered strength from imagining Sean shrieking as she watched him bleed out on the cold basement floor.

Chapter 11

Friday, August 31st

A golden sun beat down on the modest group of people walking between the headstones while birds sang from the cemetery's carefully manicured trees. The intense heat was unusual, even for August, and the funeral-goers all fanned their faces with the memorial pamphlets as they sweated through their black clothes. The chirping sounds added a casual lightness that juxtaposed the macabre mood of those gathered at the final resting place of Richard Logan Thompson.

"How are you feeling?" Sam asked as they trailed behind the mourners making their way to the gravesite.

It was everything she could do to keep from crying. Every muscle was sore, and her chest was tight, filled with a depth of sorrow she hadn't expected. Her stomach threatened to expel her light breakfast.

"I feel like I'm barely holding it together." She swallowed hard. It felt like a lie. Was she barely holding it together? Or was she doing better than she thought was appropriate?

"I'm sorry." He wrapped an arm around her shoulders and pulled her close as they walked. "I got you."

"Thank you," she whispered.

Lucia still felt shocked by Rich's death. It was a terrifying experience. But something was missing. She was sure that if she didn't break down crying, it must mean there was something wrong with her. Did she not have enough empathy? She was sure she had plenty of empathy, but she was torn.

She still remembered every day Rich had struck her. She also couldn't forget his lack of remorse for the physical and emotional abuse. The controlling behavior and possessiveness. On top of it, he cheated often and made it out to be her fault. In her youthful naivete, she let him gaslight and isolate her. She had allowed him to hurt her.

Until she didn't anymore.

Although she never really faced everything that happened so she could heal, she had worked hard to move on and set new, higher standards for her life. Meeting Sam had made keeping those standards a hell of a lot easier. Since she had fallen for him and settled into a relaxed, low-drama relationship, forgetting Rich had been easier than she'd expected.

It was as if he had already been dead to her for a year.

Lucia could no longer ignore Rich's existence as she stepped through the cemetery toward his gravesite with Sam by her side. She would never have a chance to say all the things she wanted or to confront Rich for all the pain he had caused her. They would never reconcile as friends, and he would never turn his life around and become the good man she believed was buried deep beneath the insecurity and pain.

He would never right all the wrongs he had committed against her and so many others. Lucia's empathy went instead to his sister and father. They were the ones who would bear the emotional brunt of his loss. Their love for him was unaffected by his earthly conduct.

Lucia mourned for them.

Standing behind Rich's family, she stayed close to Sam throughout the rest of the proceedings. She fidgeted, uncomfortable in the old, knee-length black dress she pulled from a dusty box in her cellar. It was the only thing she owned that was remotely appropriate to wear to a funeral.

Rich's extended family members cast her a few curious looks, but his father, Liam, had been focused on his son's burial. Rich's mother, Beth, had died in a car crash when Rich was still in high school. Liam always blamed her untimely death as the reason Rich had turned to drugs. Unbeknownst to the father, the son had already begun using and dealing years before his beloved mother passed.

It wasn't for the money, Rich had once confided to Lucia. His parents had plenty of money. The people he worked for made him feel like he was good at it and said they needed him. Besides, the risk of getting caught had given him a rush he couldn't get enough of.

Today, Rich's eulogy was given by a high school friend that Lucia didn't recognize, but he was a better choice than the myriad shady figures who hung around Rich for "business."

One face was missing from the family lineup, and it surprised Lucia. Natalie, Rich's sister, was intelligent, beautiful, and, above all else, kind. And she loved her big brother dearly. Lucia had come to love her like a real sister, and she knew it must be a cold day in hell for her to miss her brother's funeral.

Clouds moved in to block the sun, much to the relief of the mourners as a Catholic priest finished the burial rites. Lucia was thankful Sam had been rather quiet that morning. He felt more like a bodyguard than a boyfriend right now, but, given recent events, she didn't mind. After most of the crowd had dispersed and Liam remained graveside, she approached him.

Without wife or child by his side to comfort him—and his own sisters and brothers instructed to wait for him back at the farm—Liam stood alone before the open grave with his hands folded, looking down into the earth as if he were considering climbing in to join his son.

"Liam?" Lucia lightly touched his arm as she walked up beside him.

The older man, who towered considerably over her and Sam, turned his head slightly but kept his gaze on the casket holding his son.

"Thank you for coming, Lucia."

"Of course." She swallowed hard, choking on the words. "I'm so sorry for your loss. Is there anything I can do for you?"

Liam said nothing, but his jaw tightened. When the older man finally turned to face her, his blue, tear-filled eyes gazed at her from a pale, clean-shaven face. He ran a hand through his salt and pepper hair. Then, without warning, he wrapped her up in a long hug. Lucia returned the strength of his embrace, surprised by the tears that fell down her cheeks.

When he finally released her, they were both crying. He turned to Sam and offered a hand. "I'm Liam."

"Sam," he said as he shook Liam's hand. "I'm sorry for your loss, sir."

Liam only nodded and cast another glance at the casket nestled in the brown earth before returning his gaze to Lucia. "We've missed you, Lucia. The horses miss you, too."

"I always think about you and Natalie. And I do miss the horses. I haven't been riding at all since the last time I visited you."

"Well, you're always welcome to come out. The horses need exercise, and I simply don't have the heart to do it right now. They're getting fat and spoiled."

"I might just have to take you up on that." Lucia smiled. "Where's Natalie?"

The lightness that had brightened Liam's face when he talked about the horses faded.

"She couldn't make it," he replied, his eyes turning toward the grass.

"Why not?" A knot of tension tangled itself in her stomach.

"She's sick with the flu. I couldn't get anybody to drive her down here from Marquette."

"I would have driven up there if I'd known."

Liam raised an eyebrow. "I couldn't possibly ask you to do that after what you went through on Monday."

The fear and adrenaline from the crash hit her again like a wave. "I don't understand what's going on," she admitted. She eyed the casket below, her bottom lip quivering. "But I'd do anything for you and Natalie."

Liam gave her another tight hug and patted her back. "I'm grateful you came today."

"Of course I came." She tried to smile as she looked up at him. "I'm just... I'm so sorry." Lucia wiped away the tears.

Liam's shoulders slumped as he returned his focus to his son's resting place.

Footsteps from behind broke their shared reverie.

Chapter 12

S am stood quietly with his hands clasped in front of him, scanning their surroundings and watching over Liam and Lucia's reunion. His Soldier instincts told him what happened to Rich was only the beginning. Today especially, alarm bells rang in his head.

The flash of a platinum watch caught the sunlight and nearly blinded him as he turned toward it. It was the man from the farm.

McNamara, Phil, Sam recalled, in his habit of reciting surnames before first names.

Phil's icy blue eyes locked briefly with Sam's before he walked past him and up to the edge of the grave. He glanced down at the earth for a moment before glancing toward Liam and Lucia.

"Liam." Phil greeted him with a broad smile, but the older man stiffened. "It's good to see you." He glanced conspicuously at the casket. "I'm so sorry about Rich. He was a great kid."

Sam moved a step closer to the group, watching Phil closely.

"Thank you," Liam said through gritted teeth.

Phil whipped his attention to Sam. "Officer Frost, right?" There was something predatory in his eyes, something that made Sam feel like he was staring down a rabid dog.

"That's right," he replied, glaring back without blinking. He wouldn't be the one to break eye contact. "You ever figure out that noise problem?"

Phil burst into laughter, breaking the mournful air of the cemetery. "Nope." He continued smiling even as his laughter subsided. "Sorry, Sam."

Their eyes remained locked for a moment longer, Sam seeking dominance and Phil seeming amused at the attempt before turning his gaze on Lucia. He grabbed her hand and squeezed. "And I wanted to offer my condolences to you as well, Luce." She pulled away, and Phil put his hand up to stop Sam before he could move in. "Do you remember me at all?"

Lucia seemed frightened. Sam stared at Liam, an unspoken question hanging in the air between them. Liam shook his head sternly, warning Sam to stay calm.

"N-no. I'm sorry," Lucia said. "It's probably been a while since we met."

"Hmmm." Phil nodded at her before leaning forward and muttering in her ear, but Sam's keen ears picked up every word. "It's probably best if you don't remember anything, Luce. People who remember bad things sometimes go missing. And the people they love? Well, they'll end up taking a trip, too. You get me?"

"Are you fucking kidding me?!" Sam closed the distance between them and pushed Phil backward.

Phil ripped his phone from his pocket, then his fingers flew over the display. He raised it and pointed the camera at Sam. "You want your career to go down in flames, Sam? I've started a video chat with my lawyer, and I'm recording."

"You stay the fuck away from her," Sam growled, failing to control his tone and his words. He could feel Lucia pulling at his arm.

"Phil?" a voice asked over the phone's speaker.

"Yeah, I'm here. Remember that cop I told you about?"

"Yes," the voice responded, hesitant.

"He just assaulted me."

"Officer Frost," the voice said. "If you can hear me, I advise you to stay away from my client. We will be filing for a restraining order against you."

Sam balled his fists and stood his ground, seething as he looked directly into the phone's camera. It was a dangerous situation for his career and for the people around him.

"I'm serious, girl," Phil said as he walked backward, still aiming his phone's camera at Sam. "You're smart enough to know what's on the line." He spun on his heel and strode away.

Sam knew the heat in his face betrayed his fury. In a matter of minutes, Phil had successfully crawled deep under Sam's skin, calling Lucia by her nickname and making a barely veiled threat against them both. He had also taken videos of them. Who the hell did this punk think he was?

"Hey!" Sam shouted, walking after Phil.

The other man turned his head and grinned broadly. "Chill out, Sam," he said the officer's first name with a chilling emphasis. "You keep that sweet little thing on a leash and make sure she does what's best for her and her family. And for you."

Phil formed a gun with his hand, his long, boney index finger pointed straight at Sam. Then his hand popped up at the wrist as he simulated shooting him.

Sam's blood turned cold, kicking his fury into a rage. He followed after Phil until he jumped into a new Land Rover. Pulling his own phone from his pocket, Sam caught a few clear pictures of Phil's vehicle and the license plate before he could drive off, his arm hanging out the window and flipping the bird.

Sam vowed he would crush this punk at the earliest possible opportunity.

Chapter 13

Sam called Dan as he drove with Lucia from the Pine River Cemetery and shared what had happened. His hands still shook as he parked in Lucia's driveway.

"Hey." She stroked his white knuckles with her soft fingers. "It's going to be okay. I bet that guy is all talk." She didn't sound very confident, but Sam admired her attempt to calm him. He said nothing as he exited the car.

Breathe, he told himself. *Just breathe.*

"Sam? Let's have lunch." The gentle smile she offered melted the edges of his anger, though its core raged against the cage of his reason.

"Okay." He forced himself to relax and followed her into the house.

Lunch was made easy by the leftover pizza from the night before, despite neither of them having much of an appetite anyway. Although a storm still swelled within, Sam had calmed considerably since they'd sat together in Lucia's kitchen.

Silence filled the space between them as Lucia pulled out plates and reheated the previous night's pizza. She appeared to be as lost in her thoughts as he was. His teeth clenched as his mind reviewed the incident at the funeral, wondering if he could have handled it differently. No matter how many times he replayed it, he couldn't find a better way that wouldn't leave him feeling just as helpless.

"Hey." Lucia's unusually cheery voice broke through his contemplative thoughts. "You know what we haven't done in ages?"

"What?" He took an unenthusiastic bite of his pizza before dumping it back on the plate.

"We haven't been to the range in weeks." She swiped both plates from the table and dumped their unfinished pizza in the trash. "Ready?"

A real smile broke his hardened face, and his jaw finally relaxed. "Hell yes! How quickly can you get changed?"

"I wasn't planning on staying in this dress all day."

"Well then, darlin', let's go," he said with an exaggerated country boy accent before hopping out of his chair and racing her to the bedroom.

His heart felt light again, and for a minute, his mind was lifted away from everything that had happened. He was here in the moment now with the woman he loved, getting ready to do something they both deeply enjoyed.

Sam had been surprised the first time she had suggested going to the range. It wasn't long after they started dating. Turned out, her father was a cop, and both parents had been in the Army. Lucia had grown up around firearms and hunting, and had participated in marksmanship competitions. The gun range was a favorite place for her and her older brother to spend time together as siblings.

She slipped off her heels and kicked them toward the door before fussing with the pins in her hair. He shrugged off his suit jacket and unbuttoned his shirt.

"What are you staring at, cowboy?" Her playful question halted his hurry to change as her silky, dark hair fell to her shoulders.

He still couldn't believe he was dating a woman who enjoyed so many of the things he loved. A relatively calm, mostly level-headed woman who was passionate, loyal, and hardworking. Her job and her past worried him initially, but he had long ago convinced himself she couldn't be blamed for falling in love with the wrong person. Hell, he had made his own bad decisions about whom to trust, and those decisions had come back to haunt him.

"Hands down, the hottest woman in the world." Sam pulled her close and ran a hand through her hair. He fought to calm his quickening pulse as her warm body pressed up against his.

As much as he loved her, there was a small part of him that remained cautious. Her desire to be completely independent made her vulnerable, and he wondered if there could be a real future with her. Whenever he was about to give up on her, she would open up a little more, offering peeks into her soul and her true character and pulling him back in.

The lace hem of the black dress only came down to her knees. He slid his hand down to the edge of the dress and pulled it up. Leaning back a little, he looked down to admire her beautiful legs. Lucia laughed softly as she pulled him toward the bed.

"Are you sure?" He stopped, raising an eyebrow. "We just came back from a funeral."

She was loving, kind, caring, and a little wilder than most women. Wild in a way that could never be tamed or domesticated. She wouldn't be bridled. She was a survivor, able to rise to any challenge fate threw at her. Sam was fascinated and enchanted, and he couldn't help but admire everything she was.

Lucia's eyes flitted away. "You..." She bit her lip and paused briefly before continuing. "You make me feel alive, and you make me feel loved. I don't want to think about death or wallow in what happened. I need to feel alive right now. I need your love." She squeezed his fingers without looking up. "I always need you."

"Lucia." Passion rose within him. He pulled her close for a gentle, slow kiss as they lay down together on the bed. "You always have my love."

She kissed him back, the warmth of her soft lips sending heat racing through his body. He ran his hands down her sides until his fingertips found the bare skin of her beautiful legs once more. His fingers slid under the hem of her dress, gliding across her warm thighs. He knew she couldn't wait much longer as she arched her body against his and teased his lips with her tongue.

He laughed softly, running one hand through her hair before pulling her in for another kiss. "God, I want you, Lucia."

"I'm yours, Sam," she whispered breathlessly as the heat overcame them.

Chapter 14

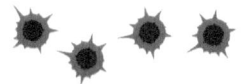

The trip to Sam's favorite, private outdoor range near Mount Pleasant was only a half-hour drive from Lucia's house. The two enjoyed a simple, satisfied silence along the way. He glanced at his passenger, leaning back in her seat and basking in the sunlight with her aviator glasses pulled down over her closed eyes. She was rosy and glowing, and she looked as beautiful now in a fitted t-shirt and dark jeans as she did when she was all dressed up.

The main road to Mount Pleasant headed straight north out of Pine River. An alternating canvas of forests and fields whipped by outside the window at fifty miles an hour until they slowed down and turned onto a gravel road. His car kicked up a trail of dust as he drove them deep into a forested area toward the private range.

After Sam parked and killed the engine, he reached over and rubbed her shoulder. "Are you sleeping?"

"Just resting." Her soft lips released the words in wisps. Sunlight and shadows danced across her cheeks as the canopy of leaves above them swayed in the breeze.

"Let's go, Luce. We can rest later." He kissed her hand before removing the keys from the ignition and getting out.

He pulled a rifle bag, pistol case, and a range bag from the trunk as she got out of the vehicle and stretched to wake herself up from her catnap.

"Did you grab mine?"

"Of course. I wouldn't leave you hanging."

She kissed his cheek before they entered the range control office. "You know, we haven't gone fishing in a while either."

He halted in his tracks and stared at her, half-stunned. "What the hell is wrong with us?"

"Hey, Frost!" a man greeted from behind a long counter. The wall behind the man displayed a variety of rifles and shotguns. "What the hell is happening, man?"

"Hey, Keller, good to see ya. Luce and I need a range day."

"Yeah, you do!" He turned a softened gaze to Luce. "I heard about what happened. Are you okay?"

"I'm intact." Her forced smile was obvious, and her downturned gaze was all the signal either man needed to realize it wasn't a topic open for discussion.

"Well, what do you want to do today?" Keller stood a little straighter and offered a broad smile.

In unison, Lucia and Sam laid the pistol case and rifle bag on the counter. Sam pulled out his wallet and dropped three twenty-dollar bills on the counter. Keller promptly scooped them up.

"We need ninety minutes of range time, two lanes, four slow-fire silhouettes, and gimme two boxes each of .40 cal and seven-millimeter rounds."

"You got it." Keller put the money in the cash register before collecting their silhouettes and ammo. He laid them out and began filling out a paper logbook with the details. "You've got lanes three and four. And you have the range all to yourselves for now." He gave them a wink before returning his attention to the logbook.

As they headed out a rear door in the building to reach the access-controlled range, Sam smelled the burned gunpowder, and his nostrils flared in response. A thousand memories crowded his mind as the pungent scents of an expended shell and gun oil invaded his head. Each memory clawed at him, fighting for his undivided attention. Visions of desert scenes, desolate highways, and crowded checkpoints flashed through his mind. He struggled to push them back, fighting to shove them just beneath the surface like he did every other day.

The sensations haunted him each time he arrived at the scene of a car accident and smelled the hot, twisted metal and the burning antifreeze. And when he saw the bloodied and broken bodies pulled from the wreckage.

"Sam?" Lucia's voice tore through the meandering trails of his thoughts like a ray of sunlight breaking through storm clouds. He didn't know how long they had been standing there, but he frowned at the worry he saw etched on her face. After walking to the table shared by their lanes, he set the bags and the case down before turning to her.

"Sorry, I was lost in a memory," he said. A hundred terrible memories.

Lucia nodded and stood closer to rub his back. He took several deep breaths, hoping to lower his heart rate and center his mind. Finally, he locked the memories back in their boxes and opened the gun cases.

First, he handed her the rifle. "All right, Artemis, goddess of the moon and the hunt. Let's see what you can do with this beauty. This is a seven-millimeter Weatherby Mark V bolt-action rifle. Then you can have your pistol back."

She grinned as she took the rifle from him, and with deliberate, clean motions, she pulled the bolt back to check the chamber for rounds, despite knowing he wouldn't keep it loaded.

Sam laughed and crossed his arms over his chest. "So, you've handled a bolt-action before?"

"Yeah, my dad has a K98 Mauser in his collection. Most of my early marksmanship training happened with that rifle." Lucia unwrapped the new passive ear protection Sam had brought for her. They looked like normal earbuds but were designed to allow conversation while effectively blocking out sounds above 85 decibels.

"Damn, I was hoping to surprise you," Sam said as he walked down the lanes to staple their targets to the stands.

She stood stock-still while he made his way back from setting up the target. He admired that he didn't have to teach her range etiquette. Her parents had practically raised her in the woods and on ranges.

He nodded his head as he took his place beside her, inserting his earbuds as she loaded four rounds and closed the bolt with a round in the catch. She pressed the butt of the rifle firmly into her shoulder and set her feet a little less than hip-width apart with her left foot a half-step forward of her right. He watched with pride when she leaned slightly forward into the buttstock and toward the target. Leaning back when firing powerful firearms often resulted in accidents.

Lucia's posture, breathing, and grip suggested military training, but that was through her family. Beyond the physical performance of firing, it was a mental game. It was everything he could do to not build an expectation for her to be an excellent marksman. He wished he could convince her to compete again.

"Aim for the 100-meter target." The slow-fire military rifle marksmanship paper target contained ten silhouettes of different sizes to roughly represent the human torso at varying distances from the marksman. The distances ranged from 50-300 meters, with the two 300-meter torsos being the hardest to hit for most marksmen.

He heard a click as she disengaged the safety lever rear of the bolt and watched her line up her target. She paused after exhaling, and the bark of the rifle shattered the stillness of the otherwise empty range. Birds took flight from the canopy of trees above them.

"I think I winged him," she said without taking her cheek off the stock.

"Yeah, you got his shoulder." He tried to hold back his excitement that she hit the target with the first shot. He maintained his composure, not wanting her to get complacent. If she became too comfortable, he might not see what she was really capable of. "Try again."

In two smooth motions, she had pulled the bolt back to eject the spent shell and pushed it forward again to load the next cartridge into the chamber from the internal magazine. For a moment, she was steady and silent. The only sound was the wind rustling the leaves of the lush treetops above them. He watched her chest closely, studying her breathing.

She squeezed the trigger.

Another shot rang through the air, but he couldn't see where she hit–or if she'd hit the target at all.

"Did you hit it?"

"I thought I did." She frowned. He appreciated that her cheek still hadn't left the stock.

"Hold on." He dug into his range bag and found his spotter scope. What did a single veteran with some extra cash do if not buy extraneous gear? He used the scope to get a look at the target, first finding the hole from the first shot in the right shoulder of the silhouette and then moving across to the left.

There it was. A dark hole in the black center of the torso shape.

Perfect.

"Damn, girl!" He lowered the scope and looked at her. "You got him!"

"Center mass?"

His skin prickled. God, he loved having a woman who understood these terms and used them so naturally.

"Yeah." He kneeled to prop up the scope and watch the center of the target. "Aim for the 200. Two rounds..."

"All right." She snugged the rifle tight against her shoulder.

Her breathing was perfect, he noted, as she squeezed off the next round and blew the right side out of the silhouette. A spent cartridge flung from the chamber as she pulled the bolt back and caught the final round. In a fluid movement, she pushed it forward and loaded the round. In less than three seconds, another shot whip-cracked the air, completely blowing out the center of the target.

"Clear it, and let's have a look." He stood up as she pulled back the bolt to eject the remaining shell. She laid the rifle on the table between them, and they walked toward the target. When they reached it, Sam pulled a quarter from his pocket and laid it over the holes she made in the silhouette. He laughed and shook his head when he confirmed all the shots fit within its circle.

"That's a fantastic shot group." He couldn't hold back a smile.

"I can't believe my grouping is still that tight after so long." Her eyes twinkled, and her cheeks had an extra glow about them.

"Very tight." He grinned, prodding his elbow into her side. She laughed and slapped his shoulder.

"Maybe it's just luck. Or Kentucky windage." She winked.

"Oh my God, Lucia, marry me," he exclaimed, only half-joking before pulling her in for a kiss. She returned his kiss, then leaned back, blushing. Sam knew he was in serious trouble. He was ready to marry her but terrified to ask in case she wasn't.

"So, come on," she prodded, changing the subject. "My .40 cal, please!"

He grinned, excited to fire off a few rounds side-by-side with her.

Sam pushed the pistol case toward Lucia and pulled his own from the holster positioned in the small of his back. He held it up for her to see. "This, my dear, is my new .45 caliber Sig Sauer 1911."

"Holy shit, Sam! When did you get that?"

"Last Friday." He realized he hadn't told her before the incident at the gas station on Monday.

"Ready to fire off some rounds? Blow off some steam?" She was as anxious as he was to fire off a few rounds.

"Okay, Luce." He leaned back a little to watch her first.

She released the magazine and pulled back the slide to ensure the chamber was clear before setting the pistol down on the table, muzzle pointing downrange. The badass woman enthralled him.

Lucia loaded eight rounds into her magazine, then slid it into the well and gave it a firm bump with the butt of her hand to make sure it was fully inserted. She pulled the slide back to chamber a round before adjusting her stance and cupping her left hand over her trigger hand as she leaned slightly forward.

There was a moment of stillness before she disengaged the safety and popped off the first shot. The recoil seemed to surprise her a little, and that surprised Sam because she had never been bothered by recoil before. Considering all that had happened and the events of the morning, she was probably a little more high-strung than usual. Regardless, her first shot tore through the head of the fifty-meter target.

"Nice shot!"

"I was aiming for center mass," she grumbled loud enough for him to hear as she readjusted her grip and posture.

The second shot hit just below the neck, and Sam watched her mouth an expletive before he held up a hand. She switched the safety on, then glanced up at him, holding the pistol angled down in front of her.

"Is the recoil bothering you today?"

Lucia nodded, eyes back on her target. "Yes, but I don't know why. I guess I'm a little jumpy. And it pisses me off."

"Remember to squeeze the trigger. Don't pull."

"Yeah, I know that."

"I think you're anticipating the recoil." He shrugged.

"I don't remember the recoil being anything like this." She sounded frustrated. It was unlike her, but he had to consider that the past week had been especially difficult for her mental state. A lot of marksmanship was mental.

"Don't worry, we have two boxes of rounds. We'll fire together, and I bet that will help you relax." He paused, trying to figure out her neutral expression. "Do you have a word?"

"A word?"

"Yeah, like a mantra word. A word that you focus on, something that centers you."

"I've never heard of that."

"Okay, so I don't want to get too weird, but it's some woo-woo shit I got into after I got back from Iraq. I was having a hard time dealing..." He trailed off, not wanting to fall into that black hole of conversation. "Anyway, I looked at everything that had happened and decided what was most important to me and how I could sum it up in one word."

She finally met his eyes. "What is it?"

"Life," he responded with emphasis. "Life is worth living, it's worth protecting, it's worth dying for."

"Okay, so what do you do with your mantra word?"

"Well, when it comes to living my life every day in a way that matters, lots of things." He lifted his own pistol, took aim at the target, and switched off the safety. "But when it comes to shooting, I use it to steady my shot. I'm aiming for the head."

"Life," he elongated the word as he squeezed the trigger. The shot ripped through the center of the silhouette's head. He re-engaged the safety and lowered his pistol.

"Wait." She shook her head. "You mean you say 'life' when you're taking a shot that could kill someone?"

Sam cringed at the way she worded it. He knew he needed to explain it in a way that wouldn't leave her thinking he was a complete psychopath.

"Luce, sometimes we don't realize our mortality or the dark gravity of death until we're forced to face it ourselves, or when it takes someone we're close to. That happened to me. I watched too many men in my unit die. Some died quickly, others died horrible, painful deaths. Others took their own lives once we were home or drank themselves to death." The corners of her mouth turned downward, and he knew the story made her sympathetic, which wasn't his intention. Sam rushed to explain it.

"When you look at someone you've known for years, and you see the light leave their eyes, the vitae gone from their limbs, some people experience an existential crisis. I did. I had to decide what life was and if it was worth living. What's the point of it all if we just end up as cold corpses sooner or later anyway? I didn't believe in God anymore, and I even stopped believing in the idea of the soul for a long time. Hell, I almost..."

No.

He would not tell her that. It wasn't the point, and he had to keep his thoughts on track.

"Like I said, I had to decide what the hell the point was to my own existence. When I visited a friend's widow and children, I realized I couldn't imagine her pain at losing her husband and the girls' pain at losing their father. But I could see why he was always eager to get home to them. They were worth everything he had to go through to provide for them the best way he knew how. He didn't plan on having kids when he joined the Army, but once he met the love of his life and they had kids, he didn't know how to do anything else. To him, his family had always been worth fighting for, worth dying for.

"It was the light in those girls' eyes that turned me around. They were eight- and six-years-old, and I knew Stacy had been struggling with money ever since Tom died. So I made it my mission to sober up enough to make

Christmas Day happen for them. And do you know what the six-year-old told me when she caught me trying to sneak all those boxes in?"

Lucia shook her head.

"She told me that her daddy said I would come. When I asked her what she meant, she said that she talked to her daddy all the time. She said he was there with her. He told her 'Sam' would come to help them when they needed it the most." He got chills as he remembered it. "Every year I visit them for Christmas and deliver presents. Sandy has me and three other guys from our platoon on speed dial for whenever they need something."

"That is really wonderful of you to do." Tears glistened in her eyes.

"Anyway, for me, I know that if I have to fire my duty weapon, it's not about my intent to take a life. It's about protecting as many lives as possible. Protecting a woman from her abusive husband, a child from a deranged parent, or bystanders when some little shit takes out his rage on a bunch of defenseless people. Life matters, innocent people deserve protection, and that's why I do what I do. I'm never firing out of fear for myself or anger or insecurity." He paused, his eyes searching the distance for the peace and assurance he suspected he might never find.

He turned and laid his pistol on the table before shoving his hands in his pockets. He nodded toward the one in Lucia's hands. "Now, if you don't have a word in mind, that's fine. It's only a suggestion. For now, you can just say 'squeeze' like a lot of pros do."

"So, I say that?"

"Well, draw it out. Say 'squeeeeeeze' as you're squeezing the trigger. It distracts you from the anticipation of the recoil."

"Oh." Understanding lit up her face as she lifted her pistol once more. "All right. I'm aiming for center mass." She got comfortable in her stance and gripped the pistol.

Sam watched her lips form the word as she squeezed the trigger, and the pistol barked its shot. He looked downrange and found a new hole had torn out the center of the fifty-meter target.

Before he could praise her, she spoke again.

"The two-hundred and fifty-meter targets." Lucia fired four more shots, rhythmically tearing out the centers of both 250-meter silhouettes.

He looked back from the target to see her standing with the pistol pointed up before her, its slide locked back to reveal an empty chamber and magazine.

"Damn." He shook his head in awe as Lucia ejected the magazine and laid the pistol down on the table so she could reload.

"Now, let's get back on the line and spill some brass together."

She blew him a kiss.

Chapter 15

The time spent at the range did wonders for them both, but tension still hung in the air between them. Lucia knew Phil's poorly veiled threats had gotten to Sam. Outside of her catnap, she eyed every shadow because he'd gotten to her too.

After a hot shower together and another steamy romp, Sam offered to treat Lucia to dinner at the local brewery, and for once, she didn't bother to fight him paying for all of it. Normally, out of sheer proof of independence, she would even insist on driving if they took her car.

Today though, after the funeral, the incident with Phil, and their range time, her aching bones and cramped muscles begged for rest. Exhausted, she asked Sam to drive. The ride was a blur. He was quiet, but she assumed he needed space to digest everything that had happened throughout the day, too.

Once they were seated in the brewery with drinks on the table and their food ordered, Sam took her hand. With the charm of his smile and passion burning bright in his green eyes, he brought warmth back to her cheeks. "Chin up, Luce. Everything's gonna be all right."

She smiled in spite of it all. Even when she felt lost and hopeless, Sam's presence and words always provided comfort, hope, and companionship. He was the only part of her life that hadn't fallen apart, much to her surprise. Despite everything in her history and all the events of the past week, he was still standing beside her.

Acting on impulse, Lucia got up and pulled Sam by the hand, leading him onto the dance floor. A country band played a two-step, and he quickly swept her into the rhythm. She leaned into him, following his lead and enjoying how close she felt to him.

"Where did you learn to dance like this?" she asked when they stopped to finish their drinks.

"Germany, actually." They paused their conversation as the waitress delivered their food to the table.

"Germany?"

"Yeah, country bars on base. Get there about seven-thirty or eight for lessons and then dance until three in the morning. Pick up some drunk chicks." A wolfish grin spread across his face, and he winked.

"Sam!" She thought back to the first night they met. The laughter, the mischief in his eyes. The instant, undeniable chemistry. And he always had a story to share. "It sounds like it was a lot of fun."

His gaze fell to his bottle, and he swirled the remaining liquid before downing it. "Life is what you make of it. I wanted my time in the Army to be a great experience, so I gave it everything I had and made the best of it."

The vision of having a family with Sam struck Lucia suddenly, but she quickly locked the smoky thought in a secret place in her heart. "We need shots." She grinned back at him.

"Shots? Wait. Why are you looking at me like that?"

"No reason." She headed to the bar.

After she returned with two shots, Sam put a hand over hers before she could throw it back.

"There's something I've been wondering about," he began carefully. "What was that note you wrote about your ex?"

Lucia looked at him blankly for a moment before she realized he was referring to her notes from Rich's emails. She pulled her glass away to take the shot, then swooped up the bottle of beer the waitress dropped as she passed and chased it.

"You were reading my notes?" She set the beer down and leaned back. She hated the idea that he might read through her stuff. Not that she felt she had anything to hide, but she had a history of her privacy being invaded when Rich reached his peak level of possessiveness and paranoia. Bristling at the thought of being with a possessive partner again, she cocked an eyebrow and waited for his answer.

"I was picking up before I came to bed and saw it. I only glanced. I didn't snoop through." He paused, fingers drumming the tabletop. "I need you to be honest with me. If we're in this together, then I don't see why you can't tell me."

Bouncing her leg nervously, she gulped the second shot before glancing at a handful of couples dancing to a country cha-cha. She signaled to the waitress for another beer.

"Have you heard much about the investigation yet?"

"Very little. I'm not privy to all the details."

"Privy?" She threw her head back and laughed. "What are you, British? Who the hell says that?"

"All right, Miss Comedian. On with it." He rolled his eyes.

"I'm so sorry." She continued to chuckle.

"The notes, Luce. Focus." He took her hand and rubbed his thumb over her knuckles. "Tell me about your notes."

Her mirth subsided as she forced her thoughts to center on her dead ex.

A sick feeling rolled through her as she thought of his body lying cold in the ground, sinking like a brick in her stomach. She squeezed Sam's fingers as the waitress set Lucia's next beer on the table. After the woman departed again, she answered him.

"I got all these emails from Rich, and at first, I just thought they were the usual shit. All that 'come back to me' nonsense. But the ones he sent over the past two months were different. They were frantic, like something bad was going down. He sent encrypted attachments. They're zip files, but I can't figure out the password to open them." She sighed and tousled her hair with one hand.

Sam clenched his jaw, probably fighting back the urge to say something until she finished.

"I think... This might sound crazy." She shook her head. "But I think he was trying to tell me something. I spent that whole day while you were at work combing through those emails and trying to figure out the password. I didn't mention it to you right away because I didn't know if it was important." Lucia saw the skepticism on Sam's face. "So, what do you think?"

"Have you told Dan any of this yet?"

"No." Lucia took a drink of her beer. She had taken two shots and had two beers since they'd arrived, but the dead man's cryptic messages muted any buzz she might have felt. "What is there to tell Dan if I can't figure out what's in the messages?" She lifted her empty palms to him. "To an outsider, the messages probably look pretty mundane. But I know what he's like; I know how he talks and writes when everything is normal. What's in these messages screams everything but normal."

"You sure he didn't just want to get your attention?"

"I'm sure." She shook her head. "It wasn't just him trying to get back with me. I mean, I think he knew what was coming, that he might die."

"You really think so?"

"I do. And he wasn't suicidal. I know that. I think he was terrified of whatever was going on with the people he dealt for."

"Did he say who he was afraid of?" Sam's eyes gleamed with curiosity.

"No. He never mentioned any names. He always said it was to 'protect' me." She recognized the cynicism in her voice but refused to stop and analyze it. She struggled to find the right words. "He was important to them because he knew everything about how they brought drugs into the area, the locations of their trap houses, the identities of the dealers."

She imagined this was the kind of information that could not only propel an officer's career, but maybe even make a dent in the war on drugs, a war that was waged inside communities and took the lives of the locals as its casualties.

"What's in your notes?"

"Well, I think he was writing to me in code. He keeps referencing these places where we spent time together, but he does it in this weird way. So I know there's something in those emails, something important. One minute he's rambling about the people who are following him, and the next, he's asking me to go to the place where we used to barbecue in the summer."

Sam flinched, but Lucia was grateful he didn't say anything. He was a great guy, but Lucia knew that no one was perfect. One of Sam's apparent flaws was his jealousy.

"Okay, so it sounds like you're on to something," Sam conceded. "But why would anyone be after him? You said he was good with the people he worked for."

"He quit." She shrugged.

The waitress approached the table. "Another round?"

Sam pushed his beer away. "Ice water, please, for both of us. And the check."

When the waitress left, Lucia continued. "Anyway, he stopped doing drugs and dealing, and he cut his involvement with every part of the process. He was out completely. I think he used to owe them a lot of money, but once I got through his emails, it sounded like his dad bailed him out."

"How much money was it?"

"Probably in the tens of thousands. Easily."

"And his dad had that kind of money?"

"Oh yeah, they have a lot of family money. The farm sustains them, but it isn't the source of most of their wealth. I don't know too much about that, but I know that, for the most part, they're wonderful people." She finished the last of her beer. "And Liam, who you met today, he would do anything for his children. And I mean anything."

The waitress came and dropped off their cups of ice water and the check on the table before heading off to another patron who was waving her down.

When she left again, Sam leaned forward and spoke in a low tone. "You need to take all this to Dan."

"No." Lucia hadn't meant for her response to sound blunt, but she didn't bother apologizing.

"Why not?"

"Like I said. Nothing to tell yet. Besides, you ever hear that saying?"

"What saying?"

She shrugged, feeling odd repeating something she had heard so many times from Rich. "Snitches get stitches."

Sam scoffed and leaned away from her. "You can't be serious."

Her stomach tightened, and her cheeks grew hot. "Why not?" She took a long drink of her water, trying in vain to control the shameful feeling crawling through her bones.

"I never thought you were the kind of person to ascribe to criminal ideologies." He turned his attention to the check, pulling out his wallet and holding it out for the waitress to take as she passed.

It stung her deeply to hear him say that. She didn't know if she was more embarrassed by the implication or pissed at him for pointing it out.

"So," he continued. "What are you going to do about your notes?"

"I don't know," she mumbled, looking away from him.

"Yes, you do." His challenge hung in the air between them. "I know you well enough, and you're not the type of person to do nothing."

"Were you there today?" She kept her voice low, anger and frustration simmering. He didn't understand. "Did you hear what that man said to me? It may have been a subtle threat, but I heard it loud and clear. And it would fucking kill me if he went after my family. If he... if he went after you. I can't do anything."

She grabbed her purse and stormed out.

Chapter 16

S am walked out of the bar and found Lucia waiting for him, the butt of a burning cigarette pinned between her painted lips.

"Are you okay?" He looked at the ground as he pulled her car keys from his pocket.

She shrugged.

He nodded and stood beside her. Leaning against the wall, he crossed his arms over his chest. She took a deep drag on the cigarette and stared into the darkness beyond the parking lot. Sam knew there was some battle raging within her. Enduring her silence and waiting for her was non-negotiable. He loved her and would be there for her when she needed him, whether that was in five minutes or five days.

Sam inched closer to her until their shoulders were touching. Her bare skin was warm, a welcome contrast against the cool evening air. He stretched his arm behind her, pulling her toward him in a partial embrace.

"Come on," he whispered, leaning in close, knowing his breath in her ear would give her goosebumps. He rubbed her shoulder and felt her skin prickle. "You can smoke in the car."

"I'm not a criminal," Lucia insisted.

"I know that, Luce." Sam squeezed her. "I wouldn't be here if I thought you were."

"Then why did you say it?"

"I didn't mean to hurt you." He kissed her cheek. "At some point, you have to realize that not doing anything won't keep you safe. You can't let them win before you've even fought."

"But Sam, didn't you hear—"

"I heard that little shit perfectly fine, but he also has my attention. And now he has Dan's attention, and likely our post commander's attention. He's on our radar, Luce. The spotlight is on him, no matter how many lawyers he buys. And he's making enemies far too fast to do anything to you."

"I'm scared," she admitted. He could feel her trembling but knew the cool evening air wasn't the reason.

"I know. But the worst thing you can possibly do is nothing. He wouldn't have made that dramatic appearance in a public place and openly threatened you if he wasn't spooked about what you might know. Do you hear me?"

She shrugged and smothered her cigarette butt before relaxing a little and wrapping her arms around his neck.

"He is scared of you. If you don't do all you can to fight against people like this, you're going to end up just like everyone else who turns a blind eye to all the darkness in our society. The ones who are too afraid to speak up, to do the right thing. And that's why these guys get a stranglehold on our communities, and everything goes to hell in a handbasket."

She didn't respond, but he held her anyway, hoping his words would have some effect. He had never seen her this scared. The girl he knew and loved wouldn't back down from a fight.

"Can we go home?" She looked up at him then, her eyes tired, their usual light now dimmed.

"Of course." He led her to the car, opening the passenger door for her before walking around to the driver's side. As he reached for the door handle, he noticed a little yellow square of paper attached to the window, its edges flickering in the light breeze.

☐☐*STAY QUIET*
☐☐*STAY SAFE*

He froze, studying it, then looked around the area carefully for any sign of who might have left it. Crickets chirped, leaves shimmered, but nothing else stirred in the darkness.

Sam pulled out his phone and snapped a picture. Then he used the edge of his shirt to carefully pluck the sticky note from the window. He opened the door and placed it in the cupholder as he lowered himself into the driver's seat. Lucia gave him a curious look and reached for it, but he stopped her.

"Don't touch it."

"What is it?"

"Evidence."

Sam texted the picture to Dan. He waited until his phone indicated the message had been delivered to Dan's phone before calling his friend. There was no answer. Sam checked his watch. It was nearing midnight. He left a voicemail describing the note and promised to bring it to the post, then shoved his phone back in his pocket before putting on his seat belt.

He kept his voice soft. "Refusing to talk won't keep you or anyone else safe." He turned the key in the ignition and shifted the car into drive. "All you'll do is enable these assholes to carry on with everything they've done to hurt others."

Lucia sighed and pressed her fingers to her temples.

"My position needs to be crystal clear to you."

"What can I possibly do, Sam?"

He didn't fail to notice the razor-sharp edge to her voice.

"I can't fight people like this. I can't stop anything they're doing to hurt people." She mocked his tone, and it rankled him. "I'm not a cop or a soldier or anyone with any power to do a damn thing about it."

"Wrong. You do have power, and you exert that power every time you choose to speak up or stay quiet."

A tense silence blossomed thick and heavy between them. She pressed her cheek against the glass of the passenger-side window and closed her eyes. The ride home was quiet, but Sam didn't mind. This asshole Phil was getting to Lucia, weakening her resolve. He filled Sam's veins with fire, and Sam desperately wanted to strangle the punk.

He centered his thoughts when he pulled into Lucia's driveway, taking a deep breath as he parked the car and turned off the headlights. Reaching over, he grabbed her hand and squeezed gently before stepping out of the vehicle.

She closed the car door behind her to follow, then froze.

"What's wrong?" He turned to her as he reached the steps.

"Maybe I'm just buzzed."

"What is it?" he insisted, hoping his voice didn't betray his agitation.

"It feels like..." She let her words trail off, and her eyes locked with his. "Like it's too still. Too quiet."

"Go wait by the car," he ordered before beginning to search around the house.

"What? Why?"

"Would you just fucking listen once without fighting me?" He hadn't meant to snap at her, but he only now realized how tired he was of constantly being questioned. All he ever tried to do was watch out for her, but she still challenged his every move and word. "Can't you just trust me?"

Lucia's jaw dropped, and she froze, her eyes wide with shock. "I-I'm sorry."

"Please, just get in the car." Sam waved her off, still seething, and began examining the front of the house. Nothing seemed out of place, but once he cooled down, he couldn't deny the uneasy feeling in his own body. He had this feeling before, the queasy sensation that turned his stomach and electrified his skin.

Something was definitely wrong.

Sam walked the perimeter of the house, careful to look for signs that anyone had been tampering with the doors or windows. If they were being followed, he had no doubt the location of Lucia's house was well known to whoever had killed Rich. And to Phil.

Seeing nothing out of place, he headed to the front of the house and tried to dismiss the feelings. Though every fiber of his being pulsed with alarm, he pushed it down with deep breaths. They couldn't afford to live in constant fear of attackers and intruders, and tonight should have been like any other night they had come home together.

Except tonight, someone had left them a message, one intended to frighten Lucia. He wished he could get her to tell Dan about the emails. If he went behind her back and told Dan without her permission, it would be a betrayal of her trust.

If she wasn't sure whether the emails were important, and she had no recollection of this Phil person, then what was there to tell Dan? If he betrayed her trust, he was sure he would lose her, and he wasn't ready to let her fend for herself. Or to risk their relationship.

As he caught sight of Lucia leaning against the car, he swore an oath that he would not betray her trust unless he believed her life was in immediate danger.

Although Phil had gotten under Sam's skin, he'd been too overt, took too much risk, and reeked of an amateur. No criminal mastermind is going to allow that much attention to be drawn to him and invite investigation into his activities.

Lucia brushed the hair from her face. Sorrow and foreboding filled her eyes.

"Did you—"

"I didn't see anything out of the ordinary."

"So it's safe to go in?"

Sam offered his hand. "It looks like it."

She accepted his hand but did not smile, and he regretted snapping at her.

When they entered the house, Sam asked her to wait by the door while he searched the first and second floors. He checked each window and every dark and hidden space, ensuring the house was secure before giving her the all-clear.

"Ready for bed?" She slipped off her shoes and threw her purse on the couch.

"I'm going to check my messages first. I'll be there in a minute."

She made her way down the hall to the bathroom and closed the door.

Sam removed his boots and jacket before sitting on the couch and unlocking his phone. He scrolled through his messages, but there was nothing new or important. Still, he couldn't shake his unease.

By the time he settled down and made his way to the bathroom, Lucia was already in bed. He poked his head into the bedroom, heard her soft, even breath, and knew she had already fallen asleep.

Anxious to be close to her, Sam quickly double-checked the doors and windows before climbing into bed beside her. He pulled her close, his mind still buzzing from the events and revelations of the day.

Looking at Lucia bathed in the moonlight that peeked between the bedroom curtains, he knew that despite everything, he really was happy. Sam hoped he wasn't a mere rebound to her and that she was over her relationship with Rich. It was hard to tell with someone who mostly kept her thoughts to herself. Yet, he didn't want to make the mistake of offering the next romantic leap with someone who wasn't sure of her own heart. Regardless of where the two of them now stood in their relationship, Sam knew there were too many things to uncover beneath the strange events of the past week.

Did Rich's last messages to Lucia really contain clues? Or was she simply reaching for something to hold on to from her ex-lover? Had Rich been pointing her to more, or had he only been trying to win her back?

Sam didn't know how deep the rabbit hole went, but he was more than happy to follow the trail through the warren if it meant he could keep her safe.

Chapter 17

Saturday, September 1st

L ucia woke alone in the morning. She rolled over into the empty spot and wished Sam was still there. Her head ached from exhaustion, and she didn't believe she'd had enough fun the night before to justify it. As she rose, her stomach turned when she remembered Sam's words: "Refusing to talk won't keep you or anyone else safe."

Lucia's nagging inner voice insisted he was wrong, and self-preservation required her to take Phil's warning seriously. What if she did speak up, and Sam or someone else got hurt? She would never forgive herself if anything happened to him. But if it was a hollow threat, then she was safeguarding criminals.

As she dressed, she finally admitted that Sam was right. She had to act, and the longer she waited to do it, the more she put off the inevitable. If there was trouble, it would come to her regardless of what she did or didn't do. Especially if these people believed she knew something. Doing nothing might mean these guys were getting away with hurting other people. People like Rich, who dealt with them, or people who were only in the wrong place at the wrong time.

In the hallway, the soul-warming scent of coffee greeted her. Sam always brewed a fresh pot when he stayed over. Most days, she woke up with him, but today he had slipped out without waking her.

Anxious to tackle the growing mountain of financial problems facing her now that she'd been laid off, Lucia kept her shower short, then made a beeline for the coffeepot. Although Sam was nowhere to be seen, she found her favorite cup waiting by the coffeemaker. Heat flushing her cheeks, she lifted the pink ceramic mug and studied the gold script.

Today is your day.

She filled her mug to the top. Glancing around as she took her first tentative sip, she found her phone was plugged in and charging beside the coffeepot. The kitchen was tidy, thanks to Sam, so she didn't have a good reason to avoid addressing her financial situation. She grabbed her phone and headed to the couch.

Naturally an introvert, she didn't usually have many notifications waiting on her only social media account. Lucia only agreed to create it on her brother's insistence so they could stay in touch. She didn't think it was helping them connect, even though she loved seeing pictures of him. He was living the life of his dreams, and she was happy for him. Beyond that, she had only used the platform to connect with her mom, extended family, and a few friends from school.

Today, her phone's lock screen was filled with notifications. Apparently, everyone who remembered her had tagged her as they shared the news about the crash at the gas station. Lucia counted five reports from various Michigan media outlets before she turned off her phone in frustration. She knew she shouldn't read the articles, despite her curiosity.

Would they even mention her? Or only Rich? She worried what they would say but knew she couldn't afford to waste time on half-informed reports and the ignorant comments that would surely be left by the lowliest of trolls.

After a few minutes of silently sipping her boyfriend-brewed coffee, she unlocked her phone again and scrolled through her contacts until she reached Dan's number.

Lucia's thumb hovered above it. Sam's words rang in her head, reminding her of a quote she had read in college: "Darkness only wins when good people let it."

Or something like that. Regardless of the exact wording, the sentiment resonated deep within her. As the daughter of two Army veterans who had become Sheriff's Deputies, she'd been raised in a household that idealized honor and integrity. Those values had gradually fallen to the wayside when she'd left home after high school. College was supposed to be the test, the fire which would reveal her true nature. It hadn't.

Now, a genuine moment of truth stood before her.

Lucia was terrified to piss these guys off, but she couldn't deny the growing spark in her soul that insisted she not back down. Whoever they were, they had killed Rich. Throughout their time together, Rich tried to protect her from whatever he was involved in, and she rarely met anyone he dealt to or worked with. It was dangerous, he'd warned, to get on "their radar."

He'd also mentioned that his boss had wanted to meet her, but Rich kept making excuses to prevent it from happening. Now she knew why.

Lucia tapped Dan's number to initiate the call.

He answered on the third ring. She struggled to explain everything that had happened, intentionally omitting her and Sam's argument.

After describing her suspicions about the oddly placed phrases in Rich's emails, Dan agreed she might be onto something.

"Keep combing through the messages," he said, excitement tinging his voice. "I'm glad you shared this with me. Keep me updated with anything you find, even if it doesn't seem important at first."

"Will it really help?" she asked, worried about bothering him with every minor detail.

"Of course. Just take notes about everything. I'll call you for an update later, okay?"

"I can do that."

"Forward me all the emails, too. I'll send them to Lansing so we can break into those attachments."

"I'll send them now." Lucia relaxed as an invisible weight lifted from her shoulders.

"As soon as I'm not neck-deep in work, we'll all catch up."

"Yeah, we need to have a barbecue," she agreed. It had been too long since she and Sam had invited friends over.

"Oh, and I think the press got wind of your name. Watch out for reporters, and don't speak to anyone about anything you find."

"Really? Reporters?" Lucia hadn't considered that possibility. She knew a few uninjured people at the gas station had spoken with the media that evening, but she had been too busy with the police and paramedics. Eventually, investigators would be required to release more details, and her involvement would be revealed.

"Yes. I'm serious, Luce," his deep voice reverberated across the line. "Don't say anything to strangers who come asking."

"That shouldn't be a problem. I hate people," she joked.

"Okay, Luce. Take care of Sam for me."

"You know I will."

When they ended the call, she stared at her lock screen. It was only 9:30. She hoped Sam would return soon.

The hairs on the back of her neck prickled as she laid her phone down on the table. Surveying the room, she found nothing unusual. But the strange sensation crawled like ice water through her veins.

A storm was coming, and she stood directly in its path.

Chapter 18

Sam returned shortly after Lucia finished her call to Dan. He came bearing breakfast sandwiches. She hadn't realized how hungry she was until she smelled the food. They sat together on the porch steps, eating their sandwiches and sipping coffee. About halfway through her sandwich, when the edge of her hunger was sated, she broke the silence.

"I did it."

Sam took another sip of his coffee. "Did what?"

"I called Dan. Told him about the emails."

His eyes brightened, and he nodded. "You did the right thing."

"I know."

"So what happens next?"

"I sent the emails to Dan. He said something about sending them to Lansing. He thinks they can break into the attachments."

"Probably."

"I wish I could see them first."

"Why?"

She shrugged. "I want to know what he wanted me to see. I want to know what was so important."

"Well," he replied, grinning at her. "Then you better get that brain to work and figure out what the hell the password is."

"I guess so." Lucia sighed. She had no idea where to start.

After they finished breakfast, Lucia answered a call from her landlord, Clark. He'd heard what happened and asked about her job. She informed him she'd been laid off until the owners reconstructed the gas station. Although he was a kind older man, she knew he was hard up for cash. He also shared that his granddaughter desperately needed a place to stay, and he wanted to give the house to her.

Lucia was stunned and heartbroken, and she asked him, rhetorically, what she was supposed to do. He told her if she couldn't make her rent in twelve days, she would have to leave within another week so his granddaughter would have a place to stay.

"Don't you have a boyfriend?" he asked. "Maybe you could stay with him."

Lucia didn't answer, reluctant to give up her independence. She had busted her ass fixing this house. She hadn't signed an official rental contract since he was a friend of Liam's, and Liam had convinced him to rent to her unofficially.

Even if she wanted to fight him, she couldn't. She always knew it was only supposed to be temporary—just until she got on her feet. Yet, with such a low-paying job, how was she ever supposed to get on her feet?

Lucia knew it wasn't fair to keep the old man on the hook, especially when he had family members to care for. She wasn't his responsibility or anyone else's. It was time to make her own way and face up to responsibility like any other adult.

She hung up the phone and returned to the kitchen. Sam had brewed another pot of coffee and started filling her cup as soon as he saw her. Lucia guessed her red eyes and puffy face gave away the fact she had been crying again. Over fresh coffee, she shared the news about the house with Sam.

"I don't know what I'm going to do."

"Easy. You can come and stay with me for as long as you need."

There was a hint of reservation in his voice, and Lucia hoped he wasn't simply being polite.

"I don't want to impose on you."

"You're joking, right?"

She squirmed in her seat. "I don't know if I'm ready for that yet."

A muscle twitched in his jaw.

"It's not that I don't enjoy being with you," she said, careful to avoid the L-word. "I just need more time to heal."

He nodded his head but said nothing.

"Wanna smoke with me?" She didn't always smoke, but lately, the stress had increased the urges for her go-to menthol cigarettes.

Lucia might resist moving in with him, but it didn't mean she was ready to lose him. Did she need more time to heal? Or was it something more? Yes. She feared feeling trapped again. But she couldn't be trapped if she didn't enter a trap.

After she smoked a cigarette and talked about her job prospects, Sam retrieved his laptop from his car and helped her work on her resume. They spent the rest of the day on the hunt for her next job. While she waited for more news from Dan—or for her brain to puzzle out the password for the encrypted documents—there wasn't much else to do.

After hours of job searching, Lucia closed the laptop and snuggled with Sam on the couch. If he was still upset over her rejection of his offer to move in, he didn't show it. She was surprised and relieved, but it made her reconsider. Maybe feeling trapped wasn't about who you were with. Maybe it was a culmination of all the decisions you made up to that point that left you feeling unable to break free or find a better life.

Perhaps taking the next step with Sam would be an important step on the road to a better life. Lucia wasn't sure, but in twelve days, there would absolutely be a change in her situation. She would either agree to move in with Sam, or she would find another place. If she found another place of her own, she thought it might break his heart.

Chapter 19

A t 7:30 on a Saturday night, there were plenty of heads to turn as Sam
and Lucia walked into the Pine River Tavern. They chose a corner
table far from any other patrons and ordered drinks and ice water. For a
few minutes, they lost themselves in their phones. Eventually, the manager
came, stepping in to back up the busy waitresses.

"Ordering any food?" She smiled at them, pencil and check pad ready.

"You first." Lucia studied the menu. She hated going first. There were
too many options, and everything here was delicious.

"I'll have the bacon burger with fries and a refill on my beer," Sam said as
he turned off the screen on his phone and placed it face down on the table.

"And I'll have the same." Lucia's empty stomach was rumbling. "And
another cider, please."

"All right. Anything else?"

"Yes. Could we talk for a second, Amanda?"

"Sure. Follow me." She gestured toward the bar.

Lucia leaned on the bar, waiting patiently as Amanda entered the order
into the POS system. The two women had gotten to know each other over
the past two years that Lucia had been coming to the restaurant.

"Everything okay?" Amanda reached forward for a friendly hug.

"Is there any chance you're hiring?"

The older woman stared thoughtfully at Lucia before answering. "Actually, yeah. I got a bad feelin' one of my waitresses is gonna quit on me. If you can start on Tuesday, you're hired."

"I can! Thank you so much, Amanda." Lucia smiled broadly as she returned to her seat. A wide grin lit Sam's handsome face.

"What?" she asked, suspicious of his humorous look.

"That's very down-to-earth of you."

"What do you mean?"

"Getting a job at a bar." He said it as if it was a charitable act. As if it were cute or humble. It was serious, and there was nothing to be ashamed of for working in hospitality.

"What else am I going to do? I was working at a gas station, and I got 'laid off.'" She used air quotes for emphasis, still bristling at the feeling he was putting her down about where she could find work. "I didn't finish college, and I really haven't done much since I dropped out." Her cheeks were hot again, and she chewed the inside of her cheek so she wouldn't raise her voice.

"Hey." Sam reached over to squeeze her hand. "Calm down. Please don't get offended by every little thing I say. I'm impressed that you're already trying to go to work, considering everything that's going on. Especially after last night."

She thought of the note. *Stay quiet, stay safe.* He rubbed his fingers over the back of her hand, and she softened under the warmth of his touch. At least a little. But she decided against apologizing for being defensive.

"I don't know, Sam. That's me: always working, always moving. I feel like if I stop, I'll be trapped with my thoughts. Like when I'm at the house alone. There's nothing to do, and I can't keep it all out of my head. I just go in circles." She ached from the alternating adrenaline spikes and crashes that had plagued her over the past week.

The bell on the Tavern entrance rang, and Lucia stiffened.

"Here." Sam stood and began repositioning the furniture. "Let's move the table a little. Yeah, like this. Okay, you sit here."

"Why?"

"Well, now we can both see the entrance. Take a look around. Don't you feel better?"

She realized she could view the entire room from her new position. Although she didn't recognize the couple walking into the bar, she relaxed when they didn't show any interest in her.

Lucia slipped her palm over his. "Thank you." A warmth sparked in her belly and flared within her. The familiar pulsing desire of her body signaled its need for Sam's touch. Their food came, and they talked as they ate—mostly about her rent situation.

Typically, she wouldn't share her money worries with him. But she was too exhausted to keep her guard up. After so long together, her finances were no secret to him. After they finished their meals, there was a lull in the conversation. Sam ordered dessert for Lucia and encouraged her to enjoy a little sugar rush. It was during the first bite of triple-chocolate cake that she genuinely enjoyed a simple moment.

The simultaneous sensations of relaxation and stimulation had her brain buzzing. She sliced off a small piece with her fork and turned it toward Sam.

"No thanks." He waved her off. "I can't keep up my girlish figure if I eat that stuff." He laughed, rubbing his shirt over his hard abs. She loved that he didn't have trouble making fun of himself, even if there wasn't anything to make poke at. He was fit, strong, and hot as hell.

"Come on," she insisted, waving the fork in front of him.

"Fine." He conceded, leaning forward. She fed him the cake, and he gave her a thumbs-up as he chewed it. "Happy now?"

"Delighted." She winked at him and finished her slice.

Lucia moved her chair closer to his, and they watched the bar fill with patrons excited for the Saturday night band. She entangled her fingers with his and rested her head on his shoulder. They sat in silence like that until she could order another beer and a shot of peach schnapps.

Sam raised an eyebrow at her. "Is that a good idea?"

"I really don't care right now." She shook her head. "I just want to get loose, ya know?"

He laughed, but she could tell he was uncomfortable. She knew he understood. Back at about the six-month point in their relationship, he had detailed to her exactly why he didn't like to drink much. She was unnerved to learn that after his last deployment, he'd sated his trauma with alcohol.

Lots of it.

She would have ordered more tequila if she hadn't known his past struggles with liquor, how it had almost taken his life and ruined any prospects for his dream of a law enforcement career. Still, she needed to relax, so one shot came after another, and the more he suggested they leave, the more she resisted.

When the band played a country song, she asked Sam to dance with her. He led her onto the dance floor, and they two-stepped as the singer crooned about waiting too long to confess his love and asking what he could have done to keep his lover.

He had been so patient with Lucia, and she couldn't believe they had only been together for ten months. It felt more like they had been with each other for years already. The thought that she could lose him made her heart ache. Yet, she still hesitated to move in with him. She didn't know if or when she would be ready to take the next step. She wished there was some sign that would tell her the right paths from the wrong paths, something that could help her avoid making all the same mistakes she'd made before.

Healing from being with a narcissist was taking much longer than Lucia expected it would. She'd thought as long as she found a good man, she'd be able to distance herself from her past and her pain. Sam was incredible, despite any little flaws that kept him from being too good to be true, but she still wasn't healed. Distancing herself from that last relationship was far more difficult than she'd imagined.

What would it take to give her the strength? So she could surrender into a leap of faith and let Sam catch her?

She pulled her cheek away from his and looked into his eyes, finding kindness and warmth. He had never put her heart, her body, or her mind in danger. He was the only person she felt safe enough around to be her truest self.

Lucia didn't feel like she knew much these days, but she knew for certain that she loved this man.

If he asked her outright, she would tell him. So far, the L-word had been floating in the air between them in the quiet, intimate moments when the rest of the world had faded away. But it had still been left unsaid.

Like now, as he swept her across the dance floor with mesmerizing ease.

Lucia knew her leap of faith needed to happen soon. He clasped her hand gently in his own, and the warmth created between them grew as their bodies inched closer together. The knee-melting way his breath tickled her ear, and his deep voice vibrated down her spine. He stole the air from her lungs.

Sam leaned in close to whisper. "Would it be wrong if I said I love having you in my life?"

Lucia tipped her head up to kiss his cheek. "I feel the same," she whispered back. She brushed her lips over his, and he led her back in tempo to finish the dance.

Chapter 20

They danced to nearly every song the band played until Lucia was fully sober again and edging on exhaustion. When they finally left, she was somewhere in limbo, caught between a tired and electrified body vibrating with passion. It seeped through her veins, pooling in her stomach and filling her with butterflies and uncontrollable smiles.

When Sam pulled her car into the driveway, she noticed a piece of paper hanging on the front door. After they walked up the three small cement steps, she realized there were dozens of cards stuck in the door jamb.

They plucked them away one by one, reading each aloud as they went. Journalists from several news organizations had asked her to call them. Sam nodded to a folded piece of paper hanging from the door. She pulled it free.

  Hey sexy,
  How have you been? We need to talk.
  Miss you...
  - Jordan
  (616)555-0099

Lucia laughed, but Sam's face turned stony. There was that green-eyed monster again. She rushed a kiss to his lips.

"Who's Jordan?"

"Calm down, big boy," she said through her laughter as she unlocked her door. She threw the cards haphazardly on the coffee table but kept the little paper in her hand. "Jordan was my roommate in college."

Sam stared blankly at her.

"My female roommate, and probably my best friend in the world. Well, when we see each other."

Understanding sparked in his eyes, and his cheeks turned red. He laughed before hugging her tightly. "Sorry, Luce. I'm an ass."

"I know." She patted his cheek in mock comfort before slipping off her shoes.

"But it's only 'cause I like you so much."

"Is that right?" She propped one fist on her hip.

"It's true. You gonna shower?"

"After all that dancing? Hell, yes! Are you making coffee?"

"If you want some."

"I always want some," she said, winking.

He laughed and playfully slapped her ass as she turned to walk down the hallway to her bedroom.

Lucia rifled through her dresser, grabbing a pair of cotton pajama shorts, underwear, and a ribbed tank top before hitting the shower. The hot water relaxed her muscles as she let it wash the evening out of her hair and off her body. She thought of Sam and how sexy he made her feel without any of the pressures other men usually exerted. Anxious to be back in his arms, she finished showering quickly.

Lucia never imagined she could have so much chemistry with one person, and so much sexual tension rippling through her body after he touched her. That very man was in her house now. The one who'd invited her to live with him. He was good-hearted, responsible, charming, and delivered mind-blowing sexual experiences she hadn't known were possible.

Lucia found her reflection in the mirror, focusing on the length of her hair and then her own dark eyes. How long had it been since she had looked Rich in the eyes? She had been in his bed, too, and now that she enjoyed a healthy relationship, the thought of having sex with her ex-boyfriend made her stomach turn. Knowing his lifeless vessel was cold in the ground only made it worse.

She didn't hate Rich but she also couldn't look back and find anything physically, emotionally, or intellectually attractive about the man. It was still eerie to think he had stood before his own mirror not so long ago, preparing himself for his day or evening and completely unaware of the speed as fate hurtled itself toward him.

In the past year, Lucia had focused on moving on, and Sam had helped her do that. He wasn't simply a rebound, though. He was the only man she could imagine being with.

When she was half-dressed, wearing only her shorts and pulling her tank top over her head, a knock sounded on the door.

"I'm almost done," she called. "A little wait will do you good."

Just as she pulled her shirt down over her torso, the door opened. Lucia turned toward the door and sucked in a breath. Her skin prickled in waves, and the damp hairs on her neck stood on end.

A sickly-thin, blonde-haired, blue-eyed woman stood before her.

Chapter 21

With sunken cheeks and her dirty-blonde hair pulled back in a ponytail, Lucia almost didn't recognize Rich's most recent ex-girlfriend.

"Cassie?" she narrowed her eyes, shocked at the state of the once-healthy woman.

"I can't believe you even remember me," she spat, her frail body shaking. "You're nothin' but a self-absorbed bitch. And it's your fucking fault he's dead. You filled his head with all this bullshit about being better. Well, I got news for ya. He didn't need to be better. He was just fucking fine the way he was. You're the reason he's lyin' cold in the ground!" Cassie's piercing screech reverberated off the tile walls.

Lucia gritted her teeth, unsure of what to do. She'd been so distracted by Cassie's anorexic appearance that another important observation had nearly escaped her notice. Ice washed through her veins when she saw it.

Held tight in her shaking right hand was a small silver pistol with a black grip.

Lucia's mouth went dry, and she struggled for words. "Cassie, what are you—"

She didn't wait for Lucia to finish her sentence. She raised the gun and pointed it at her.

Lucia weighed her options. She could try to talk Cassie down, or she could make a move. Unfortunately, she had little faith in the first option. They had never liked each other. Cassie had hated her guts because Rich refused to leave Lucia for her, and he'd still talked about Lucia after he and Cassie moved in together.

The second option presented an enormous risk. All Cassie had to do was pull the trigger, and Lucia would be dead in seconds. She guessed it was a 9mm. At least it wasn't a cannon of a .45. Some people survived 9mm gunshot wounds. Hell, one of Lucia's favorite rappers survived several shots at close range.

Each millisecond seemingly crept by in her mind, but she made the decision almost instantly after staring down the barrel of the pistol.

She leapt forward, closing the distance between them in a single stride. Grabbing Cassie's gun hand, she pushed it up and away from their bodies while stepping into the woman's space. With a rapid, fluid motion, Lucia delivered a palm heel strike to Cassie's nose, breaking it instantly.

Before she could strike again, Cassie caught Lucia's wrist and attempted a head butt. She missed, then tried to twist her gun hand out of Lucia's grip.

"Sam!" Lucia screamed as she fought with Cassie, surprised by the emaciated woman's strength. There was no answer, and it drove a spike of fear through her heart.

"You killed my man, so I killed yours, bitch!" Cassie's maniacal smile stretched across her pale face. Lucia twisted her hand free and jabbed Cassie in the left eye first, then drove her fist into the woman's throat as hard as she could.

The gun clattered to the floor without discharging as the blonde clutched her throat with both hands. Her eyes went wide as she struggled to breathe, her brain sounding alarms over the pain and sudden lack of oxygen. Lucia hooked one of her heels behind Cassie's knee, then grabbed her by the shirt and pushed her backward. Cassie fell on her back, her head slamming against the powder-blue ceramic tiles.

Lucia fell upon Cassie, straddling her torso before pounding her balled fists into the woman's face. She hit Cassie over and over again until the woman stopped moving. Lucia's muscles burned, begging for rest by the time she finally stopped. She sobbed as she forced herself to stand.

Cassie's face was red and purple, swollen and covered in cuts and scratches from the silver rings on Lucia's fingers. She groaned softly in pain, but no words escaped her battered lips.

Rage filled Lucia as Cassie's words repeated in her mind. In her blood-lust, Lucia hoped those would be the last words she ever spoke.

She didn't have time to question her ill will. Sam had been in the living room, and now he wasn't answering. If Cassie had killed him... No. She couldn't think of it.

Searching around the bloody bathroom in a daze, she spotted the gun near the toilet. Lucia lifted the pistol with trembling hands and found the safety was still on. She wondered if that explained why it hadn't accidentally discharged when it dropped to the floor.

She heard the hiss of Cassie's ragged breath and focused on her. As the adrenaline wore off, her arms sagged, and her heavy legs protested with pain as she rolled Cassie to her side so she wouldn't choke to death on her own blood. Then, she stumbled out of the bathroom and into the hall, steadying herself with her free hand against the wall.

She spotted Sam lying face down on the floor, and her heart stopped in her chest. He'd fallen between the kitchen and the dining table just outside of it. His torso was visible, but his legs were hidden behind the kitchen cabinets. The sight of his still body resting so near to the spot where they'd shared breakfast that morning paralyzed her.

Lucia forced her legs forward and raced to his side. She hesitated to touch him as she knelt beside him.

She was too terrified that he might be gone.

Before she could steel herself to check Sam's pulse, a high-pitched whimper came from the kitchen. Peeking around the corner of the cabinets, she was shocked to find a fat Rottweiler lying on the floor.

"Penny?" she asked. The dog stared up at her, tilting its dark head, but didn't move from Sam's feet. Lucia was sure it was Rich's dog. "Up, Penny. Come, now!"

The dog whined, reluctant to leave her post. Her dark eyes were worried and sad as she trotted to Lucia. She forced herself to reward the dog with pets and rubs behind her ears before commanding Penny to sit and stay. She was instantly grateful that she'd raised Rich's dog for him.

Turning back to Sam, Lucia studied his body and noticed blood in his hair but no pooling or streaks on the floor.

"Sam," she whispered, fighting back tears as she pressed her fingers to his carotid artery. Feeling one bump and then two more, she exhaled a ragged sigh of relief.

"You're going to be okay, Sam," she said louder as she grabbed her phone from the coffee table.

She checked his pulse once more as she unlocked the screen. It was strong, steady, but slow. "Stay with me, Sam!" She hoped saying his name would help him come to consciousness.

A sob escaped her throat as she dialed 9-1-1 and pressed it to her ear. With her free hand, she rubbed his back, believing her gentle touch might rouse and comfort him.

She composed herself and swiped at the tears on her cheeks when a woman's voice answered after two rings. "9-1-1, what is your emergency?"

Chapter 22

S am sat on the couch as a paramedic examined the spot on his skull where Cassie had struck him with her pistol. After the police arrived, a search found a broken basement window, likely her point of entry into the house. It looked like Cassie had been there for hours before they returned from dinner, staying hidden until she could sneak up on Sam and pistol whip him before going after Lucia.

At the kitchen table, Lucia sat with Dan for questioning. Her muscles ached, and her hands trembled after her adrenaline crashed. He asked her to walk him through the events and fill in the gaps, repeating his questions and sending her exhausted mind to the brink.

"Dan." She cut him off mid-sentence, leaning forward to lock eyes with him. "I thought he was dead," she whispered, new tears blurring her vision. "She told me..." she stopped to bite her lip so she wouldn't sob aloud. Lucia didn't want Sam to hear her breakdown. "She said she'd killed him."

She covered her mouth with one hand and lowered her head as she cried. Dan reached forward and rubbed her shoulder, trying to comfort her.

"It's okay, Luce. He's okay. He's a little concussed, but he's going to be all right. Considering there was a gun and a dog involved, he got out of this in pretty good shape." He sighed. "It's clear she came here to kill you. Once we start digging, I bet we'll find she's connected to everything. Between us, I think Cassie's behind it all, especially after what she told you."

Lucia leaned back and grabbed another tissue to dab at stray tears. "You really think so? What about that guy, Phil?"

"His name comes up clean. He's big money out of Detroit, and his dad is a principal at the top commercial real estate company in the state. He's got a hotshot legal team that's already filing complaints of harassment."

"What about his threats?"

"They aren't direct, especially without us knowing whatever it is he thinks you know. If you knew something severe enough to put him away, then you might be placed in a protection program. Have you opened any of those attachments yet?"

"I still haven't figured out the password. What about the guys in Lansing?"

"They're working on it." He sighed and dropped his pen on the table.

"So, how does Phil connect to all this?"

"You don't see it?" Dan asked.

She shook her head.

"Listen, we think he's Cassie's new boyfriend or something."

"What? Why? That doesn't sound right."

"I'll question her and ask as soon as…" he paused. "If. If she wakes up."

"Is she going to be okay?" Her heart thudded a little faster in her chest. She was torn between hating the woman and not wanting to be the reason she died.

He snorted. "Yeah, she's in intensive care. She'll probably be in the hospital for a while. You crushed her trachea. And her face… well, her face is pretty fucked up. You're lucky that we know you, that Sam is a cop, and it's already evident this was self-defense. If you'd killed her on the spot, we'd be having a very different conversation. But I still need you to prepare."

"Prepare?"

"Luce," he said in a low voice. He looked around before leaning in closer and placing a hand on her arm. "We have to be able to prove it was purely self-defense. Do you have a lawyer?"

"What do you mean? She attacked me in my home!"

"I know. Calm down. I'm on your side. But for all anyone knows, you invited her over, you two got in a fight over Rich, and this is a case of assault and battery gone too far."

"That is NOT what happened!" Lucia snapped.

"I know that, but a judge won't. Right now, we have to be ready for her word against yours. But you have something she doesn't."

"What's that?" she asked, wiping the tears from her face.

"Sam." Dan threw a thumb over his shoulder, pointing in the direction of the couch. "He's also a victim and a witness. So don't worry. Just take steps to protect yourself. Do you have a lawyer?"

"No." Her head was fuzzy, and her vision blurry. "Of course I don't have a lawyer."

"It's okay. We can figure all that out tomorrow."

"All right." Lucia resigned herself to the overwhelming helplessness settling in her bones. She wasn't afraid of scrutiny, but it still made her uneasy. She had heard too many horror stories about ambitious prosecutors who cared more about their success rates than real justice. "You really think this is all over?"

Dan tossed up his hands. "Maybe. Don't you?"

She shrugged and grabbed a fresh tissue. "I don't know. I never thought Cassie would be capable of this. And what would that guy want with a girl like her? If he's a clean, rich kid, then why her?"

"I can't say. That's why we need her to wake up. There are too many unknowns, and I'm hoping when she wakes up, her world will be too fuzzy to coordinate any lies. As for why she attacked you, sometimes people snap when they're in mourning. They're looking for the easiest target to blame, and, for Cassie, that was you."

She could only nod, averting her tired gaze toward the table.

"The investigation isn't over, but I'm pretty confident, based on what happened here, that she might be the one behind it all. The crash, the threats, the notes. Attempting to murder you. She wanted revenge for Rich's death."

"So what now?"

"There will be more questioning, more interviews. Keep your ringer on, and expect to spend plenty of time with me at the post."

"How can I get a new job with this going on? I'm supposed to start waitressing at the Tavern on Tuesday."

"Someone just tried to murder you." Dan shook his head. There was an edge to his voice, and she could hear he was losing his patience. "Get some perspective. Is your phone bill due anytime soon?"

"Two more weeks. Why?"

"Just want to make sure I can get a hold of you. What about rent?"

"Same. About two weeks."

"What's your plan for that?"

"There's not much I can do, so I guess I'm moving. Not sure where I'll go."

"Are you serious?"

She looked up and found his dark eyes were hard. "What? What do you want me to do?"

He nodded his head back toward Sam. "I don't know if you've figured it out yet, but that man loves you." His hoarse whisper was barely audible.

Heat radiated across her face.

"You have support, a place to go, and someone to help you get on your feet again. You will not be homeless." His hard eyes softened when he looked at Penny. "One last thing. You said you know this dog?"

"I do," Lucia said as she reached down to pet Penny, who now lay quietly on the floor beside her. "She was Rich's dog. I helped raise her from a puppy."

"You wanna keep her?"

"Yes, please," she replied quickly, holding his gaze. "She didn't hurt anyone. She didn't even growl at me. It looked like she was protecting Sam."

"I love Rots. I grew up with one."

"So I can really keep her?"

"I don't see why not since she didn't attack anyone. I mean, I have to check and make sure there's nothing we need to do officially."

"I think the guarding behavior was from her training. Cassie probably cued her to guard Sam, even though she might have been trying for something... worse."

"I haven't had to deal with anything like this in an investigation yet. For now, she's yours. Be prepared in case I'm ordered to take her, okay?"

"Thank you, Dan."

"Maybe it will help to have a mean-looking dog around."

Lucia shook her head and smiled at Penny. "This girl ain't scary. She's nothing but a sleepy couch potato."

Catching movement in her periphery, she turned to find Sam staring at her, still holding an ice pack to his head. She put on her most sympathetic smile. Although he briefly returned one, it didn't reach his eyes.

She hoped now that Cassie was in custody, this would be the end of all the madness. If it wasn't, she didn't know how much longer Sam would stick around.

Chapter 23

Dan needed more time to collect evidence from Lucia's house, so he asked her to pack some clothes and stay with Sam until his team finished. She packed as much as possible since she'd be ending her lease soon anyway.

"Are you sure about keeping the dog?" Sam shot a wary glance at Penny laying perfectly still on his kitchen floor. Only her eyes moved, tracking his every action. It clearly put him on edge.

"Yes, Sam. She's a good dog. She's protective, but she's also very obedient. I don't think she would have hurt you. It looked like she was guarding you."

"If you say so." He rubbed the back of his neck.

"Sam," she said, reaching out and taking his hand. "She's fine. I like you, so she'll like you too." Lucia gave him a wink, but he seemed unconvinced.

He grumbled under his breath as he retreated to the kitchen for a glass of water. "Why do you want to keep your dead ex's dog?"

The unexpected question stabbed at her insides. It was still hard to think of Rich as being dead. It hadn't quite cemented into her worldview yet. And she didn't feel like keeping the dog was some extension of any desire to hold on to Rich.

Lucia loved that dog. She was the one who had raised Penny and worked through her obedience training. The young Rottie became another point of contention between her and Rich over his laziness and inability to follow through on commitments.

"It's not about him," she said softly, her gaze drifting. Silence fell between them only briefly before her voice returned with strength, and she met his eyes again. "I raised this dog, Sam. His dad paid for Penny, but I raised her, I trained her, and I took money out of my own pocket for help when I couldn't train her alone. Really, she's always been my dog. But my landlord doesn't allow animals, so I couldn't keep her with me."

Lucia felt Sam searching her eyes for some shred of deceit, but she held her ground.

"Your time off is ending soon. Having her around would make me feel safer."

He shook his head and turned his attention to his phone. He sat back down on the couch in his high-ceilinged, open living room. His spacious, new-build home was situated on twenty-five acres of mostly wooded land. It featured more bedrooms and bathrooms than she thought necessary, even for a family. Its open floor plan and large windows hinted at big money, but it was all purchased with money he'd earned during his deployments and through carefully investing his military pay. He had exceptional financial savvy.

Lucia crouched next to Penny and pet her back. The dog whined and stared at the door.

"I need to take her for a walk."

"Okay." Sam sighed. "Let me get my shoes on."

"No, it's okay." Lucia waved at him to sit down as she dug into one of her boxes near the front door.

"Are you sure?"

"Dan said he thinks it's over, right?" she asked as she pulled a leash from the box and clipped it onto Penny's collar.

Sam relaxed in his recliner. "That's what he said."

"Then I think I can walk a dog alone. Let's call it a test walk." She headed for the sliding glass doors that opened to the deck at the back of the house.

Lucia's heart ached as she crossed the threshold and closed the door behind her.

As she walked farther away from the back deck, she embraced an undeniable truth about her past. When things got tough, she ran. She hid. She avoided confrontation, and she avoided facing her problems. Had she ever stared down the things she feared most? It wasn't even the physically frightening parts of life that made her run; it was the emotional parts.

Like accepting Rich's proposal. She'd been too frightened to tell him no, afraid that her rejection would send him off the deep end. Instead of confronting the truth head-on and speaking up for herself—saying out loud that she didn't want to marry him—she hid it behind a mask of conditions and excuses.

Conditions for their marriage included a big wedding, an expensive dress, and transporting all her friends and family. Liam was more than happy to foot most of the bill, and Rich's "job" made him believe he could afford to pay the rest.

Then she introduced the condition that they had to coordinate with her brother Robert so he could attend. Before she knew it, Rich had made friends with him online. Being an easy-going person, Robert gave his blessing and said he would make sure he was there, regardless of the date.

Finally, Lucia pulled the card she never wanted to pull. She told him she needed to have her parents there. And for that to take place, she would need to reconcile with them. For too many years, she'd avoided them out of shame for her relationship. Reconciliation, being fully on her own shoulders, would never happen before she was ready.

This final condition served its purpose of keeping her out of a marriage she had no intention of actually going through with. Unfortunately, it also kept her from reconnecting with her parents. Although Rich, Liam, and

Robert all pushed, she would come up with every excuse to avoid trying to make things right with them.

Now she was hiding from her parents and from Sam. Instead of staying inside and working through whatever was bothering him, she had opted to walk the dog. She didn't know if she was ready to begin confronting the emotional conflicts.

She fled from the true depth of her feelings for Sam and her fear of losing him. It wasn't hard to want to hide since she was still uneasy about the situation with Cassie. When Dan said he thought she orchestrated all of it, Lucia should have felt relief because Cassie would now be in custody. But relief had not come.

Penny barked, breaking Lucia from her thoughts, then bolted into the darkness beyond the ambient light from the yard lamps. She tore the leash from Lucia's hand.

"Come on, Penny," Lucia grumbled, jogging after the dog. She glanced back to find they'd walked farther than she intended.

She now stood at the edge of the woods. Ominous shadows stood like sentinels beneath an outline of thick forest canopy, warning of nocturnal creatures, danger, and the unknown. Still, it would have been easier for her to wander the pitch-black forest than to go back to the house and talk through the hard things with Sam. Now that she acknowledged her problem, she also knew she had to do something about it.

She loved Sam, and running from him would only push him away. If that happened, she would regret it for the rest of her life.

After calling into the darkness three times, Penny finally came loping back with a gnarled stick in her mouth.

"Are you finished, girl?"

Penny dropped the stick and gave Lucia a canine smile that gleamed in the ambient light as she trotted to Lucia's side. She picked up the leash and turned back toward the house, steeling herself for whatever words needed to be said when she returned to Sam.

Chapter 24

Sunday, September 2nd

When Lucia walked in through the sliding glass doors into the living room, Sam stood up from his recliner. The guilt from asking about the dog being her ex's had been ransacking his brain ever since he'd asked it. Not that he believed it was an unjustifiable question, but because of the hurt that had filled her eyes. There was so much he didn't know because he didn't like to hear her talk about her old life with that jerk.

Once, when Lucia was drinking, she admitted Rich had hit her on several occasions. Sam had been furious with Rich and furious with her for staying with him for so long. His aversion to hearing about her life with Rich meant Sam was missing out on her history. If he could learn to relax a little, he would learn more about the woman he loved.

"I'm sorry," he said as Lucia hung the dog's leash on a hook next to the front door.

After a long silence, she turned to him. "It's okay. You didn't know."

"I didn't mean to make you feel bad." He swallowed all the other things he wanted to say but couldn't yet.

"I don't want you to feel threatened." She rubbed her palms against her jeans. "He's dead, Sam. And I've been living as if he didn't even exist for a long time now."

Sam was speechless, stunned by her directness.

"He never held a candle to you. I didn't love him the way I love you."

Just when he thought he couldn't be more shocked, she surprised him again by finally saying the one word that had been for so long reserved.

"That's right." She threw her hands up in the air for effect. "I said it. I love you. I've never loved anyone like this. What we have is real. There aren't any conditions, there isn't any placation. There's no requirement that I have to say it to make you happy. You're the only person I could ever be real with. And you're the only one I've ever wanted to stay with."

Words escaped him, so he closed the distance between them in a single step and drew her into a passionate kiss.

She pulled back from him. "Are we okay?"

Sam whispered in her ear. "I love you, too."

The next morning found the lovers entangled, reluctant to rise after an emotional evening and the love-making that followed. Lucia buried her face in a soft pillow as Sam softly traced his fingers along her back.

"You're so beautiful," he said between kisses on her bare shoulders.

She grinned, her face still stuffed in her pillow.

"I can't stay in bed anymore." He pushed himself up. "I'm going to start the coffee. You want anything special for breakfast?"

Lucia cast her fuzzy gaze and a satisfied smile his way. "I can't even think of eating right now."

"All right. Bacon, eggs, and toast. Got it." He stood from the bed though she pulled at his arm.

"No, stay," she groaned.

"Get your sweet ass up." His voice was playful and teasing. He quickly dressed and disappeared from the room.

She sank back into her pillow to savor rest for a little while longer, pulling the covers over her head. A few minutes had passed when the aroma of coffee and bacon crept through the air. When the smell of food hit her, her stomach growled, so she pushed herself out of bed. Her appetite provided her the motivation to pull on cotton shorts and a tank top.

She sat at the kitchen table and checked her phone while she waited for Sam to finish cooking.

"You spoil me." She beamed a smile at him as he placed a mug of hot coffee in front of her. "I'm going to have to start cooking so you don't think I'm only with you for the food."

Sam's bright laughter broke the air, adding to the warmth of their morning together as he set their plates on the table and sat down.

"I'm used to taking care of people." He sipped his coffee. "I actually hate living alone."

"That is the oddest thing I've ever heard anyone say." She chuckled as she wrapped her hands around the hot mug.

"I got used to it in the Army. I always thought I couldn't wait to get out and live alone so I'd only have to take care of myself. But now that I'm out... I guess I miss it." He looked down at his plate for a moment before picking up his fork. "Let's eat."

Lucia devoured her bacon before attacking the rest of her food.

"What do you wanna do today?" He asked between bites.

Lucia chewed a forkful of eggs to blunt her hunger before answering. "I don't know. I have to call Amanda and see if I really have the job." She spooned some eggs on top of her toast.

"Are you okay?"

"You mean after... after last night?" Her gaze remained on her food as she spoke.

"Yeah. After that."

She swallowed and set her toast down to grab her coffee mug, hugging the warm ceramic with her fingers. "I was so scared that I was going to lose you." Her voice was barely above a whisper. "Sam, I wanted so badly to end her when she told me that she…" She let her words trail off, sipping coffee instead of finishing her sentence.

"You can't be blamed for that." He nodded in understanding. He leaned back in his chair and crossed his arms over his broad chest. "Eventually, the intensity of those feelings fades. And if it happens again, I bet you'll have a lot more mental clarity next time."

Lucia shuddered at the vision burned into her brain of Cassie's swollen face and her own hands covered in the woman's blood. She grabbed the coffee pot and refilled both their cups.

"Thank you. For listening, I mean."

"Of course." He reached up to squeeze her hand as she came back to the table. He smiled before sipping his coffee and reading something on his phone.

Lucia picked up hers and found a message from Liam on her lock screen.

I may have a buyer for Tess, but she needs a few rides before they come out. I know things are tough right now, so I'll give you 20% of the sale if you help me get her ready.

Her heart lifted, and she turned to Sam. "I got a training job!"

"A what?"

"Liam needs someone to refresh one of his horses before he brings out buyers."

"Oh." He looked confused. "And you do that?"

She texted Liam back before answering.

Yes, that would be amazing! Thank you! When will the buyer come? Can I get started today?

"Yep," she said, returning her attention to Sam. "I used to work for Liam as a trainer. Part of the farm's income comes from breeding, boarding, and training horses. I also made money in extreme riding competitions. Liam always let me keep the pot because more wins meant more sales, training contracts, and stud fees."

"Okay," Sam responded slowly. "I'm sure this isn't as easy as it sounds."

"The horse he wants help with was raised on the farm and trained by me." She shrugged and glanced at her phone, anxious for a response. "And when she goes to her new home and the money transfers to Liam, he'll pay me twenty percent."

"How much will she sell for?"

"With her bloodlines? Anywhere from twelve- to fifteen-thousand, depending on how they negotiate."

"No shit?"

"No shit," she said, smiling ear-to-ear. Then, with a sense of gravity welling in her chest, she said, "I really need this."

"I know," he said softly. "Just remember, you're safe here with me. You don't have to try to do it all on your own."

Lucia cringed inwardly, even though she knew he was right. Day by day, she would work harder to accept this new step with Sam and stop running from his helping hand.

"I know." She leaned over the table and kissed him. "But it'll feel amazing to make a good chunk of cash on my own."

He nodded. "So, what's next? What is 'refreshing?'"

"Basically, she hasn't been ridden much for a few months, so I need to ride her and go through everything she was trained on to ensure she's well behaved. I texted him back that I'm ready to start today."

"Do you need anything from me?"

"Could you watch Penny?" she asked, hopeful.

"Yeah, no problem. We could probably use some time to bond anyway. Right, girl?"

Penny lifted her soft brown head and stared at him happily from her cozy spot on the rug in the living room and wagged her tail.

"Thank you," she said as her phone buzzed. She looked down and read the message.

We don't have a date set. Maybe in a week or two. You're welcome to come as soon as you can.

"All right, hon. He said I could start. I'm heading to the farm." She kissed him goodbye and bounded out the door, excited about starting this new chapter of her life.

Of course, that could only happen if the last chapter was closed.

A dark inner voice whispered that her past wasn't through with her yet.

Chapter 25

Trepidation filled Lucia as she pulled her beat-up, faded black sedan in front of the grand white stables. Green trim and shutters around the stable's office window complemented the sharp traditional lines of the structure. It was a dream barn that any equestrian could fall in love with. Four years later, it still looked as magnificent as it had when she'd first come to the farm.

Dust and the scent of horses mingled in the air, greeting Lucia as she exited the car. A nostalgic comfort welled up within her. As she walked up to the stables, she glanced beneath the sign reading "Pine River Equestrian Center" and admired a pristine flower bed filled with yellow roses in full bloom.

Where you planted the roses...

Lucia could hear Rich's voice speaking the words she had read in his many cryptic emails. She paused to study them but didn't notice anything out of place. The roses were mature now, having grown from small stalks into bushes since she'd planted them. What was it about the roses that he wanted her to know? She decided to keep an eye out in the barn for anything Rich might have left for her.

After meandering through the barn for a few minutes, Lucia found nothing. Two aisles split the barn, both flanked by rows of box stalls on each side. The main barn could hold forty horses, but Lucia found it was mostly empty. Operations had apparently slowed since she'd left. Not that she was the best trainer or barn manager in the area, far from it, but they'd always stayed full before. Liam had let her run the equestrian side of the farm after she moved in with Rich and had shown potential. He liked to focus on the crops.

Sunlight blinded Lucia as she left the shadows of the main barn and continued to a smaller structure behind it, which had been the original barn on the property. It had eight stalls, and each big box stall led to its own small paddock, allowing the horses to run at will. Thundering hooves resounded through the air and vibrated the ground.

She watched as Tess bolted toward her from the far end of the paddock, her head held high and ears pitched forward. The horse's bright grulla coat gleamed in the sunlight as her cantering hooves flung sand and dust into the hot, still air. Lucia met her in the stall and wrapped her arms around the horse's dusty neck in a tight hug. Tess's wide nostrils sniffed at Lucia's clothing before she snorted and shook her large head, flinging the long tendrils of her black mane.

Although the mare's coat was mostly clean, Lucia took the time to carefully groom her anyway. It was a bonding activity and necessary since so much time had passed since her last visit. If she could get a job training horses full time, it would be a dream come true. Unfortunately, unlike other trainers, she didn't have a high-priced education or an Olympian background to add any serious credentials to her resume. Liam was the only one who gave her a chance to manage a farm, and though she had done it well, she highly doubted anyone else would offer her the opportunity again.

Once she had Tess saddled up for a trail ride, Lucia led her to the practice arena and walked beside the horse as they navigated various obstacles, such as small jumps and barrels. The mare was excited but not nervous, much to Lucia's relief. Nervous horses were often easily spooked by objects they were already well-acquainted with, especially if the horse hadn't been worked in a while.

Aside from the thump of Tess's hooves through the soft sand and the squeaking of the leather saddle as she walked, the only other sounds came from the birds in the trees nearby, chirping angrily at some disturbance. Lucia guessed it was one of the barn's mama cats she'd seen stalk off while she was saddling up.

"All right, girl," she said, halting Tess. She picked up the slack in the reins and mounted. She kept her spine straight as she pressed her foot into the stirrup and gently lifted her leg over before lowering herself into the seat. Tess, to her surprise, did not start moving immediately as many rusty horses did. Instead, the mare waited for Lucia's cue. After a few more moments spent testing the horse's patience and being satisfied with the results, she cued Tess to walk.

As Lucia relaxed, she savored the familiar, warm sensation that overcame her body and mind. It felt good to be back in the saddle again, and her cheeks ached with an uncontrollable smile. In less than a half-hour's time, she felt happier and more fulfilled than she had in the past year. All the stress from the incident at the gas station, the threats, and the confrontation with Cassie melted away as she cued Tess into a slow, controlled canter along the perimeter of the arena.

The practice of riding was especially soothing. In the saddle, she felt alive, like she was in tune with the universe and the world around her. It was the place where her mind became relaxed and at peace enough to think clearly about everything happening in her life.

While Lucia refreshed the horse on her training and first-level dressage movements, she thought of Sam. Her mind untangled everything she'd been struggling with, but especially her relationship. Sam wasn't Rich, but she apparently needed more than just time to heal. She also needed to face everything that happened rather than pushing it away, as she acknowledged the previous evening.

It was time to stop running and hiding from everything, even the things that scared her.

That was as true for the present as it was for the past. She didn't feel secure yet that the threats would stop now that Cassie was in custody and incapacitated in the hospital.

Considering the fact Cassie had come to her house to kill her, Lucia realized that staying quiet hadn't resulted in staying safe, despite what the note left on her car had suggested.

Her muscles still ached from the fight, but Lucia was all the more indignant because of it. Cassie didn't get to win. Lucia would not permit that awful woman to stall her life or stop her from doing the things she loved.

Admittedly, it had been easy to stay quiet before since she didn't know exactly what she was supposed to be quiet about. Despite all that, Cassie had still come after her, and Sam could have been killed.

What did being quiet give Lucia except the sickening feeling of cowardice?

Lucia noticed Tess beginning to sweat and cued her to halt near the gate before dismounting. Untying the girth, she heaved the saddle onto the fence but left the pad on Tess's back to help her cool her down slowly.

They'd done enough work for today. Although Tess had been well-groomed, she was clearly out of condition since only twenty minutes of riding had left her sweaty and panting. Lucia walked her around the arena a few times until the mare's pulse rate had lowered and her breathing had calmed.

After she groomed Tess and returned the mare to her pasture, she put away the saddle and decided it was time to take action. She would start facing her past instead of running from it. There was no better place to begin than here, where she had planted the roses all those years ago.

Chapter 26

Lucia exited the main barn and turned to face the sign and the narrow flower bed beneath it. Tall yellow rose bushes sprouted from the dark soil, pushing aside the red mulch from the bases of their thorny stems. The flower bed ran parallel to the steel siding, a rectangle made of two rows of traditional red bricks to outline and protect it from wandering footsteps.

She realized she'd been holding her breath while she surveyed the flowers. A swimming feeling in her stomach sparked nausea as she stared at them. Her conscious mind tried to pull whatever thread was being shaken by her subconscious.

"I planted the roses at the barn," she murmured to herself. But she had checked the barn and nothing was out of place. Every nook and cranny she knew of was empty, save for startled spiders.

Crouching, Lucia leaned over the flower bed and slid her fingers beneath the mulch, pressing down into the soft, moist soil. After exploring as far she could reach without getting a face full of thorns, she sighed because nothing felt unusual. She didn't discount the possibility that something was buried a little deeper.

She blew a slow breath out, frustrated by the cryptic clues.

Something tickled the back of her hand. When she looked down, she breathed an expletive when she spotted a beetle crawling over it. Instinctively, she jerked backward and lost her balance. Grasping for anything, she grabbed onto the bricks outlining the flower bed for support. They were strong and solid enough that she was able to immediately right herself.

Except for one brick.

One of them had wiggled loose, scraping and thudding against its neighbors when she had grasped at them. Putting her knees on the ground for stability, Lucia leaned over and studied the backside of the decorative barrier. A single inner brick in the middle was partly hanging out.

She tugged at the edges of it with the tips of her fingers, and it came free without a struggle. She couldn't see anything immediately. Reaching her hand inside the shallow hole left by the brick, she discovered a plastic package taped inside.

Her fingers picked at the thick tape, struggling because the hole was too small to put her other hand inside for leverage. With a tug, it finally came loose, and she nearly lost her balance again. It was a zippered, plastic freezer bag folded around a tiny object. The duct tape attached to it looked new. She guessed Rich had sent her the first email with the hint about the roses just before or immediately after he hid the package.

She gently pried the tape off the package so she could unroll it. Inside, the rectangular object was rolled up in several layers of paper towels. For a moment, she studied it, worrying over what Rich had hidden.

The sound of a diesel engine broke her focus, and she quickly crammed the bag into her jeans pocket before replacing the loose brick. As a truck door slammed, she fixed the soil of the rose bed. Footsteps crunched along the gravel path behind her.

"Lucia?" Liam asked, his steps slowing.

She put on a smile and turned her gaze toward him, wiping her dirt-covered hands on her jeans as she rose and hoping he wouldn't ask about the conspicuous bulge in her pocket.

"Hey, Liam." She gave him a quick hug before pulling back and crossing her arms over her chest. She tried her best to play it cool, but she nearly trembled with excitement from the find.

"Is everything okay?" He raised an eyebrow as he surveyed her clothes.

She looked down and realized that her hands and jeans were covered in the black soil and red mulch of the flower bed.

"Oh, yes. I just saw some weeds and thought it would be a shame to leave them. The roses are so pretty this year. I'm surprised they're still growing," she said, honestly.

A sad smile lifted the corners of his mouth. "You wouldn't believe it, but Rich tended to them himself this spring. He spent his own money and everything, even asked me if I remembered exactly what kind you had planted here."

Spikes of guilt twisted in her chest. "Wow, that's..." She wondered if Rich had needed an excuse to spend time at the flower bed so he could hide the package or if he had actually cared about what she left behind. Or both.

"Don't worry, Lucia. It's okay. I know what happened with Cassie and what she said. It's all bullshit. She's so drugged up that her head is permanently entrenched in her ass."

Lucia was shocked. Liam was the kind of God-fearing, love-thy-neighbor, righteous person that everyone else could only pretend to be. She had never once heard him cuss in the four years she had known him.

"I'm sorry—" he started.

"No. It's okay." She offered a sly smile. "I never expected to hear you say something so sharp-tongued."

He had been like a father to her. Kind, patient, and loving, but always in a fatherly way. One of her reasons for staying with Rich for so long was her attachment to Liam.

"I wish things could have been different." He forced a smile, but his eyes squinted against the agony. He turned and walked toward the house. "I'll see you later, Luce." He waved without looking back.

"Goodbye," she said, barely loud enough for him to hear. Pain wrenched her insides. They would forever be tied through the connection of his only son, the child he had to bury too soon.

Her eyes stinging, Lucia made sure the area around the flower bed was cleaned up and the mulch resettled before she headed back to her car. Dark clouds swallowed the golden sun and lightning raced across the sky as she turned the key in the ignition and took one last look at the main barn.

It was time to find out what Rich had wanted her to know.

Chapter 27

When Lucia returned, she found Sam chopping vegetables and a fresh pot of coffee brewing, filling the air with dark, fragrant scents. She was grateful for their shared love of caffeine as she breathed deeply.

"Hey." She greeted him with a kiss on the cheek before leaning against the counter.

He turned to smile at her. "Want lunch?"

"I'm starving," she admitted. Smelling the fresh peppers he was slicing made her stomach rumble.

"So, how'd it go with the horse? Did she dump you?" he teased while he chopped veggies to make one of his complex but delicious veggie-full salads. It was the perfect lunch on sweltering August days. Especially when Lucia's body was vibrating with excitement, too tense to handle a heavy meal.

Lucia dug in her pocket and pulled out the freezer bag, holding it up for him to see.

"What's that?"

She gently placed it on the counter before answering.

"Remember the clues I thought Rich was leaving me in those emails?"

"Yes," Sam said tentatively, pausing his meal prep to face her. He crossed his arms over his chest, his smile fading.

"Easy, tiger." She shook her head in warning. Picking up the bag again, she passed it to him. "I looked all over the barn because I thought the hint about where I planted the roses meant whatever I was supposed to look for would be there. But it was literally in the flower bed, behind a loose brick."

Sam glanced from her to the bag and back again. "This was hidden in the flower bed?"

Lucia nodded and reached past him for a slice of green pepper to munch on.

"What is it?"

She shrugged. "I don't know. I haven't had a chance to look yet."

"Well—"

"Tell you what," she said after finishing her pepper slice and grabbing a handful of cherry tomatoes. "You finish lunch, and I'll try to figure it out."

"Okay. You don't want to call Dan?"

"Not until I know what to tell him."

"Just text him. Now," Sam said firmly as he returned to the cutting board.

Lucia pretended not to hear him as she sat at the table. She pulled the object from the bag and unwrapped it. It was like taking apart a Russian nesting doll, but instead of dolls, she was unwrapping layer upon layer of store-brand paper towels until, finally, the object was exposed.

A tiny black thumb drive sat on Sam's dining table.

"Shit." She immediately thought of the password-protected attachments in her email. She brought her laptop to the dining table, losing energy as she worried about the thumb drive being encrypted too.

She plugged the drive into her computer and waited for it to load. Her thoughts drifted to the yellow roses. There were implications in Rich's care of the roses, but more so in the cryptic messages and mysterious package he had hidden. He was a man cast as a lost cause, irredeemable. Before he died, he had sought to leave something else behind. Perhaps to make up for all the years of delivering poison, but he was too late to turn his life around. The speculation was too heavy to bear. Lucia's tangled emotions welled up within her, threatening to swallow her mind.

The final, loud spitting of the coffee maker as it choked forth the last of the hot water through the filter snapped her out of her dark thoughts. She poured herself a cup, taking a careful sip before setting it on the tabletop and reseating herself.

"Anything yet?" Sam's voice broke through the still air, easing her tension a little.

"My crappy computer takes forever to load these things."

"I could get you a new one," Sam offered as he placed their plates and silverware on the table and took the seat next to her.

Lucia gave him a side-eyed look as she pushed the laptop aside so she could eat while the thumb drive folder opened.

"You know better. I can't take your money like that. Besides, I should receive a pretty nice check from helping get Tess ready for sale."

Sam shrugged and started eating.

"But I apprec—" Lucia stopped as the folder for the thumb drive finally popped open on her screen.

There were more little folder icons than she could count. Their titles were dates ranging from eleven months earlier to within a week of Rich's disappearance in June.

Sam glanced at the screen. "It looks like he was stockpiling data. What do you think is in the folders?"

"I can't imagine. Apology notes? Apology videos? All the emails I haven't read? Notes with the names of the people he thought were following him? I don't know what to expect at this point. Maybe he knew Cassie was out for my blood." Shrugging, she double-tapped her touchpad and tried to open the most recent one.

A dialogue box popped up and prompted her for a password.

"Dammit." Lucia sighed, then picked up her fork and stabbed at her salad.

"Let's figure this out together for a change," Sam offered. "Was there anything special you two did? Some really significant place or memory?"

"I've been trying to think of things like that. Everything was always about him and what he wanted. I've tried variations on the farm name since we lived there. I've tried his mom's name, then all his family members together and individually, about a hundred ways."

Sam was quiet for a minute, and Lucia appreciated the time to think it over. She hoped the same password would work for the folders and the email attachments if she could figure it out. Perhaps Lansing had already broken through the encryption.

"What's his favorite number?" He scraped the last of his romaine and avocado from his plate and chewed it as he took over the laptop.

"Seven, I think."

"Let me read the emails."

"Ugh." She didn't imagine it would be healthy for their relationship, given his tendency to be jealous. "Are you sure?"

"Yes, I'll put on my cop-hat and try to be objective, okay?"

"If you say so." She opened her browser and clicked on the tab that showed all of Rich's messages. "But I'm telling you, I've gone through them more times than I'd like, and I still can't figure it out."

"That's okay," Sam said, gesturing as if he placed an invisible hat on his head. Then he tipped it to her. "Let the police handle this, ma'am."

She laughed at the exaggerated bass of his voice and the mock-heroic expression on his face. Leaning toward him, she slid her arms around his neck and played along. "Oh, officer, please save me! Rescue me from all the emails and paperwork!"

To Lucia's delight, Sam's deep laughter resounded, and he hugged her and kissed her neck. She kissed him on his cheek before pulling back and giving him space.

"It's all yours then, trooper." She couldn't control her smile as she pushed the laptop toward him. If he hadn't joked around and eased the tension, she didn't know if she would have let him read the awkward and often confusing emails from her ex.

She finished her salad, trying not to worry about what Sam was reading. Or what he was thinking.

Chapter 28

S am tried to detach from the part of himself that loved Lucia as he read the emails, but he was relieved to find the recent ones were just as cryptic and bizarre as she had described. Probably more than she'd let on. Thankfully, there wasn't actually much to spark his jealousy.

As he examined the messages, he found Rich's sign-off was the only constant that stood out from the ever-evolving and chaotic rants. It was mundane, sticking out like a sore thumb amid the paranoid and enigmatic ramblings.

Remember: I Miss You.

To an outside observer, it might appear as if Rich was simply trying to convince her to come back, but Sam had learned enough about him to know better. Her ex was the kind of guy that wanted to make a woman think that she needed him rather than the other way around. He wasn't sentimental, gushy, or romantic. Instead, he hid any emotion beneath a protective barrier of aggression and apathy, bastioned by his narcissism.

The oldest emails, where Rich was trying to win Lucia back, did not have attachments and did not sign off with "Remember: I Miss You." In fact, they didn't sign off with anything. Rich wasn't the most accurate writer, mostly forgoing punctuation and capitalization.

Was it too obvious? Perhaps, but it was worth a try, and he didn't need to bother Lucia over it unless it worked. Sam wanted her to relax and trust him.

Opening Lucia's downloads folder, he scrolled through the attachments. He double-clicked the most recent file, dated only a few days before Rich's father reported him missing, and the password prompt box popped up on the screen.

With careful consideration, he began entering possible passwords based on his hunch.

The first, second, and third guesses at the password failed, but on his fourth attempt, the folder opened.

By the thumbnails alone, he knew this was far more serious than a guy trying to win his ex-girlfriend back. Sam's skin tingled.

"Lucia."

"Hmm?"

"Look at this." He repositioned the laptop so she could see the screen.

"You got it open?!" she exclaimed, her dark eyes wide with surprise.

"The password was in the sign-off. 'I miss you' without spaces and the number seven. He really did try to make it easy for you to figure out."

"Holy shit, you're a genius!"

"Probably not, but thanks anyway. See? At least in this first folder, it's not pictures of you or him. It doesn't look like it has anything to do with you."

He watched as she squinted at the thumbnails and the color drained from her face. "I need to see," she said, locking eyes with him.

Sam nodded, unwilling to deny her that. He set a fifteen-minute timer on his phone. When it went off, he would have to call Dan so the detective could send the password to the guys in Lansing.

Dan would also need to review these folders.

Before he saw them, they needed to satisfy their curiosity. He couldn't look away entirely. Sam opened the first picture in gallery mode so he could simply tap the directional keys to view each of the pictures in the folder.

When it loaded and filled the screen, Sam's blood ran cold, and Lucia gasped.

"Oh my God." She rested a hand on his arm and trembled beside him.

In the photo, a man knelt with his hands behind his head. Two men stood at his back with pistols. There was no emotion visible in their pale faces. Sunglasses perched on top of their heads, the camera had captured both gunmen's unobscured–and identifiable–faces, as well as that of the cowering victim.

"Shit." Sam shook his head. "Where did you say you found this?"

"Hidden in the bricks around the rose garden, in front of Liam's barn. I saw Liam just after I found it, but I'm sure he didn't see me take it. He mentioned that Rich spent a lot of time tending to the roses this spring. I think he was preparing for this."

He studied her, aching inside as he recognized the horror on her face.

"You don't have to look anymore," he said, taking her hand in his and rubbing her knuckles gently with his thumb.

"No. I need to see." She pulled her hand away, then interlaced her fingers together and held them against her chest.

"Okay." He nodded and tapped the right-arrow key.

The next picture was the first in a series of six taken of a young girl, probably in her early teens, being raped and beaten by several men. His stomach turned as he flicked through the pictures, but he willed himself to stay strong for Lucia.

"I'm going to be sick." She rose and left the table. Sam followed her into the kitchen and wrapped his arms around her.

"I'm sorry," he murmured into her hair. "I shouldn't have let you see."

Lucia leaned back. "I'm not fragile. I just... I've never seen anything like this. Is this really what Rich was involved in?"

Pain and anger mingled in her eyes as she looked to him for answers.

"It's pretty clear." He squeezed her hand. "I want to go through as many as possible. As many as I can stomach, anyway."

"Why? Why not let Dan do it?"

"Do you really think Cassie is behind any of this?"

Lucia hesitated, then she shook her head.

"Neither do I. I'm looking for any familiar faces, anyone we might recognize, that we might have met before."

Like Phil.

He sat down at the table again with a fresh cup of coffee and began flipping through the pictures, examining each closely for any people, buildings, or landmarks he may recognize. Lucia sat beside him but often turned her face away. When he did glance at her, there were tears in her eyes. All the pictures were difficult to look at, often featuring executions, rapes, and vicious beatings. A few files were videos, but he knew she couldn't bear to watch or hear them. He'd save those for the guys in Lansing.

Most interesting to Sam was the sheer number of photos that clearly captured faces. He flicked through all eighty-three pictures in the current folder, each time-stamped and taken in May of that year, about three months earlier. He hoped more information was embedded in the raw files.

While a handful of the photos were too dark to make anything out, the vast majority clearly showed situations ranging from drug and weapons trafficking to gang rape and murder. There was also evidence of sex trafficking and possible kidnapping. Some of the victims looked vaguely familiar, and he was sure at least a few matches could be made if they were cross-referenced against missing persons databases like NAMUS.

Something odd about the angle of the photos piqued his interest. The pictures were often taken from about the height of the torso or the waist and were rarely centered or neatly aligned.

"Oh, shit," Sam said as the epiphany dawned on him.

"What?"

"I think he took these pictures with a hidden camera." His confidence in the idea didn't fully sink in until he spoke the words aloud.

His timer hadn't ended, but he couldn't wait any longer. He dialed Dan's number.

"Hey, man. I may have made a huge break here. Can you find out whether or not Richard Thompson was somebody's Confidential Informant? Yeah, seriously. Then come over to my place. You have to see this."

Chapter 29

Lucia wrapped one arm over her stomach while the other trembled at her mouth as she paced back and forth through Sam's kitchen. She knew the images she had seen could never be burned from her mind's eye. The pictures of torment and death were now ingrained in her memory. They would haunt her when she closed her eyes, but they would also be there every time she had to decide whether to speak up.

Saying nothing or refusing to aid the investigation would only silence the victims. She knew she needed to be strong to help bring some degree of justice for what they and their families had endured.

"I'm sorry you saw this, Luce," Sam said again as he leaned against the counter and placed a warm hand on her shoulder. She flinched away.

"Sorry. Just..." She struggled for the right words. "I'm rattled. I can't believe he was involved in all this."

"Sometimes people start small, and before they realize it, they've fallen too far down the rabbit hole. Basically, they feel trapped doing things they never imagined they were capable of."

Penny barked and trotted toward the door near the kitchen, nearly tripping Sam as he answered it. A knock sounded, then a voice.

"Open up! Police," Dan called out. He could never resist an opportunity to tease them.

Sam opened the door, and the men greeted each other.

"How are you?" Dan asked Lucia as he stepped inside, his eyes filled with concern.

"I'm okay." It felt like a lie, but she didn't want anyone to worry about her right now. He needed to focus on the people in the photos. "Would you like a cup of coffee? It's fresh."

"Sure, that'd be great."

Sam led him to the table and brought the computer out of its automatic sleep.

"So, what's going on?" Dan pressed, clearly eager to hear why they'd asked him to come.

"We figured out the password." Sam watched as Lucia set Dan's cup in front of him.

"Sam figured it out," she corrected him. "Apparently, I was too close to see it. And now I feel like an idiot."

"You're not an idiot," Dan chided her. "The password?"

"The one we needed to open the attachments in the emails. And," he pointed to the thumb drive lying next to the computer, "the encrypted folders on that thumb drive."

"What thumb drive?" Dan's dark eyes were stern, flickering between Sam, Lucia, and the thumb drive.

"I found it this morning," Lucia said as she set Sam's mug in front of him and took a seat on the other side of Dan. "I went to Rich's dad's farm because he's paying me to help with a horse. I told you about what I thought were hints in the emails. One of them referenced where I planted roses."

"Right." He nodded, unblinking.

"I planted roses in front of the main barn years ago. So I checked inside the barn, but there was nothing. But then I looked around the flower bed, and I found it hidden behind a loose brick. You wouldn't see unless you knew exactly where to look."

"Then how did you find it?" Dan raised an eyebrow as he sipped his coffee.

"Honestly?" Lucia felt her cheeks warming. "I was crouching down to peek in the rose bed when a beetle crawled on me. I freaked out and lost my balance. When I grabbed the bricks, one came loose." She glanced away, shaking her head.

"What's on it?" Dan jerked his head toward the drive.

Sam double-clicked the folder they had already reviewed and opened the pictures in gallery mode. The first picture, featuring the man on his knees with the two men pointing pistols at the back of his head, expanded on the screen.

"What the hell?" Dan muttered, his eyes filling with horror as he examined the photo.

"Nearly all the pictures have faces," Sam said. "Most are easily recognizable. But this stuff is dark as hell, Dan. Everything illicit activity you can think of is on here."

"How many?" Dan muttered. He shook his head as Sam scrolled through the pictures.

"Eighty-three in this folder, but we haven't even touched the other folders yet."

"Why not?"

"Keep scrolling. You'll see. This kind of stuff will fuck with your head," Sam explained. "We gotta get this sent off to Lansing. Maybe the analysts can extract more information from the raw files."

"No doubt about it. I need the drive. What's the password?"

Sam slid him a scrap of paper.

"That's it?"

He nodded, hoping Lucia wouldn't still feel foolish for not figuring it out.

Dan started to say something but stopped himself.

"I don't think Cassie goes this deep." Sam gestured to the photos on the laptop screen.

"I agree," Dan said. "Plus, I have an update about her." He held up his hand as a signal for patience when Lucia perked up. "First, I can tell you both that the medical examiner agrees that Rich's death was not a suicide. And Rich didn't die in the crash. He was dead for at least two hours before it happened."

"Shit," Lucia whispered, her gaze falling to her hands clasped together on the table. "How?"

"Not yet." Dan shook his head. "Next, Cassie was down in Tennessee when Rich disappeared. She headed down there after they broke up. That was about a month before he was reported missing by his father."

"So she wasn't involved with his death?" Sam leaned back in his chair, tapping his heel on the floor as he processed the new information.

"At this point, we don't have anything to connect her to Rich's disappearance or death. She was only back in Michigan for about three days before she came after you."

"How did you find all of this out?" Lucia asked, incredulous.

"We had to contact her next of kin and found her mother. She filled us in on a lot of details. And it matches up with her digital trail."

A sick feeling rolled through Lucia's stomach. "Does that mean Cassie isn't the person who left the note? And maybe she's not Phil's girlfriend?"

"There's nothing at this point to verify or eliminate those possibilities."

"Damn," Lucia muttered, folding her arms on the table in front of her and then resting her head on them. It felt like they were back to square one.

Someone out there hadn't wanted her to share whatever she might know. Now she'd found what Rich had left and shared it with the police. Since the person who'd threatened her wasn't Cassie, who was now in custody, it meant the person who'd left the note was still out there. In her mind, that person had the face of Phil, the man from the cemetery. The memory of his voice sent a wave of goosebumps across her skin.

Chapter 30

The dueling sounds of grunting, moaning, and metal clinking against metal pulled Shelby from her restless sleep. The shadows of the basement greeted her first, the only light coming from a single 40-watt bulb over the stairs.

As her eyes adjusted, Shelby peered to her right without turning her head. It was Sean. He had been favoring a girl he called Missy. She'd introduced herself as Mel, but he didn't like it. Mel was scared, but she wouldn't fight him. She gave him what he really wanted by letting him see the fear and pain in her eyes.

The second and last time Sean had come for Shelby, she had looked away, avoiding his gaze at all costs despite his demands for it and the abuse he delivered for her refusal. She needed to escape soon because she wouldn't live much longer if she remained defiant. But if she wasn't a free woman, she didn't want to live at all.

She wasn't sure how many days had passed without daylight or moonlight to tell in the dim, damp space. They'd marched all the girls upstairs for a group shower at one point, but from what she could see through the edges of the living room curtains, it had been night. Shower time was supposed to be a chance to bathe, but it turned into a terrifying and humiliating experience. The things she'd been forced to do itched and bubbled beneath her skin, and they would always be there, branded into her memory.

They'd only been fed a few crackers each day. Correction. That was all they had given Shelby. The other girls were more compliant, so they received more food and better treatment. They were being trained like little Pavlov dogs. They submitted, accepted cues, and did what they were told or, increasingly, cued to do. She almost lamented that she didn't have the strength to play along and go through the motions, at least enough for Sean to let his guard down around her.

She was too defiant, and he'd punished and starved her for it.

Now that she was fairly certain of the men's general patterns, she was ready to try to escape. There was no more waiting. In a few more days, she would be too weak to run. She was sure the lack of movement, food, and water had already deteriorated her muscle strength. Even if she didn't make it far, even if she faltered, no man would ever take her again.

She was committed. Escape or die.

On the first day, after Sean punished her for the attempt to run past the man in charge, she started planning. After he left and the other girls had dozed off, Shelby had maneuvered her legs so she could pull herself to a stand. Each hand was cuffed, the links resting around the pipe so that none of them could use their hands. The pipe wasn't far from the ground, so she couldn't rise to her full height, but it was enough for her needs.

Sean had peeled her shorts off and tossed them aside, but with her agile legs, she'd been able to retrieve them, grasping them in her toes and getting them to her. Thinking back to the little yoga she had practiced with Lauren, Shelby kept her breath calm as she squatted on one leg. Pulling her free leg up, she bent her knee and brought the shorts to her hands.

Inside the right front pocket was a handful of black bobby pins. When she had left her apartment, she had stuffed them in her pocket in case she needed to pin back her hair while she worked. In this moment, those pins might save her life.

On that first night, she hadn't been ready to escape, so she stuffed the pins under the edge of the mattress so she could easily retrieve them later. Then, she threw her shorts back in the pile, hoping Sean wouldn't notice.

Any chance she found to flee would have to be carefully evaluated. She couldn't fail because a single failure would be absolute. So she waited. Although there were a few chances when she could have run, such as when the men took them to shower, she couldn't risk it.

While she was confident she could outrun Sean and Matt, she wouldn't be able to outrun bullets. Both were armed, and there hadn't been a situation yet when she could slip away without being noticed.

The current moment presented the perfect confluence of urgency and opportunity. She needed to try before she lost more strength, and her captors had become complacent. Shelby was also confident she understood their patterns of activity. Once Sean had sated himself with Mel's "company," he would have a beer and eat something. Listening closely each evening, she heard the sounds of glass and plates rattling after he had left the basement. She was sure he would be hungry tonight, just as he had been each of the other nights.

Escape or die, she reminded herself.

Sean gave a final grunt as he finished with Mel. For a minute, he lay there on top of her, one large hand cupping a bare breast. When he moved again, Shelby closed her eyes and breathed slowly, as if she were sleeping. She heard him rise and listened as he stepped close, then tapped her foot with his.

Without moving, Shelby continued her slow breathing. Although it felt as if she had to wait an eternity, Sean finally walked away, and she waited as he climbed the stairs. He opened and closed the basement door, then his footsteps thumped through the kitchen above.

Straight to the fridge. Glass bottles clinked together. *That's right. You deserve a drink, you sick son of a bitch.*

She opened her eyes slowly and let them adjust again before studying the three women to her right. Mel shifted uncomfortably, sobbing lightly, but she would pass out soon. Soundlessly, Shelby grabbed the cold, rusty pipe with both hands and pulled herself up. She rose, hunched over, and continued to grip the pipe to keep the links on her handcuffs from rattling against the metal.

Wiggling one foot and balancing on the other, she dipped her toes between the edge of the mattress and the wall and squeezed her bobby pins between them. With determination and patience, she squatted on her standing leg and lifted her free leg that held the pins pinched between her toes and the pad of her foot.

Easy, she silently reminded herself, careful not to say anything aloud. Her body was shaking, but not from lack of movement. Every time Sean had left them alone, she had risen, bent her knees, and moved as much as she could, despite being handcuffed to the wall.

Shelby brought the toe-full of bobby pins to her waiting hand. As she unclenched her toes, most of the pins dropped, but her eager fingers caught three of them.

She paused, looking around to ensure the others were still sleeping, then used the keyhole in the cuffs to unbend one pin until it formed a right angle. Then, turning the pin between her fingers, she hooked the straight end into the keyhole of the left cuff and bent it into an L-shape.

Shelby raised it into the half-light that filtered into this corner of the basement and examined it. Her heart, calm up to this point, began to beat faster. She was so close.

Perfect.

She dipped the bent tip of the pin into the keyhole and scraped around until she felt it catch against the simple locking mechanism. When she twisted the bobby pin in the lock, the cuff on her left wrist popped open. Her head buzzed with excitement over the unexpected success, and she carefully lifted the cuff from between the wall and pipe, not wanting to make any noise that would wake the others.

Although Shelby fully intended to send help, she didn't trust the others to be quiet or strong enough to slip away with her. She worried they would do something foolish, and they'd all get caught. And if they got caught, they would be punished. Severely. But if one of them didn't escape, none could be rescued.

Once she had the cuffs away from the wall, she used the same bobby pin to pick the cuff off her right wrist. It took a few more tries since she didn't have as much dexterity in her left hand, but she finally got it.

In less than thirty seconds, she was free to dig her shorts and tank top out of the pile they'd been thrown into and pull them on. Once she was clothed, Shelby tucked the bobby pins into her right front pocket and shoved the cuffs into the left one. They could be used as a weapon if needed.

Sean and Matt had removed the dead man from the basement the day after the women arrived, but the chair he'd been tied to remained. Shelby gently lifted it now and placed it beneath one of the blacked-out windows. The window was narrow but easily big enough for her to slide through. She stood on the chair and silently rotated the old swivel lock.

With one last look at the others sleeping on the dirty mattresses, Shelby silently vowed she would return for them with help.

Then she tilted open the window and pulled herself through.

Chapter 31

Cool, wet grass chilled Shelby's bare skin as she pulled herself through the window. She stayed low once she was out, and quietly closed the window behind her. Her racing heart felt like it was going to burst from her chest, and she took several deep breaths while surveying her surroundings.

A billion stars glittered in the velvet sky above and the moon shone brightly. It was nearly full, and there wasn't a cloud in the sky. Since they'd been kept mostly in darkness, Shelby's eyes adjusted easily to the night. The soft grass felt good against her bare feet, but she knew the comfort was only temporary. For the moment, fortune favored her.

She turned left and moved along the side of the house at a crouch, waiting until the sound of her blood rushing in her ears quieted before she continued. Once she could hear clearly, she decided no one knew she was gone.

Yet.

Inching around the corner, Shelby found the driveway where she had come in. It was brightly lit by a floodlight. She couldn't go that way. It was too risky. Once they realized she was gone, they would look for her out front and along the roads. Trying to remember how they had come in when Tom had dropped her off, Shelby estimated that 25 minutes of driving time from Mount Pleasant meant it was unlikely she could make it back there by morning. At least not without being seen.

There was another town nearby though, if her bearings were right. She and Lauren had driven through it on their way up from Flint. She couldn't remember the name, but she remembered seeing a Michigan State Police post. At the time, she had commented about hiding her weed where the sun doesn't shine if they got pulled over. The girls joked about it, but their trip had been rather uneventful. Boring even.

She ached for boring now.

Shelby turned around and moved the opposite way along the side of the house toward the back. Edging around the next corner, she found the backyard was blissfully dark. She studied the sky and found the Big Dipper, its stars twinkling their light toward her from across the vast galaxies between them. Tracing the constellation with her eyes, she found the tip, pointing faithfully to the North Star.

I think it's east, she reasoned before sneaking past the corner. She reached the eastern edge of the house, then paused to weigh her options. There was a small open area between the house and the barn, but the floodlight from the front cast a cone of light through it.

Shelby didn't know what time of night it was, but she didn't want to take any chances. If anyone were looking out the windows, they would easily see her. She chewed her bottom lip and followed the edge of the light with her eyes. There was a point where the shadows overcame the light, a cross-section of darkness between the house and the barn. If she stuck to the shadows, she might be safe.

The woods would be her safety, as her captors would likely expect her to be on the roads. Thankfully, she hadn't heard any dogs since she arrived and was sure they didn't have any to send after her. She guessed no one had managed to escape before.

Lucky me.

She took a deep breath and stayed low as she rushed across the open space, staying within the boundaries of the shadows. In less than a minute, she slipped into the safety of the woods behind the barn.

Shelby traveled east through the shadows of the woodline, walking slowly to keep from making too much noise. Once she could no longer see the lights from the farm, she relaxed a little. Her heart still thudded in her chest, but the farther away she traveled, the more hopeful she felt.

At least until she couldn't go east anymore. The woods cut north along another hayfield, and if she were to continue east and a little south to reach the town with the state trooper post, she would have to cross the field. Just beyond the field, she could see a road. The only reason she could see it was because it rose above the fields around it, and the glittering dew collecting on the grassy shoulders reflected gently in the bright moonlight.

She crouched just inside the edge of the treeline. The debris on the forest floor hurt her feet, so she sat down in the leaves and rubbed them while she estimated the distance through the hayfield to the road. On the other side of the north-south running road was a cornfield thick with six- and seven-foot-tall stalks.

She needed to get into the field as quickly as possible. Although the hayfield was tall and ready for cutting, it wasn't tall enough to hide her from the headlights of a car, even if she lay in it. She estimated about 200 meters between her position in the woods and the safety of the cornfield on the other side of the road.

The moon seemed to shine brighter as she moved from the woods and into the hayfield. She crouched and prepared to sprint. Looking north, she saw nothing but darkness. Glancing south, she found the same.

There wasn't a streetlight or a car's headlight anywhere in sight. Only the chirp of crickets and the occasional chatty owl greeted her ears. More creatures might skulk through the darkness beyond her vision, but as long as they left her alone, she wouldn't worry about them. She would much rather be vulnerable to the predators of the countryside than the human predators who lurked within the constructs of civilization.

Shelby sprang from her crouch and sprinted across the hayfield. She hadn't expected the rough ruts left by tractor tires, which slowed her pace considerably. She looked left and right as she approached the road, but all was quiet.

All was dark.

She took long strides across the road, the wind rushing in her ears and her bare feet slapping across the still-warm pavement. When she reached the ditch, she cleared it with a small leap, then bolted between the even rows of corn. She ran deep into the field before letting herself slow to a walk.

The long sprint had winded her. Starved and dehydrated, her body wasn't ready for any of this. Her head swam, so she fell to her knees in the dirt. She needed to catch her breath and desperately needed water. The tall stalks whispered around her as she stared at them, the slight breeze tickling their long leaves.

As her pulse slowed, Shelby stood again and touched the tops of the cornstalks. The upper leaves were wet with midnight dew, as the grass at the farm had been. She pulled a long leaf down and gently licked the dew from it.

It was a mistake she instantly regretted. A burning sensation overwhelmed her tongue as the sharp leaf sliced into it. Determined to drink, she tried again, pulling another leaf down and pinching the edges together to funnel the dew. It worked, and she dripped the dew into her mouth without cutting her tongue this time, providing a little of the hydration she desperately needed. Shelby sipped the dew from the leaves as she walked in between the rows, and it helped her regain a little energy.

Shelby froze when a roaring engine shattered the stillness of the night air. She listened for a split second before realizing it was heading her way.

Bursting into a sprint, she forced her legs to carry her to the forest beyond the cornfield as the vehicle sped closer along the road.

She slipped into the woodline and dropped behind a large pine tree, clapping a hand over her mouth to stifle her panting. The roaring hit its loudest point as it passed, and the vehicle–obscured by the corn–continued without stopping. There was no flash of spotlights, no sign that anyone had seen her–or that anyone was looking for her yet.

Shelby squeezed her eyes shut and dropped her hand to the ground to steady herself. Exhaustion crept through her aching muscles, but she opened her eyes and forced herself to stand again. Exiting the forest and stepping into the dirt perimeter of the cornfield, she searched the sky until she found the Big Dipper and the North Star once more.

At her current speed, she didn't know how long it would take to cross the fields and forests before she could reach the state police, but she had to keep going until she did. Time was not on her side if she would keep her silent promise to Mel and the others. She was determined to not fall asleep until she reached the troopers.

Shelby would not stop until justice had been meted out.

Chapter 32

Monday, September 3rd

At nine in the morning, the mid-Michigan air was cool for late August. Although surrounded by the Great Lakes and dotted with over 11,000 smaller lakes, the area lacked the oppressive, suffocating humidity of more southern states. Lake Michigan cooled the winds that came east from Wisconsin and the rest of the Midwest. The sun was bright in the cloudless sky, and Lucia savored the earthy, dewy morning air as she ran alone along the road.

Earlier, Sam had decided to work through all the pictures from the thumb drive and Lucia's emails with Dan. She no longer had the stomach for it and opted to go for a run instead. She wasn't a star runner, but she enjoyed it anyway. Her parents had raised her and her brother on fitness, always insisting they strive for peak physical condition.

After high school, Lucia had stopped running for a while but quickly realized she needed it. Running cleared her head and got her blood flowing. During college, she struggled with her weight once her parents no longer compelled her to exercise anymore. Her roommate, Jordan, was a track and field competitor at Ferris State and one of the most caring people she'd ever met. And she pushed Lucia to get her health back on track.

A natural extrovert, the beautiful, down-to-earth young woman had quickly taken Lucia under her wing. She helped build Lucia's confidence, got her to socialize, and put her back on a path to fitness. Lucia's new habits had formed through a bond of friendship. These days, she ran at least three times a week when it wasn't snowing—and when people weren't crashing cars through gas stations where she worked and trying to kill her.

Sam's house wasn't visible from the road, hidden behind a wall of trees and a winding half-mile-long driveway that might cause passersby to think it was a dirt drive into the state game area. For Lucia, it was perfect. It gave her space to breathe and a sense of privacy. She also enjoyed running the main highway out in the country. The shoulders of the road were generous, and there was plenty of traffic to see her if something happened.

This morning, she would aim her run away from town rather than toward it, hoping to find more peace than if she strayed too close to the edges of Pine River. Outside of town, the huge country blocks were perfect for a four-mile stretch as they skirted nothing but forest and farm fields for miles. The occasional farmhouse dotted the landscape, but most were empty at this time of day during the work week. Farmers tended their lands and livestock, while others worked jobs in Mount Pleasant, Midland, or Saginaw.

Gravel crunched under her running shoes as Lucia jogged out of Sam's driveway and turned west along the busy highway. After about a half-mile, she headed north on a faded gray asphalt road surrounded by cornfields. She slowed to put her headphones in, confident the road was empty enough for her to safely run along the narrow left shoulder.

As she fell into rhythm with an early 2000s rap song, she spotted a vehicle coming down the road toward her. Glancing at the shoulder, she noticed the ditch was becoming steeper as the marshy, forested area near the corner of the road gave way to cornfields. Near many fields in the area, the long ditches provided a buffer and caught the rain runoff between the roads and the crops, supporting irrigation. Now that it was late August, the corn stood five- to six-feet tall in most places, sometimes higher.

As the vehicle approached, Lucia slowed her jog to a walk and took her earbuds out. She moved as far away from the road as she could without falling into the ditch. Stopping to catch her breath, she propped her hands on her hips while she waited for the little black Jeep to pass by.

Instead of speeding by her as any random vehicle should out in the country, the Jeep slowed to ten or fifteen miles per hour as it approached. Two men inside stared at her curiously. There was a sudden pinch in her stomach, and her mouth went dry as she locked eyes with the driver. She waved them on, forced a smile, and stepped off into a jog once they passed her.

When she glanced over her shoulder, she saw them continuing to the stop sign at the main highway, so she put her earbuds in again. She tried to get back into her zone and shake off the eerie, icy feeling that still gripped her heart.

In a lull between songs, Lucia heard the roar of an engine. She spun, and her breath caught in her throat when she saw the Jeep was coming up behind her and driving over the centerline. She plucked out her earbuds and followed them with her eyes, trying to keep the fear from her face. Fear encouraged predators.

"Can I help you?"

The man in the driver's seat was older, too thin to be healthy, and had black hair, brown eyes, and a mustache. "Hey, aren't you the girl that worked at the gas station in town? The one where the crash happened?"

"Maybe. Why?" she answered, rubbing her thumb over her earbuds.

"Lucia?"

She froze, her blood running cold as the alarm bells clanged in her head.

The man took her silence as confirmation and flashed a smile before slamming on the gas. She watched, frozen, as he blocked her path with his vehicle. The emergency brake cranked as the Jeep stopped. Then the man jumped out and faced her.

Her skin prickled as her brain pumped adrenaline into her blood, ready for fight or flight. He stood straight, and his head nearly cleared the top of the lifted Jeep Wrangler. His height, combined with his anorexic body shape, gave her the impression of a snake in a man's form. He wore an old black concert t-shirt with letters too worn to read, black denim jeans, and weathered black cowboy boots. For a moment, the two stared at one another, deadlocked in understanding. He was here to take her.

The dark-eyed man took a step closer.

Chapter 33

Lucia spun on her heel, ready to run back toward the highway where there would be plenty of people to see her. Then she saw the other man. It appeared he had gotten out when the Jeep turned around at the stop sign and had been silently approaching her while the driver distracted her. Now, the passenger was less than fifteen feet away. She paused only a moment before spinning to her right and running.

She leaped across the ditch and cleared it. As soon as her feet hit the other side, she bolted, fleeing into the cornfield. She kept her head low and sprinted in between the rows of corn, heading east as fast as her adrenaline-fueled legs could carry her. Behind her, the men shouted, and she could hear their clumsy bodies barreling through the corn stalks.

Having grown up in a small town like this one, Lucia spent much of her youth playing with her friends in the cornfields. As long as they didn't destroy any of the stalks, the farmers never minded. As children, they had learned how to navigate the fields both day and night, swift and silent like little redneck ninjas.

She willed her legs to move faster, ducking the sharp-edged leaves and jumping over fallen stalks as she went. Being shorter meant she had the advantage, as a taller person would have more corn stalk leaves to contend with. The edges left tiny, painful slices in human flesh.

Soon, Lucia only heard the sound of her own body whispering through the towering stalks and the wind rushing in her ears. But she didn't slow until she broke through the edge of the cornfield and onto a freshly cut lawn.

There was a faded turn-of-the-century red barn, a two-story farmhouse to match, and a rusted 4x4 pickup in the driveway. Cars buzzed past on the highway, but it was at least 100 meters away, and she hesitated. Her chest heaved in ragged breaths as she considered her options. She had seconds to decide whether to approach the house and hope the driver of the pickup was home and willing to help. Or she could run to the road and try to flag down a car before her pursuers caught up with her. The second option was riskier because people might not stop as they may have twenty or thirty years ago.

Hearing the rustle of cornstalks behind her, she sprinted toward the house and banged on the door. It opened after a few moments, and an older man appeared at the threshold. He was a stout, appearing to be in his late sixties, and wore a plaid shirt and a John Deere hat. Thick, white hair topped a sun-weathered face set with gentle brown eyes.

"Please, sir." She kept her breathless voice low. "Please help me, please let me in!"

"What? Why? What's going on?" Suspicion filled his expression as he glanced around her.

"Please!" She began to cry. "I'm being chased by two men, and I don't know who they are!"

He moved back from the door a bit and gestured for her to enter. "Come in, but I'll warn ya; I got a gun. I'll use it if you try an' rob me."

Lucia bolted inside the house, trembling violently as she entered the living room. She slumped to the floor and covered her mouth to keep from crying aloud.

My phone! she thought as her adrenaline crashed. Her earbuds had been ripped out at some point and were probably somewhere in the cornfield now, but thankfully she still had her cell phone.

Ripping the band from her arm, she wrenched the phone from its grippy rubber casing and struggled to unlock it.

"You weren't shitting me, were you?" The older man kept his voice low. He engaged three locks on the door and peered out the window at the top before picking up his shotgun from the corner behind it.

Uncontrollable tears rolled down her cheeks as she stared up at him. "I'm calling 9-1-1 now," she whispered. He nodded toward the couch, gesturing for her to hide before he walked into the kitchen.

Lucia kept herself beneath the windows as she moved through the living room, then crouched on the floor behind the old blue couch and started the call. There was just enough signal to connect, and within seconds, a dispatcher answered. Lucia hurriedly explained her situation.

"Two men are chasing me!" she cried into the receiver, struggling to keep her voice quiet.

The old man returned from the kitchen with his double-barrel shotgun in one hand and an envelope in the other. He dropped it on the floor in front of her and pointed. She recited the address on it to the dispatcher. According to the envelope, her new friend's name was Patrick.

Patrick sat down on the couch with his shotgun across his lap, one knee bouncing rapidly. He didn't rise until Lucia told him the police were on their way. He nodded, then stood and peered out a window before moving around the house again.

While he was out of sight, Lucia stayed on the line with the dispatcher, answering every question imaginable and more about how the events had transpired, including descriptions of the men and their vehicle.

There was a banging on the door, and the dispatcher asked Lucia to verify it was the police. Terrified, she crept from her hiding place and glimpsed through a crack in the curtains over the living room window.

"Lucia Sorenson?" a woman's voice called out, sounding tense and serious.

A wave of relief washed over her when she saw the flashing lights of state police cars and officers in blue uniforms standing on the porch, hands perched on their duty weapons.

Chapter 34

Lucia rested her head on the one empty space on Dan's messy desk. He said he had cleared that little space just for her after he was told she'd been picked up. The troopers made the initial reports, but she still needed to be debriefed by Dan.

"Okay, Lucia, I think that's everything." He rubbed his fingers absently through his short, black hair. "I need you to swear to me that you're not holding anything else back."

She lifted her head and glared at him. "Seriously? After everything, why the hell would I hold anything back?"

"Listen, I get it. You're frustrated, but I need to know that you're not keeping any secrets. You should have told me about the emails right away. So, if there's anything else like that, anything at all, you have to tell me."

"You're killing me, Dan." She shook away the tears that threatened to fall. "Why don't you believe me?"

"Lucia," he said, lowering his voice as he leaned forward. "We've been friends for almost a year now. I do believe you, but sometimes you make decisions on your own about what is or isn't important without letting anyone else in on your thoughts. You can't do that anymore. It could mean your life." He paused, his eyes flickering to Sam, who was talking to another officer outside Dan's office. "It could endanger other lives, too."

His gaze locked with hers and probed for any tell that might give away what she was thinking, but it was useless. She couldn't think of what else she could tell him. The emails were all she had, and she hadn't even had the smarts to figure out the password. That was all Sam's clever work.

"All right," he said with a sigh as he leaned back in his chair. "One more thing."

"Anything, Dan," she responded sincerely, hoping he would relax and have a little faith in her again.

"What about the other clues he gave you? Have you figured them out yet?"

Lucia held his gaze. "I... I haven't even thought about the other ones. After we saw the pictures, I just... it was too hard to consider anything else after that."

Dan nodded and tapped the desk with his pen, concern apparent on his face. "Are you okay?"

"I mean, yes. I'm fine, I think. But those people. They're not okay. They're..."

"Stop, Luce." Dan cut her off. "The farther you fall down that rabbit hole, the harder it is to get out."

"I'm sorry," she whispered, trying to chase the images from her mind.

"Don't apologize. The clues. What do you think they mean?"

"No." She shrugged. "I was working on it, but so much has happened."

"Can you remind me what they are?"

"There are two more after the roses. The second said something about where we liked to go out and grill. But we did that in a lot of places, like everybody else."

"Right. What's the other one?"

"Where he burned our names. But it's not ringing any bells. I don't know what that means."

"Well, take some time, get some rest, and keep thinking about it. If you remember anything, text or call me."

"I don't think I'm going to have much of a choice about resting." She tilted her head toward Sam.

"And please don't go running off on your own anymore. Not until we're sure this is over. Okay?"

"Yeah." Her stomach turned at the thought of being out in the open and defenseless again. "Not any time soon."

"Sam," he called as he ran a hand through his short hair.

"Are we good to go?" Sam asked as he walked into the doorway. Seeing how anxious he was to speak with her, she knew he must have raced to the post immediately after Dan called him. They hadn't been able to see each other until Dan finished debriefing her.

"I'm going to see if we can extend your vacation time," he said to Sam before turning back to Lucia. "Can you go grab a cup of coffee or water for yourself while I fill him in on all the details?"

She nodded, thankful Dan would relieve her of having to retell the morning's events. Again. At least until she and Sam got home. Lucia brushed her fingertips down Sam's arm as she passed. He paused, then surprised her with a tight hug.

"I can't let you go anywhere alone, can I?" he teased, whispering in her ear. "I'm so glad you're okay." He kissed her cheek gently before walking into Dan's office.

Dan closed the door behind Sam. Had there not been a room full of cops looking at her, she might have stayed close to listen in on their conversation. Instead, Lucia strolled over to the mini-lounge and poured herself a cup of black coffee before sitting at one of the little round tables. Carefully, she sipped the steaming hot liquid as she tried to push back all the hurried thoughts fighting for space inside her head. There was a mountain of darkness growing within her mind, feeding on her prolific problems.

It was eleven o'clock in the morning, and it already felt like she had a full day behind her. How could so much happen so soon after the morning had begun? The room spun, so she stood and steadied herself first before walking calmly to the women's bathroom so she could vomit. When she came back after rinsing her mouth and cleaning herself up, she caught sight of the post lieutenant heading into Dan's office. His face was stern, and his cold eyes only briefly glanced at her before he closed the door.

Sitting back down, she thought about the emails from Rich and what the other two clues might mean. She wondered if there were more hints that she was missing but shook the thought from her head. She needed to focus on what she did have rather than speculate on what she didn't.

Lucia was supposed to be the one good at puzzles, the one who had the right combination of book and street smarts that gave her a leg up on the average person. Lately, she seemed to falter. Maybe she wasn't as smart as she'd thought she was. Instead, she felt pretty damn useless.

It was time to step up.

She walked out of the break area and onto the main floor. Finding the nearest cop, she relaxed a little when she recognized him. He was one of Sam and Dan's friends, and he had been out with their group when she and Sam had first met.

"Chris?"

"Hey, Lucia," he said, turning to her with a smile. "How are you holding up?"

She shrugged. "As good as I can, all things considered."

"Yeah." He nodded. "You're a tough woman, though. You'll be all right."

The compliment surprised her. "Thank you. Really. Do you have a pen and a piece of paper?"

"Sure." He pulled open a drawer filled with a chaotic heap of stationery, writing utensils, and other office supplies. "Pretend you didn't see that," he said with a laugh. After taking out a small notepad, he grabbed a handful of pens and passed the bundle to her.

She accepted the bundle and smiled. "Thank you."

"Sorry, some of them don't work."

"No problem, I'll toss the ones that don't and bring back the good ones."

He smiled politely before returning his attention to his computer.

Sitting down in the break room again, she found a pen that worked after tossing three useless ones and began writing out what she knew about the remaining clues. It was evident they were related to specific places, as the clue about the roses had been. Probably places she hadn't visited since she and Rich broke up. She wondered what she would find at the other locations.

Lucia wrote the first of the two other clues on the notepad.

1. Where I burned our names.
- ???

Lucia didn't have any idea what Rich had meant by this, but she knew it was important because it was one of the three phrases he repeated over the last fifteen or so emails he had sent. She resigned herself to letting her subconscious sort it out and wrote out the second clue.

2. Where we used to grill out.

There were three places she could think of right away where they had grilled out, whether with friends, Rich's family, or by themselves. The first place was at the farm, right out front on the expansive lawn between the house and the road, but that seemed too obvious. It looked too risky to put two clues so close together.

Isn't it too risky? If the same area holds two different things for me to find? She pondered the possibility and wrote "the farm" beneath the clue.

Next, she jotted the names of the other two places they'd usually grill out.

- *Pine River City Park*
- *Riverside Campground*

Any other places she could think of were ones they'd only visited once or twice.

We.

Lucia hated "we" when she thought of Rich because there was no "we" with a narcissist, not in the context of any kind of relationship, romantic or platonic. With everything that had happened, she still hadn't sorted out her thoughts and feelings about him.

After all the things left between them, some good but mostly bad, she had never wished him any harm. Despite all the bullshit he put her through, she felt sympathy for him. She never imagined he would die so young, and especially not in the way he had.

Until she'd found out it was his body in the driver's seat of the car that crashed through the gas station, she had a tiny well of hope tucked away in her mind for him. It was a hope that he would straighten up and lead the kind of life his father always wanted for him. Then, to hear of his death and to know her gaze had fallen upon his lifeless vessel after the crash without realizing it until later... It was too heavy to carry in her heart.

A gentle hand squeezed her shoulder, and she wiped stray tears from the corners of her eyes before turning. Sam stared down at her. Behind his sympathetic expression, she recognized a touch of sadness. Worry was evident in the deep furrow between his brows.

"I've got four more days off." He forced a smile, and she forced her own despite her concern for him. This was not the time or place for sharing and caring.

"Great," she replied, her voice cracking. "Can we leave now?" Her hands trembled, but in his presence, she knew she was safe. Sam would always catch her.

"Yes." He released her shoulder and grabbed her hand. "Let's go home."

Home, she repeated silently as she collected her things.

Chapter 35

Lucia forced herself to take a bite of pizza. Sitting with Sam on a small bench on his back deck, she stared off into the woods. She didn't feel like eating after the morning's incident but knew she should. Her stomach grumbled, evidence of her physical hunger, but her mind wasn't at ease enough to enjoy it.

"What's wrong?" he asked.

"What isn't wrong would be a shorter list," she said before she could stop herself. "I don't even want to think about food."

"I'm sorry."

"For what? Sam, don't apologize for anything." She put down her pizza and faced him squarely. "You are the reason I'm okay right now. I'm safe, and I'm alive. I even believe that everything might be okay. Eventually. Hell, you're the reason I ran for my life, the reason I'm ready to fight."

He remained silent as she threaded her fingers through his.

"Thank you." She kissed him on the cheek.

He let her linger, then kissed her lips and ran his free hand through her dark hair. "What do you want to do?"

"I'm not sure, but I don't want to just sit here. I can't think when I feel confined."

"I know." He squeezed her hand. "That's why I asked. You said you're ready to fight, so what's your next move, Rocky?"

She grinned at him as an undeniable warmth sprung from within her. Everything about what they shared was simply right. It wasn't all cupcakes and rainbows, but it was perfect all the same.

He was the only person who truly understood her.

Lucia drew a piece of folded paper from her pocket and handed it to him. She had torn it from Chris's notebook before returning it to him on their way out of the post.

"What's this?"

"Dan wanted me to think harder about these clues since the one I *did* figure out provided a cache of evidence. So I tried to write my way through them. You figured out the password, so it's my turn to be smart now. Is that okay with you, genius?" she teased.

"I'm not sure, Luce. You know how competitive I get." He gave her a wink and stood. "Let's follow your instincts on this."

"You're serious? We're going to do it?" She hadn't thought he'd be on board, considering it involved her ex.

"Yep. Let's hunt down whatever we can. Anything you think of, lay it on me." He paused, offering his hand. "We'll figure it out together."

Lucia couldn't control her smile as she placed her palm in his.

She hated the idea of taking her cop boyfriend to the places where she used to spend time with Rich, the unapologetic criminal who intentionally harmed the community that had nurtured him as a youth. But she knew this was a necessary part of her journey to help her let go of her past.

With Sam by her side, she would incinerate the memories that lingered like poison in her mind.

"You're amazing." She beamed at him as they went into the house and got Penny ready to go with them.

"What's our first stop?" he asked as he pulled his pickup truck to the end of the driveway. Penny panted excitedly in the back seat, happy for the ride.

"Well, there are only two places–possibly three–I want to check out."

"Why 'possibly three'?"

"Because the third place is back at the farm. I don't want to bother Liam by wandering all over his property. It's too soon since..." Lucia stopped herself.

Since he buried his son.

"Agreed," Sam said, clearly understanding what she had hesitated to say. "He needs time to grieve. We can't go looking there unless you're sure."

"Exactly."

"So? What are the other two?"

"Pine River City Park and Riverside Campground."

"Where to first?"

"The city park. It's small, there aren't many places to hide anything. It almost feels too small, but I figure it's easier."

"Sounds good," he said as he pulled onto the highway and headed east into Pine River.

Within ten minutes, they were walking hand-in-hand in a loop around the park. The playful squeals and laughter of children filled the area, giving Lucia a surreal feeling after the dark events of the past week. The crash that could have killed her, watching her ex-boyfriend's casket lowered into the ground, and the attempted kidnapping had all happened while other people were happy, entirely unaware of the pain and trauma around them.

She and Sam walked the park several times, on and off the paved paths, peeking through all the nooks and crannies. Penny was as energetic as ever, her tongue flapping happily as they wandered.

Despite the search, a piercing feeling of insignificance consumed Lucia. The world was so vast and filled with so many complex lives. It nearly overwhelmed her as they approached the playground for the third time. How could so many people be so oblivious to the suffering of others?

Like the people in the pictures on the thumb drive she'd found. Lucia had only seen flashes of the hell so many poor souls had been through, and it had already become harder to smile, more difficult to live in the moment. Each flash of happiness with Sam was swiftly followed by an undercurrent of guilt that swept through her like a riptide. How could she be happy when so many others were suffering?

But she couldn't feel that when she looked at these children, these innocent young souls carefree in this quiet moment and entirely unaware of the greater horrors of the world. They should be cheerful for as long as they could.

"Luce?" Sam's voice broke through her macabre train of thoughts. The gravity of the darkness weighed on her soul and exhausted her.

"I'm sorry. I don't feel well." She leaned her head against his shoulder.

"Let's go back to my house. Until you're feeling better."

"No." She shook her head. "I just want to get through this. I won't feel better until I do something useful."

"Okay." He rubbed her back. She was surprised he didn't offer an argument over her "useful" comment. "Do you see anything that strikes you as out of place?"

Lucia stopped as they neared the parking area again. They'd been around the park three times, and there wasn't anywhere to hide something where it wouldn't immediately be found by strangers.

"If I was meant to find anything like the thumb drive, it's not here." Her shoulders slumped forward.

"Perk up, buttercup." He kissed her cheek and led her to the truck. After opening the passenger door and helping her and Penny in, he closed it and leaned in through the open window. "Where to next?"

She couldn't stifle her sigh, discouragement suffocating her ambition. Without Sam here, she didn't know if she'd bother with the wild goose chase. "Riverside."

He jumped in the truck and turned the key in the ignition. The engine roared to life, and he hesitated before pulling out of the park until she pointed right. He pulled back onto the main highway and turned east.

Sam was her rock, picking her up when she was down. She did the same for him when he needed it. They needed each other.

"Tell me where I'm going." He squeezed her hand. For his sake, she would try to regain some of the energy she lost at the little park.

"We need to get on Riverside Drive and head north. So take a left on Main Street and a right on McGregor."

"I know that route."

She was sure he did. Hell, he had driven around here as a cop more in a year than she had in almost four years.

It wasn't long before they were traveling north on Pine River road. It followed the river, winding its way through forest and farmland. For a while, Lucia leaned back in her seat and closed her eyes, enjoying the warmth of the sunlight on her face, the gentle wind from the open window teasing the dark strands that fell from her messy bun. The dips and rises along the curves and straightaways offered a country rollercoaster and lulled her into a peaceful state of mind, countering her earlier wave of depression.

What could be better than appreciating a beautiful afternoon with this man? she wondered as she stared at Sam. If only she hadn't been chased during her morning run, or if Cassie hadn't tried to kill her, and her ex's car hadn't crashed through the gas station. Maybe then she might be able to enjoy a normal, relaxed day.

When she opened her eyes again, Sam turned his truck into the Riverside Campground.

The sight of the little country campground fractured her calm, a bolt of unease striking her heart.

Chapter 36

"Here?" Sam asked, pointing to a parking spot near the boat launch.

"Yes," she replied quietly.

He parked in the shade and hopped out before reaching beneath the seat to grab his back holster and his 1911 Sig Sauer. He expertly kept it hidden from the myriad campers and locals who came down to the river to fish, swim, and barbecue.

She got out of the car and clipped a leash on Penny before glaring at Sam. "What?"

"Why do you need it?"

"Whoa. Annie Oakley here suddenly has a problem with firearms?"

"I don't have a problem with firearms," she said, mocking his formal term. "I don't understand why you need to bring it with you right now. Here, in a public place filled with kids and families. They won't hurt us, and no one's coming after me here."

The smile melted from his face as he finished attaching the holster before sliding his favorite pistol into it. "Let me break it down, Luce. We're hunting down clues given to you by a dead criminal who was essentially the X-O of trafficking operations around here. I'm not taking any chances after someone tried to kidnap you. This morning!"

"Okay," she shrugged. "I guess. But what's an X-O?"

He sighed. "The guy who's second in command."

"Oh," Luce replied. She thought for a moment, considering her understanding of Rich's former position when they were together. "Why do you think he was second?"

"What do you mean?" Sam looked up as he pulled his black t-shirt down over his back holster. "That's what Dan's intel tells us."

"I guess it depends on who you compare him to." Lucia shifted her weight, uncomfortable with offering contradictory information. "This was his town, and he was in charge of the entire area around Mount Pleasant. He reported straight to some guy in Detroit."

The expression on Sam's face turned grim.

"Are you sure?"

"When I was with him, yeah." She shrugged.

"God, I hope you're mistaken." He shook his head and offered his hand to her. "We gotta be careful, all right? The Sig is just in case. I'm not taking any chances anymore."

"Okay." Lucia nodded, trying to take comfort in the fact that he was ready to protect her. Her slight correction about Rich's previous work had clearly unsettled him, and it worried her. She looked around before gently tugging Penny's leash. "We have to cross the river."

Sam pointed to the grills in the grassy area just north of the boat launch. "Not there?"

"No." She shook her head. "We brought a small charcoal grill and had our own spot."

They walked to the banks of the Pine River and looked over the adults and children who crowded the boat launch. Then they took off their shoes and left them on the bank before rolling up their pant legs and stepping into the water. There was a sandbar, and they used it to cross the river. The river bottom had changed little since her last fishing visit earlier in the summer.

Lucia led the way, trying in vain to keep a happy, splashing Penny focused on following her and Sam across the shallowest point. She was grateful they could cross. Often, spring and summer floods would change the bottom of the river.

The rushing river came up to their knees, soaking the bottoms of their rolled pant legs, but the sand was easy on their feet. They crossed quickly after getting Penny focused. After several careful strides, they pulled themselves up the steep bank on the other side.

"Hey," a voice called to them from the water. Lucia turned to see a group of three tween boys and two girls swimming in a deep hole. "Where are you going?" the oldest-looking boy asked.

She chose her words carefully. What on earth could turn a twelve-year-old boy away? "We're going to study the damage porcupines are doing to the trees along the river."

"Oh, cool! You know, we all hunt. I could get those porcupines for you."

Sam answered before Lucia could. "You have a small game permit for that, young man?"

"Are you DNR?"

"Nah, I'm just a statey."

"Yes, sir, I have a permit. Just not with me." The boy grinned, and his friends laughed.

"Well," Lucia interrupted. "We're on a no-kill mission for the DNR right now, so you stay here with your friends and look at the trees around the launch if you want to help."

"Hey, do we get paid?"

"No, but if you want to keep hunting in your lifetime, that should be payment enough for working to protect and heal the ecosystem. Right?"

"Yeah, I guess so." The boy looked disappointed and returned to directing his friends about what to dive for next.

As Lucia and Sam walked away, she could hear them sharing stories about porcupines between their dives as they competed to reach the bottom of the hole they were swimming in.

They navigated upstream along the riverbank nearly 150 meters until deep, thick woods and undergrowth surrounded them. They often needed to use the game trails that wandered away from the bank, only to wind back to it at another point. At one point, the trail found the river again and offered a panoramic view of the water and an open, grassy bank. A single, rotted oak stump crowned the clearing at the edge of the bank, all that remained of the massive tree that once towered over the water long ago.

"It's beautiful here," Sam said.

She loved how the sunlight streamed in rays through the thick forest canopy and glowed on top of the water. The late-evening sun always made wild places like this even more magical.

"It really is." Lucia relaxed and absently rubbed at her sore cheeks. She was finally smiling again.

This hidden spot along the banks of the Pine River was one of the few areas where Rich would relax and be himself, dropping the facade of the badass drug dealer he had so eagerly adopted. Even after they broke up, she had come back alone to ruminate on her life. It was a place where she could be free of life's pressures and drama. She could finally just exist for a little while.

Small birds sang from the full, leafy branches, and herons fished downstream, spreading their long wings and preparing to take flight should the humans dare too many steps in their direction.

"It's also a great fishing spot. The river is deep and freezing here. And perfect for trout."

There was something in the way he paused, the sparkle in his eyes that flushed her cheeks. He held her gaze for a moment before she turned away, nervous about how vulnerable these quiet moments made her feel.

Lucia handed Penny's leash to him before she started searching around the stump. Sam stayed close to her side and watched.

"What are you looking for?" he asked.

"You can't see it, but I know it's here."

"What's here?"

"Shhh," she hushed him as she dug her fingers into the soft green moss at the base of the stump. When she lifted them, she held a thin nylon rope in her palms. She wrapped it around one hand and gently pulled it up from the earth as she followed it to the water.

When all the rope had been freed from the ground, she pulled harder and watched the string tighten at the edge of the bank.

"Okay. Really, Lucia. What is that?"

"We would keep things under the bank. It's hollow under here. We'd put six-packs of beer down here, or sometimes mini coolers with food or... mementos."

"Mementos?" Sam asked, and she wished she hadn't mentioned it. It was still awkward to talk with him about her ex, even if it was possibly relevant to the crazy events happening now.

"Yes." She set her feet and pulled harder on the earth-covered nylon. "Rich proposed to me by putting the ring in a box we kept at the end of this rope. He had me pull it up from under the bank."

"He proposed? You two were engaged?" Sam asked, the shock obvious in his voice.

Lucia cringed. "He asked, and I told him to hold on to it." She stopped pulling the rope so she could turn and look at him. "I told him as soon as he gave up all the shit he was doing, I would say yes. He didn't take me seriously and constantly nagged me about 'saying no' until I left him. Now, back to the present." Her gaze returned to the water. "There's definitely something on the other end of this, but either it's stuck or really heavy. Or both. Would you help me?"

He dropped Penny's leash and grabbed the rope as she fretted over what he thought of her. Was it bad for a career cop to be dating a woman who had been the main squeeze of a bona fide criminal? She guessed they would dump kerosene on that bridge when it was time to cross it. Hopefully, they would watch it burn together and roast marshmallows over the flames.

"Wait," she said as she sat down at the edge of the bank. Lucia hooked her foot under the string and pushed it forward. She hoped it was the best angle to dislodge whatever was under there and let it float out so they could draw it up. "Okay, now pull."

Her thighs burned as she leaned on one hip and awkwardly pushed against the thin nylon rope with the soles of her boots. There was a hollow thud from beneath the bank, and the string gave. All she could imagine was a big cooler filled with Rich's most precious things.

Something snapped under the bank, probably a branch, and whatever was tied to the end of the rope finally floated freely out into the water. At first, it looked like a massive log with a flannel cloth stuck to it. She kept pulling until it rolled. Then she saw it wore a human face and had swollen legs, arms, hands, and fingers.

Chapter 37

S am pulled Lucia away as she shrieked. The scent of waterlogged, rotted flesh washed over them like a wave. She scrambled away from the edge and trembled in his arms. Every detail stood out clear as day to him, from the pallor of the corpse's skin to the way its short, black strands of hair swirled in the water around its head, pointing downstream with the gently flowing current. He knew she would remember each of these little details as well, especially late at night when sleep refused to come.

"Holy shit."

The shrill screams of children broke the momentary stillness, and Sam whipped his gaze downstream to find the group of kids from earlier had quietly followed them. He sprang into action, tying Penny to a tree to keep her from investigating the corpse so he could usher the kids away and force them out of the river. The memory of being downstream from a rotting body might scar them indefinitely, but it would be more scarring the longer they stayed in the water with it.

As soon as Sam had gotten the kids to climb up the opposite bank and go back to the campground, he heard Lucia get sick behind a tree, contaminating the crime scene. Not that there would necessarily be any fresh evidence. It would be a lot of work for the Medical Examiner to learn how long the body had been there and whether death had occurred in that location. The cause of death might be obscured.

Water, a necessity in life, was a cruel captive to the dead. There was no chance of identifying John or Jane Doe right away. It was difficult for an untrained eye to tell if it was a man or a woman. The only thing immediately clear was this person had been an adult, and surely someone out there had prayed their loved one would come home alive. There was always someone who cared, someone whose hope would be extinguished and their world shattered when they received the news that their loved one had been found like this.

He called Dan immediately and shared the find. Dan sent out the coroner and a swarm of state and county police to the scene in minutes. Sam was thankful when the county cops took over, as he had struggled to keep all of the prying eyes away from the site on his own. There were too many people there who had been trying to enjoy one of the last weekends before school started. They'd been drawn to the scene by the kids' screams after they caught sight of the corpse that Lucia had dislodged from beneath the bank.

She stayed close but had been forced to step aside while he conferred with other officers and gave his statement to Dan. She had to give a statement to Dan too, alone, and that bothered Sam. He knew Dan believed she didn't have anything to do with putting a dead body under the riverbank, but too much had happened to exclude her entirely from suspicion.

The extent of Lucia's involvement in her ex-boyfriend's drug dealing and other activity, as evidenced by the photos, would be questioned. An overzealous prosecutor seeking to force her to spill her guts might find some charges to levy against her to attempt to force a plea deal. Worse, a prosecutor like that might not want to wait long enough for the investigation to pan out entirely before pressing charges against someone like her.

Lucia was now the only known person still alive who could be connected to the criminal activities demonstrated in the photos, and to the dead body they had just found. At least until the techies in Lansing ran the photos through facial recognition software and attempted to make matches against law enforcement databases.

Sam hoped they would make this job a priority. They needed to find some other living people to arrest before the system started looking at the woman he loved as a serious suspect. Before they could press charges, arrest her, and drag her off to jail. It would be years of fighting to clear her name, if not a lifetime. He couldn't watch that happen to her.

He wouldn't let it happen.

"Sam," Lucia said, her voice barely above a whisper, breaking his train of desperate thoughts.

"Hey." He reached out for her hand as she approached him. She'd finished giving her statement to Dan, and Sam untied Penny's leash from the tree and prepared to leave. Lucia looked like she was going to be sick again. Her icy skin shocked him as he intertwined the fingers of his free hand in hers. "Are you cold?"

"Yes." Her soft skin was pale, and pain swirled in her dark eyes.

"Have you ever seen a dead body before?"

"Outside of a funeral home?" Her eyes met his, and he noticed the shimmering tears that threatened to fall. She simply shook her head in response, then paused. "I guess, maybe at the gas station when the crash happened. But I'm not sure who was unconscious and who was..." She trailed off, the last word trapped in her throat.

She was a tough woman, but she was also compassionate and empathetic. He didn't believe it was in her nature to rejoice in death or harm to other living creatures.

He squeezed her hand as they walked back to his truck. "We're all done here. We'll see Dan again later tonight."

She groaned her response and ushered Penny into the back seat of the truck before climbing in and pulling the door shut. "I know Dan's our friend, but I don't want to see him anymore. Not right now."

"We'll get through this." He wished there was something more he could say to comfort her, but the right words didn't come. It pained him to see her like this. He watched as she put on her seatbelt and sank back into the seat.

"Take me home, Sam."

Despite the situation, he couldn't help but smile as he climbed up into the driver's seat. He loved the thought of them living together. Maybe when all this was done and things normalized again, she would stay. If she chose to stay, he was ready to ask her to take the next step.

"Lucia," he said her name softly. He turned the key in the ignition but didn't shift it into gear right away. Her tired eyes still looked forward. "Don't worry about getting another apartment next week. Just stay with me. If you hate it, then in a couple of months, I'll help you get your own place. But for now..."

Sam's gentle proposition broke off as he caught sight of something beyond Lucia that sent his pulse racing. He froze for a split second before his brain started pumping adrenaline, and he swung his door open. Leaping out, he bounded around the truck and ran toward the crowd of people gathered just beyond the police tape. The faces of men, women, and children twisted with confusion as he ran toward them.

"You, in the back! On the ground!" He was shocked to hear his voice didn't sound like his own in that brief moment. It was harsher and more panicked. Yet, in plain clothing, nobody in the crowd gave way. He was losing time.

"Move!" he shouted with his command voice, pulling his badge out of his pocket and flashing it in front of the crowd. People darted out of the way after seeing his badge, but they moved in various directions, and the scene fell into chaos. Some ducked, some stepped left or right, and others bolted toward their vehicles.

"Son of a bit-" Sam started to curse but bit it off when he spotted him again. "I need assistance," Sam shouted at the nearest retinue of officers. "I've got a suspect fleeing." He pointed at a man with black hair and icy blue eyes who jumped into a new, jet-black Corvette.

One officer drew his weapon, but Sam stopped him. "Bystanders," he shouted above their resulting screams at seeing a gun drawn. People were running toward their vehicles, and that included running in front of the officer who had drawn his sidearm. There was too much risk that a bystander would be shot.

He heard Dan shouting from behind and turned to warn him. "We need to stop that vehicle," he pointed as the Corvette peeled north from the campground's entrance, spewing gravel as it left. More screams added to the clamor, and Sam guessed that flying gravel had struck them.

"Call it in. We need to chase him down."

Dan sent two county cops in a car to chase down the Corvette before asking dispatch to coordinate assistance in the chase and prepare for spike strips. "Okay, we'll get the car, but you better be right about this. Who was it?"

"The man from the funeral," Sam said through gritted teeth. He hadn't realized he had been clenching his fists until he felt something wet on his curled fingers. Bringing up his hand, he spotted blood dripping from where his nails had cut into the palm of his right hand.

"What man?" Dan demanded.

"The one who threatened Luce." Sam saw her approach them from the corner of his eye and cringed, knowing she could hear them. "It was McNamara."

Chapter 38

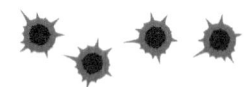

Lucia sat with Sam on his couch in silence, wishing there was some way to incinerate her memories from the past week. Penny rested quietly on the floor at their feet, her back slowly rising and falling with her breath, and Lucia knew the dog was finally sleeping after an exciting day.

Sam had been holding her close and rubbing her shoulder with one hand. His other hand held his cell phone, waiting for an update. When it buzzed, he unlocked his screen and read the text. He only sighed.

"Who is it?"

"It's Dan. McNamara's nowhere to be found. Too many curves along the river, and so many roads off Riverside Drive. He may have taken some other route once they lost sight of him up by Mount Pleasant."

"Didn't they get a helicopter?"

"Took them too long to get up here," he said, dropping his phone on the arm of the couch. "Too much forest cover to see anything."

"Did they catch the license plate?"

"Well, look at you, detective Lucia."

She frowned. She usually appreciated his teasing. But not today.

"Yes, and no," he finally responded to her question. "The plate was a fake."

"Seriously? Who the hell is this guy?"

"He's deeper than you should ever be involved with."

It pained her to have him caught up in all of this. The further things went, the scarier they became. At first, it seemed like she was the only one who needed to worry, at least until Cassie surprised them and gave Sam a concussion. Now that someone had attempted to kidnap her, and Phil had been at the campground watching them after they found the body, she knew things were far more dangerous for everyone.

"They sent guys out to investigate the house where I first saw him, but it's empty now. And his lawyer is already threatening a harassment suit."

This guy was scary to begin with, and he became more frightening by the day.

"What do we do?" She asked, though no answer would make her feel safe again.

"We have to help Dan however we can. But you can't help if you're exhausted, dehydrated, and starved. Can you at least drink some water?"

"I will." She sat herself up and reached over Penny to pick up the glass Sam had placed on the table for her. She sipped slowly and tried to calm her stomach.

"Want to eat?"

"I don't think that's a good idea."

"Well, we can lie here until you fall asleep."

"Sorry, I just—"

"I know, Luce. I get it." She looked up and found his gentle green eyes filled with compassion. He squeezed her to him and kissed her hair. She loved when he did that. It felt close and kind, not overly sexual or predatory. "We have to wait. Maybe now that he's been chased, this Phil guy will back off for a while. Well, aside from his lawyer's threats, anyway. He's claiming his client wasn't at the campground at all."

She nodded, blinking back tears. With a half-sob, half-sigh, she leaned her head against Sam's chest.

His phone buzzed again. "Dan says to keep your chin up," he said after reading the new message. "He wants you to remember that you have friends, and they won't abandon you."

Lucia smiled at that and regretted saying she didn't want to see him. She knew she was lucky to have met Sam and made his friends her own. That they were all cops was especially fortunate, as she was trying to change her life and associate with better people. Although she hated the idea of being away from him, she was still flighty, like moving in with him would mean the end of her freedom. It was ridiculous, but what she knew and what she felt were two very separate things.

"What are we going to do?" she murmured, not realizing she had said it aloud until it was too late.

"About what?" Sam asked sleepily.

"I don't know. Everything."

"As soon as Dan lets us back into your house, we should pack it up and move your stuff here. Then we lie low until the right people are in jail, and we can start living again."

Lucia tensed, and she knew he could feel it. "I don't think it's that easy."

He said nothing for a moment. When he finally broke the silence, tension filled his voice. "What's not that easy?"

"I don't want to invade your space."

"Dammit, Lucia. You've got to be kidding me right now. Please tell me you're not serious." He pulled away slightly so he could look at her.

Her cheeks burned, but the fire in her chest burned hotter. She was about to speak when her phone dinged. Unsure of the right words to say to Sam, she focused on her phone instead.

It was Jordan.

I'm in town. Can we meet at the Tavern?

"Who is it?" Sam asked, his voice darker than she was accustomed to. It stabbed a little at her insides to hear it.

"Jordan. She wants to meet up. Listen, I'm sorry about saying it's not a good idea. There's just so much going on, I can't get my head on straight right now."

"That's the understatement of the year," he scoffed, but she could hear his voice softening so she ignored it.

"Let's go see my best friend." Lucia slid her hand over his palm and squeezed. "I've told her all about you, and she can't wait to meet you. Besides, that will be an easy step for me today. And then we can work on what's next, okay?"

"Okay." His eyes lit up as his cheerful demeanor resurfaced.

She texted Jordan back.

Great! Is 5 too early for dinner?

Chapter 39

S helby was vaguely aware of the pain that radiated from her left leg as she returned to consciousness. She opened her eyes, then shut them tight again when she was blinded by the afternoon sun. The physical agony became more intense as the dull ache flared into a sharp, stabbing sensation that radiated through her bones.

She screeched, her throat too dry to let out a full scream, and her eyes flew open. Her gaze locked onto the culprit: a young coyote biting at her calf. Startled by her sudden movement, it released her briefly before snapping its maw closed on her leg once again, sinking its fangs into her flesh.

Kicking with the other foot, Shelby tried desperately to free her injured leg, but the coyote snarled and shook its head, refusing to let go. Grabbing at the earth around her, Shelby wrapped her fingers around a thick, heavy object. She got a good grip, then flung it forward as hard as she could. The other end connected with the coyote's head, temporarily forcing its teeth even deeper into her flesh, but then the small canine released her. It yelped as it loped off into the woods, glancing back at her twice as if it were considering whether to try again.

Sitting upright, her chest heaved with shuddering breaths. She realized she still held the object she'd hit the coyote with. When her eyes finally focused on it, she found it was a thick, smooth branch. It was about four feet long, two inches in diameter, and almost perfectly straight. Although it was long dead, it was hard rather than rotting, as she might have expected. She decided it would be her walking stick and her weapon to get her the rest of the way to the state police post, however long and far she had left to get there.

The wound in her leg beat out a steady, stomach-curdling throb, but she knew she had come too far to stop now. Besides, Sean and Matt would have been out looking for her first thing this morning when they went to the basement and realized she was gone. She was too weak when she left, and the activities of the night had taken a heavy toll, between rushing and hiding or dealing with the anxiety that flooded her every time she heard a car drive by or voices when she passed through the woods behind a private home.

She didn't dare go to any houses, not trusting anyone who might be associates of Sean or his boss. Every stranger was a possible captor, and as much as she had previously distrusted the police, they were the only ones she would trust now. The only ones, she prayed, that could provide safety and keep the men from taking her back and killing her this time.

Shelby grabbed a handful of dirt from the forest floor and clenched her teeth as she smothered it into the wound. The dirt was dry enough to clump the blood and slow the bleeding. It was something she had done as a child when she had hurt herself while playing. There hadn't been anyone else to take care of her, so she learned the fastest, dirtiest ways to field dress her wounds. Dirt was an easy fix that not many people knew about. For now, it was a decently safe quick fix, considering she didn't have enough clothing to spare for a makeshift dressing.

Using the stick to force herself to a stand, Shelby looked around, careful to stay quiet, though painfully aware that her screech and cries during the fight with the coyote could have caught the attention of any passersby or other predators. She alternated between moving and resting, and the last time she rested, she had fallen asleep without intending to do so.

Shelby knew she needed the rest. Her body was screaming at her for water, food, and sleep. But this had to be the final push to get to safety. She hoped the post wasn't too far because she didn't know how much more mental or physical strength she had left.

She was sure she was south of the little town where she had seen the state police post because she had finally come to the river that split the town in half. Crossing the river as closely as she could to the town without coming near any houses, she was careful to stay out of sight and away from the road. She refused to take the risk of being seen by the men she knew were looking for her.

She needed to get to the cops and take them back to the farmhouse to rescue Mel and the other girls. Especially the young one that was being brainwashed.

If you can figure out how to get there, dumbass, the evil little voice in her head quipped.

Shut the fuck up and march, she snapped back.

With a groan, she took her first step forward, walking toward the edge of the forest. All night she had continued to head east until the woods gave way to fields again. As she reached the edge of this block of forest, she hesitated. Reluctant to leave the safety of the trees, she realized there weren't any other wooded areas connecting her current spot with the area to the east. As she looked across the open field full of potatoes and toward the road due north, she realized the houses were no longer densely packed together. In fact, there was plenty of space between them.

I'm finally on the outskirts. She was careful to keep her excited thoughts unspoken. Regardless of how close she might be, silence was still her safest bet.

Following the road farther east with her eyes, Shelby recognized a small, square, red-brick building. It looked almost like a one-story house, except for the US and Michigan flags properly hoisted in front of the building and the blue and gold state police signage near the road. More obvious was the 60-feet-tall red and white communications tower snugged to the side. Her breath caught in her chest. She had finally made it.

It was now or never.

Gripping her hand on the middle of her walking stick, Shelby took a deep breath and steadied her nerves. Seeing the road again had made her anxious, but seeing the police post had steeled her against her fear—and the hot streaks of pain that clawed through her left leg.

Shelby bolted from the woodline, taking long, fast strides across the rows of potatoes. Each step she took with her left leg was excruciating, and her speed was broken too soon from a sprint to a walk. Using the stick to help her, she limped through the potato field. Although she tried to avoid stepping on the rows, she was still limping too fast to avoid them entirely. Each time she stepped on a potato plant, she was thrown off balance, and her good ankle threatened to roll, but she moved as fast as she could.

As she reached the edge of the field, her energy had fallen to its lowest point. Starving, dehydrated, and injured, there was nothing left in her tank. The field gave way to the freshly cut, dry lawn that surrounded the parking lot and driveway of the police post. She stepped from the field into the grass and limped slowly toward the building, tears burning her eyes and blurring her vision.

Almost there, Shelby, you can do this. Prove them wrong. She didn't know who she would prove wrong, but her self-talk worked well with her defiant nature, and she needed every mental edge to make it across the final 100 meters of her journey.

Thinking back to the land navigation training she had started to learn with the Army recruiters in their open-door, Delayed Entry Program training classes on Wednesday night, she knew that she averaged eighty-one steps in 100 meters. Of course, she hadn't been injured when she'd created that baseline.

Only eighty-one steps, she guessed, to reach the main entrance of the post, which was luckily on the side of the building facing her. Each step beneath the hot August sun sapped a little more energy as her bare feet flinched against the dry, prickly grass. Her throat tightened, and her body begged for water.

There was a flash of reflected sunlight as the glass door opened. She had counted to step forty-three when a uniformed officer emerged.

Shelby tried to yell, but her words only hissed from her throat. Her tongue felt like sandpaper, but she licked her lips and tried again. Still, nothing. The officer had paused and was staring down at a phone in his hands. He was a trim man, and she could tell even from this distance that he lifted weights. For that, she was thankful, if not a little intimidated. His uniform was the reason she would risk seeking his help.

She bit down hard on the side of her tongue and groaned. Although she tasted blood, the bite had also drawn a little more saliva, and she swallowed both to wet her throat.

"Help," she finally croaked, though still much more softly than she'd hoped. It was painful to try to yell. She swallowed more of her blood and pushed through the pain in her throat to try again. "Help!"

The officer's head jerked up, and he looked around. It took him a second to adjust his eyes to the harsh afternoon sunlight, but then he saw her. Shelby let the stick slide from her fingers and fall into the grass as her chest tightened and a lump formed in her sore throat.

Not yet, she told herself. *Hold it together. Stay calm. For them.*

She wanted to have the strength, the calm, and the clarity to tell the officers everything they needed to take immediate action. They had to save the other women and send Sean, Matt, and their boss to jail for the rest of their lives.

But as the officer started running toward her, Shelby couldn't keep the tears from falling any longer. She reached her arms out to him, mouthing the word 'please' since she couldn't speak it. When he reached her, the world spun and her vision faded as she collapsed into the safety of his arms.

Chapter 40

Lucia exhaled loudly as she held up her phone and read the new message.

When will you be here?

She understood her friend was worried about her, but it had already been a long day.

All she wanted to do was cuddle on the couch with Sam and relieve the tension hanging in the air between them. It was only quarter after four, forty-five minutes before they were supposed to meet up.

"I think Jordan's worried about me," she said, rising from the couch so she could freshen up and get ready.

"She's right to be worried," he muttered absently as he scrolled on his phone.

"Hey," she whispered, kneeling in front of him and placing her crossed arms over his knees. She pouted her lips. "Are you mad at me?"

"No," he grumbled.

"You sound mad."

"I've said what I needed to say."

"And, you were right. You are right. It's just a whole mess of stuff that I have to get over. I need to take it one day at a time." She paused, grabbing his phone from his hands and tossing it to the other side of the couch. "You're the only person I can imagine being happy with. You do make me happy, and I want to be with you. I love the thought of living with you, even if it does scare me. As we move forward, can we just take it one day at a time? Please?"

She was delighted to finally see his expression soften. "Yes, Lucia." He pulled her up from the floor and into his arms. "I can't deny you anything."

"Hmmm," she gave him a sly look. "Can I please have your truck?"

"I'll need a little more for that."

Lucia tilted her head up and kissed him, teasing his lips with her tongue and opening to him when he returned her kiss. She ran her fingers through his hair, then pulled away, leaving him wanting more.

"Can I please have your truck now?"

"Keys are on the counter," he said with exaggerated satisfaction.

She laughed and kissed him once more before jumping up.

"Can we get ready and head out a little early?"

He cocked an eyebrow at her and held his palms up.

Lucia leaned down and kissed him passionately, dragging her nails gently against his scalp and down his neck before pulling away. "Please?" she asked, breathless.

"Anything you want," he said with a smile, his eyes still closed. "Let's take the Vic."

We're on our way. Be there in 10.

Lucia texted Jordan from the passenger seat as Sam steered his late-nineties Crown Victoria, a retired blue police cruiser, east onto the highway. She donned her reflective aviator sunglasses he'd bought for her on their first trip to Lake Michigan together. The sunglasses were her favorite thing she owned, not just because of the way she looked in them but also because of the way Sam stared at her when she wore them.

Another text from Jordan buzzed her phone in her lap.

What are you driving?

Lucia tapped out a quick response.

Blue Crown Vic. Doesn't matter, we'll meet you inside. Sit at the bar and get a drink.

When she glanced up again, Sam was staring at her in that way she loved, the way that sent the butterflies into a frenzy. She couldn't help but smile back, outstretching her arm over the center console to hold hands with him. When they touched, a tingling warmth swept like a river through her blood.

She raised the back of his hand to her lips and kissed him, letting her glasses slide down her nose ever so slightly so he could see her eyes. His smile widened, but he quickly turned his eyes back to the road before letting go of her hand and patting her leg playfully. They flirted and messed around as he drove into town. She was careful not to distract him too much, but she loved to tease him, knowing it would pay off later when they were alone again.

He couldn't hide his smile despite his best efforts, but as they crossed the bridge over the Pine River and the Tavern came into view, his smile disintegrated, and the color drained from his face.

Chapter 41

Time seemed to slow. Lucia turned her gaze forward and watched as a black Jeep drove straight at them. It was in their lane, and she caught her breath when an arm extended from the passenger side window and pointed a pistol toward them.

"What the—" The sound of crunching glass cut off Sam's curse. The Vic swerved as he ducked his head. "Get down!" he barked at her as he crouched low in his seat. He could see just well enough to maneuver the car around the oncoming Jeep. It barely missed hitting them head-on as they passed, and she slid down in her seat to get her head below the dashboard.

She peered up and noticed the windshield now sported circular, webbed patterns from left to right. Were those impacts from gunshots?

Two more crunching sounds made her duck again. The engine roared as Sam jammed the gas pedal to the floor, drowning out the Alice in Chains song playing on the radio.

Sam wove through traffic as fast as he could, and Lucia was whipped side to side. The shots were coming from behind now, and she realized the Jeep must have turned around to chase them.

"Call 9-1-1," Sam shouted above the sounds of splintering glass, honking horns, and the Vic's engine. Lucia grabbed for her phone but didn't find it in the seat. She frantically searched the floorboard with her hands, finally locating it. She fumbled as she dialed 9-1-1 and activated the speaker function so Sam could hear the call too.

"9-1-1, what is your emergency?" The operator's voice was barely audible despite the speaker being at full volume.

"This is officer Samuel Frost of the Michigan State Police. I'm off-duty and being shot at. Heading east-bound on M-46 in a blue 1998 Crown Victoria. At least two men in a 2014 black Jeep Wrangler are following my vehicle. They're firing shots at my vehicle."

Lucia ducked as another volley of fire peppered the rear window. She didn't understand why the glass hadn't shattered into a million tiny pieces yet, then remembered the Vic was a retired police vehicle.

"Alert state and county immediately. I'm heading for the Pine River State Police Post."

As they reached the edge of the official city limits, two more shots impacted the Vic, eerily similar to the sound of large chunks of gravel hitting the car. The operator said something that Lucia couldn't hear as Sam floored the gas and passed another vehicle. Traffic was tight, with only one lane in each direction and a middle turning lane. They hadn't traveled a half-mile since first being shot at, but she knew Sam would head straight for the post as soon as he could get around the drivers ahead of him who were oblivious to the silenced gunfire.

Another spray of gunfire hit the back of the car right before Sam slammed on the brakes and yanked the steering wheel right. Her body whipped left with the centrifugal force as the car went into a slide. The engine roared once more, driving straight briefly before he braked and spun the car in a 180-degree turn.

"Stay down," Sam shouted as he reached under the seat, then opened his door. Too curious for her own good, Lucia slowly peeked from her hiding place. They were at the station. Sam had managed to drive in before spinning the car around to face the highway. His fellow state police officers were already waiting for him.

She watched as the driver of the black Jeep jammed on his brakes and failed to stop before hitting the spike strip the troopers had laid out for them. There were two simultaneous pops as the front tires caught the spike strip. The Jeep spun sideways and came to a sliding stop. The driver's side faced the cops, and the passenger side faced the hayfield on the opposite side of the road.

With more than a dozen guns trained on them, the men held their hands up and waited for orders from the police. Then, one of them said something to the other that wasn't audible to anyone else. Without warning, the passenger bolted from his side of the car and sprinted through the hayfield.

A trooper shouted orders to the Jeep's driver, and he complied perfectly. He stepped out of the vehicle, dropped his weapon on the pavement, then lay face down on the asphalt with his hands behind his head and his legs spread.

Lucia shook with fury as she watched the passenger run across the field.

"Why aren't they shooting these assholes?" she growled, flinging open her door.

"Stay in the car," Sam snapped, gesturing for her to get back in her seat. She hated being stuck and helpless, but not as much as she hated how they weren't blowing holes in her attackers.

She knew it was the same Jeep and the same men who had chased her that morning. God only knew what they would have done if they had caught her, but the fact that they'd shot at her and Sam gave her a pretty good idea. Surprisingly, she was more furious about how they'd endangered Sam's life too.

Her hands trembling and her heart pounding as she watched the officers put handcuffs on the driver. Furious, she wanted to ask what was being done about the other one, but the sound of a small engine cut through her blood-thirsty thoughts. One ATV flew past the cars and across the road, bouncing the uniformed rider as he crossed the shallow ditch. Two more troopers followed close behind one another.

The police had blocked off the highway in either direction and diverted traffic. Movement closer to the Jeep caught her attention, and she watched as two officers hauled the driver to his feet and walked him toward the post. Lucia opened the car door and stood, glaring at him. His face was bruised and bleeding. She hadn't seen what transpired to give him the injuries, but she didn't care. Her heart still thudded in her chest and adrenaline coursed through her veins. She needed action, some form of release as it spiked.

Lucia sprinted toward him, her right fist clenched and drawn back, ready to strike. A strong arm caught her around the waist mid-stride and pulled her off her feet. She locked eyes with the driver for only a moment before one of the officers redirected him, putting him in the rear of a blue and gold cruiser. She needed him to know that she wanted his blood.

"Stay back!" Sam commanded, pulling her back to the car, restraining her until she couldn't fight him anymore.

"He needs to pay," she said as her eyes started to sting. "They tried to kidnap me, they..." she choked on the words as the tears started falling against her will. "They tried to kill us." Her voice was barely above a whisper as she fought the breakdown that was coming. She was crashing as the adrenaline dissipated.

"They'll pay, but you cannot attack them. If you do, it could ruin everything we need to put these guys away."

That revelation did help sober her, but it still crushed her spirit to feel so helpless, so impotent in the face of persistent violence. Every fiber of her being vibrated with the urge to fight, to neutralize the threat. Effectively shackled by the knowledge that her interference would impede the justice system, Lucia clenched her jaw and paced on the far side of Sam's old Vic.

At first, she could only think of the things she wanted to do to the men who had nearly killed her and Sam. There was a deep-rooted urge for primal, defensive violence. Although it surprised her, she didn't try to suppress it.

He walked away to speak with Dan and the post commander, occasionally pointing at his car and Lucia. Her eyes drifted between the three cops while they talked until the buzz of small engines caught her attention. The other troopers had run down and captured the Jeep's passenger. After bringing him back, they put him in a separate cruiser, far enough from his friend and angled so they couldn't see or communicate with each other.

"Luce?" Sam's voice broke through her haze. "Can you come over here? You need to be debriefed."

"Again?" One clear look at the bullet impact points all over his car renewed her willingness to go through the process yet again. She steeled herself and walked over, rolling her shoulders to relieve some of the tension in her back.

"Are you ready to give your statement?" Dan asked when she approached.

"Yes. But I have a question."

Dan nodded. "Okay."

"Where's Jordan?"

Chapter 42

What had begun as an afternoon trip to the Tavern for an early dinner with Lucia's best friend from college had ended in yet another long "interview" that felt more like an interrogation. When Lucia finally stepped out of Dan's office without an enthusiastic farewell, she looked around the room but didn't find Sam waiting for her as usual.

He wasn't at his desk and, after a brief walk, she realized he wasn't in the lounge either. Coming back to the work floor where most of the officers' desks were located, Lucia took Sam's seat, leaned her head on his clean desktop, and closed her eyes.

"It's like she's a wife already," an amused voice whispered from across the room. Lucia didn't bother looking up. She couldn't think about that now while her thoughts still revolved around her latest interview with Dan. She felt like she did everything she could to cooperate because she really wanted to help. Now she was thoroughly exhausted and had nothing left to give.

Right as they finished, an officer had poked his head into the interview room and explained that there was no evidence that Lucia's friend Jordan had ever been at the Tavern. Dan promised her that as soon as procedure allowed, he would tell her whether the two men who tried to kidnap her were in any way connected with Jordan.

She prayed there was some misunderstanding and Jordan was sitting at the Tavern bar at that very moment. Yet, her instincts warned her that

Jordan wasn't at the Tavern. The men had played her over text, and that's why they were waiting for her. That's how they knew to look for Sam's car instead of Lucia's. She had texted Jordan, telling her when they were coming and exactly what they were driving. They had driven right into an ambush, one intended to kill her. But how had they known about Jordan?

Lucia couldn't help but worry for her friend, especially since an officer had come to tell Dan that a young woman had arrived safely at the hospital to recover. The girl, Dan had explained in hushed tones without too much detail, had shown up at the post shoeless, dehydrated, malnourished, and claiming that she'd been kidnapped and sexually assaulted. Repeatedly. Lucia shivered at the thought, especially when he said the girl swore she recognized the Jeep.

A door opened along the exterior wall of the room with enough force to shake the drop ceiling tiles and Lucia, along with everyone else, turned her head at the commotion. It was Sam, leaving the post commander's office with his jaw clenched and his shoulders tight. He strode toward her and motioned for her to follow him as he approached. She did so without question, peering behind him in confusion. Commander Evans stood in the doorway of his office, nearly filling the frame. Tall, grim, tense.

They left the post in silence and stepped out into the last orange rays of evening sunlight. She heard him exhale as he walked away from the post for several yards before halting. His hand slid into his pocket to retrieve his keys, then he looked at his car and sighed. "I have to get this thing to the body shop."

"They do windshields too?"

"They do all kinds of glasswork. I can't drive it like this."

"Hey," a voice called from behind. "Evans told me to drive you guys back home."

Lucia and Sam turned to find Chris walking toward them with keys in hand.

"Thank you," she said, grateful they didn't have to figure out a way home on their own.

The drive back was quiet, though Sam, sitting in the front seat of the cruiser, shared small talk with Chris about trucks, weather, and baseball.

Lucia gazed out the window, eyeing the Tavern as they passed it. There were a few cars she didn't recognize, but most were regulars, and there was a single state police cruiser. She guessed they were still looking for witnesses in the area. She reminded herself that they had already looked for Jordan and hadn't found her there.

When Chris dropped them off, they found a cheerful Penny waiting for them behind the front door, panting and wagging her tail so hard it hurt when it hit Lucia's leg. She took the excited dog for a quick walk before returning to find Sam lying on the couch with his eyes closed.

"I'm sorry, Sam," she said sincerely. He said nothing, his eyes remaining closed, and offered no indication he'd heard her.

A lump rose in her throat. She sat in a recliner next to the couch, blinking back tears. Even though she couldn't have predicted any of this would happen, she knew it was essentially her fault that Sam had been concussed, threatened, and now ambushed and shot at. If she wasn't in his life, it could be boring, normal, and mundane.

It sure seemed like he was a hell of a lot safer without her around.

Her heart hurt as she stared at Sam. He was only a couple of feet away, but the distance felt more like miles. She wanted so badly to hold him and hear him tell her everything was going to be all right. The time she spent with him had been the best of her adult life, and she'd been looking forward to so much more with him.

Just as she was finally growing accustomed to the idea of living with him, her past was now rearing its ugly head, keeping her from moving forward and healing. Realization struck her, and suddenly she didn't know if it was logic or fear that gripped her heart. Perhaps her hopes of a future with Sam had been unrealistic.

Maybe a girl like her, with her stupid mistakes and troubled past, didn't deserve to be with a good man like Sam. If her fears were right, he was way out of her league. He deserved a normal woman, a woman whose presence wouldn't endanger his life.

Dan had warned her she was obviously a target and in danger, and so were the people she loved. There was a strict process to approve protective measures for someone in her situation and because they didn't understand why she was being targeted, they couldn't yet submit consideration for her to be in the program. She left Dan's interview with the understanding that ensuring her safety was up to her and Sam, and she'd need to call 9-1-1 if anything else happened.

What was worse than not knowing what might happen next was the feeling that Sam was quietly slipping away from her. The strangest sensation of being utterly alone washed over her. Was there anywhere she could belong? Looking back at the last six years of her life, she had always felt alone. Like it was only her against the world.

Maybe it was always meant to be that way. Not everybody got to live a picture-perfect life, so why would she be special?

Lucia swallowed the pain, shoving it down into a deep, dark corner of her soul and locking it away. For now, she needed to embrace the resilient independence she was raised with. If she really needed help, she could suck up her pride and turn to her family. Especially her brother. If she was right, he was currently an embassy guard somewhere in Europe, and she hoped he might have enough leave to come home.

Her phone buzzed, and she picked it up and activated the screen. There was a message from Dan.

You can go back to your house when you're ready. I finished everything as fast as possible so you could get back in and prepare to move.

"Dan said my house is clear," she announced. "I need to start packing." She rose from her chair and walked toward the door.

Sam sat up on the couch, stretching and yawning before he spoke. "Give me a second."

"You don't have to come," she declared, unable to veil the hostility in her voice.

"What are you talking about? Of course I'm coming."

"Well, something's wrong, and you're not telling me. You're holding back, and I can't take it. Either tell me what's going on, or there's no point in moving all my shit in here. We don't need to play games."

Sam stood up and moved toward her, stopping at arms-length. He shoved his hands in his pockets, his eyes sad. "I'm just tired."

"If you're not going to be open with me, then we're wasting oxygen."

"My commander," Sam said abruptly before she could walk away. "He's worried, with everything that's happened, that maybe you're involved with more than I know. He said I need to be careful, or you'd be bad for my career. Or..."

"Or what?"

Sam shrugged. "We could have been killed today, Luce. He's worried."

"Am I really being blamed—" She broke off when he closed the distance between them and kissed her. At first, she was shocked, then she pulled back. "Oh, no. No, no, no. You can't just kiss me and make—" He took her in his arms and drew her close, kissing her more passionately.

She relaxed against his body, and her legs turned to jelly as he swept away her cold resolve with a single, hot kiss. Stars glimmered behind her eyelids as she savored the taste of mint gum that lingered on his warm lips. Finally, he released her. Her head was swimming and her heart melting as he led her back to the couch.

"I'm sorry, okay?" He pulled her close, and she rested her head on his chest as they sat side by side. "It doesn't matter what anyone says. I'm not going anywhere. I'll be right here with you. We'll see this thing through to the end, together."

Lucia wanted to apologize, but the words wouldn't come. She thought she had locked her hopes away only minutes ago, but they had resurged. The walls she thought she'd put up crumbled beneath the warmth of his kiss and the sincerity of his words. She didn't even realize she was crying until he wiped the tears from her cheeks with his thumb. The dam broke, and she leaned against him, letting them run like a river.

He sat there quietly, alternately running his hand over her hair and rubbing her shoulder. There were no more words between them for the rest of the evening. Instead, the understanding they would start moving her things into his home the next day was left unspoken. She couldn't deny that she felt safe with him. Safe and supported.

She knew he loved her, and, with absolute certainty, she knew that she loved him too.

Chapter 43

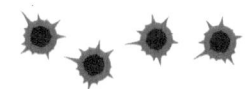

Tuesday, September 4th

L ucia woke before Sam and took Penny for a walk in the dewy morning air. When she returned to the house, she made coffee, bacon, and pancakes–without burning anything for a change. When Sam finally entered the kitchen, she wrapped her arms around his neck and kissed him. He drew back, a curious look on his face, and she forced a smile.

"What's wrong?" he asked, rubbing her shoulder.

She shook her head and gestured to the table where she'd set his plate. "Nothing really. I'm just tired. It's all so much. I don't even have the energy to think right now."

Sam nodded and sat down. "Thanks for breakfast." He caught her hand and kissed it, gazing up into her eyes with a gentleness that almost made her legs weak.

"You always make breakfast." She squeezed his fingers before turning away to grab her own plate. "I figured it was my turn."

They ate in relative silence, though he used his charm to keep a smile on her face. A grin here, a wink there, a little more flirting, and she melted for him like always. She felt like crying tears of relief for the pleasant morning but held them back.

After they finished breakfast and washed the dishes, Lucia's phone buzzed in her back pocket. She tugged it out and lit up the lock screen to find a text from Liam.

Potential buyer will be here in two hours. Can you get Tess ready? Put her in the trail saddle and give her a ride before they get here.

Lucia texted back immediately in the affirmative. The money would go a long way now, especially since she felt so guilty about Sam's car. Perhaps she could help repair it or at least contribute to the down payment for another. He still had the truck, but she knew how much he loved his old Vic.

Once she'd showered and dressed, she found Sam sitting in the living room reading a book, with Penny lying quietly at his feet. "Liam texted me about a buyer coming soon, so I have to take Tess for a trail ride. They'll probably want to test ride before they sign the sale contract and pay Liam, so I need to make sure she's ready."

Sam laid his book on the side table and glanced up. "Give me a couple of minutes, and I'll be ready to go."

"No, it's probably going to be a few hours. You'll be bored to tears."

"So? It's not safe," he insisted, shaking his head as he stood.

"Why not?"

"Well," he started, but she cut him off.

"The area is crawling with cops, and the two guys who ambushed us are in custody."

"Yeah, but–"

"Please, Sam. Please relax. There's no way that any more trauma can be crammed into a twenty-four-hour period. Besides, I need time to think about everything."

He looked skeptical and, if she wasn't mistaken, a little hurt.

"I'm going to be trail riding, and unless you want to go for a ride too, you won't be able to be with me the whole time anyway."

Sam sighed as he wrapped her in his arms. "Are you sure you're going to be okay?" he whispered in her ear.

"Yes." She kissed his cheek. "If any place is safe for me, it's Liam's farm."

"What about last night? Are we still good?"

Lucia tilted her head to stare into his eyes before giving him a deep, slow kiss.

When she pulled away, they locked eyes, and she nodded.

"Together," she echoed the words he had said the night before and held up her pinky finger.

He grinned and hooked his pinky with hers before kissing her once more.

As she walked out the door and waved goodbye to Sam and Penny, she relaxed. She was confident that things were starting to look up again.

When Lucia pulled up her car in front of the main barn, she noticed Liam's truck in front of the house. Considering it was only nine in the morning, she was sure he'd be waiting in the barn as soon as she came back from her ride. If everything went well, the buyer would take Tess for a ride, love her, sign the sale contract, and pay Liam. Lucia would go back to Sam with a couple thousand dollars to help him out and even treat them to a nice dinner. Heck, maybe she could finally afford to swallow her pride and go back home to Newaygo and make things right with her parents.

There was one more thing on her mind as she pulled her .40 Sig Sauer from the glove box and tucked it in the back holster she had borrowed from Sam. She pulled her loose t-shirt over it before exiting the car and heading for the barn. Even though she was here about horses and money, she still thought about the last clue Rich had left.

Where I burned our names.

What the hell was he talking about? Lucia cringed as she realized she was finally starting to think of him in the past tense. It was uncomfortable and nauseating as the epiphany rested in her mind.

Still, the last clue plagued her. She had found two already, and even if Dan and the others thought that capturing the men from the Black Jeep would calm things down, she wasn't convinced. Something instinctive compelled her to keep searching until there weren't any threads left to follow.

Whether it was foolish didn't matter. Maybe the clue wasn't even related to the evidence she found before, but about her and Rich instead. It seemed unlikely, but the series of events over the past week would have seemed impossible just ten days ago. She had to admit there were things about Rich she didn't know. As much as she thought she knew him a year ago, maybe she didn't actually understand the person he had become before he died.

More emotionally pressing was the fact that seeking out these clues was essentially the last thing he'd asked of her. She didn't feel right denying a dead man his final wishes, even a man she'd already given so much of her life to.

Remember where I burned our names?

Nope. I sure don't, Lucia thought.

Tess nickered as soon as she saw Lucia and trotted up to the gate, eager for the attention. Lucia wanted to savor this last ride. She loved Tess, but she didn't have the facilities or money to own a horse, especially when she was in between jobs and, potentially, homes.

She had faith that Liam had researched the buyer already, and buyers with this kind of money to spend on horses had a presence in the community and reputations. He wouldn't sell any of his horses to people who had abusive or neglectful reputations. One day, Lucia hoped to have her own farm and her own horses that she could raise and train her way.

Before that could happen, she needed to figure out how to get there. The first step she could see was to do her job today and get the horse ready for the buyers. She would make a little money to start the next chapter of her life. From every indication, that next chapter would be spent with Sam, and the idea of that increasingly warmed her heart.

As Lucia finished grooming Tess's shiny honeycomb coat and combed her long black mane, she let her thoughts swirl around what weeks and months living with Sam would look like. While she had resisted the idea before, she couldn't imagine how it would be drastically different from how they lived now, spending most nights together between their two homes. One home would consolidate the financial burden and give them both room to save more money.

After saddling and bridling the mare, Lucia led her out of the barn toward a long lane between two pastures that led into the woods. The forested area of the farm was mostly to the north and was adjacent to state land, meaning there was plenty of room to ride without ever touching a road. The trail she took today was her favorite, and she hadn't been on it since she'd broken up with Rich.

She was thankful her old saddlebags were still in the barn because she needed them to take her Sig along with her on the ride. She tied the pistol securely in the inside pocket of the right-side saddlebag where it wouldn't be seen. Although she felt safe for now, she would not go without her pistol anymore if she could avoid it.

Nine days ago, she had refused to carry it, never wanting to deal with the trouble it might cause if she needed to go somewhere that prohibited firearms. Now, after all that had happened, she loathed the idea of feeling helpless again, unable to defend herself in the face of danger. Next, she would figure out how to carry while running.

On her last run, if she hadn't turned in time to see the man coming up behind her, would she have been able to escape or outrun him and his companion? She might be dead or, worse, a captive to men who did the kinds of things she had seen in the pictures.

She mounted Tess and seated herself in the black trail saddle, silently swearing she was done watching life from the sidelines. There would be no more waiting for rescue, waiting for others to step up and help her. The people who waited for others to take action gave away their God-given power, and she would no longer sacrifice that power or her integrity.

Leaning the reins forward over the mare's withers and cueing with her legs, Lucia let Tess break into a bouncy trot before transitioning to a relaxed, rocking canter. She was pleased the mare still remembered their favorite trail. For a moment, she allowed her mind to drift aimlessly.

Memories rushed back to her, splashes of the sights, the smells, and the feel of the wind against her face as she and Rich had once raced their horses down this same trail. All the giddy feelings of love and attraction mixed up with the adrenaline from the race always guaranteed they would use the picnic blanket that was rolled up behind Rich's saddle. That was back in the early days of their relationship, before she knew about the extent of his drug use and before she quit college to move in with him.

Now the trail was overgrown, its lush trees stretching their branches overhead like grasping arms. No one came through here anymore, she realized with a touch of disappointment. It was possible no one had ridden this way since Rich's little sister had gone off to college in Marquette. Grass had grown up over the two-tracks, and in another couple of summers, the trail would be but a ghost of a path. Now it was a place haunted by nothing more than broken memories.

Lucia spotted the sprawling, twisted old oak before long. She slid down from the saddle to view the ancient tree. It had to be hundreds of years old, and she was amazed it still seemed to be growing. This tree was the king of

the forest. Something around the side of the tree caught her eye. It took a
moment to process what she saw before she realized she had finally found
the last thing Rich had left for her on this earth.

Chapter 44

Lucia dismounted and loosely tied Tess's reins to a nearby sapling. Moving around the grand oak, careful not to trip on its thick roots rising from the dark soil, she rounded the side and found a wood plank nailed into the tree. The flat, round piece of wood had been sliced from a different tree in a way that beautifully showed its rings, but it was the writing on the plank that stole the breath from her lungs.

A few years back, Rich had tried to direct his energy into the hobby and business of wood-burning. It didn't last long before he decided it wasn't as fun or lucrative as meth or heroin, so he dropped the hobby. Apparently, he had still retained enough of the skill to use it for one final message.

Lucia,
Save them.
Save yourself.
- Rich

It was a peculiar thing to read, and more peculiar was that it had been artistically burned into the wood in simple calligraphy. The ends of the letters curved and waved, and Lucia never could have imagined how a harmful action such as burning could be harnessed to create such art, to draw the eye, to bring to a single medium both life and destruction.

This is what he'd meant. He had burned their names into the plank and placed it in a spot where he couldn't have known for sure that she would visit. Rich's choice had been a leap of faith, a gamble, and possibly the only other safe place remaining where he could hide anything. Although the plank itself was a hint, it wasn't what he wanted her to find.

The massive old oak was where she and Rich had often picnicked together, and sometimes they would hide things in one of the tree's many hollows. As the plank was nailed, it covered one little hollow they had used most often. Anyone looking wouldn't know there was something behind it unless they knew exactly where to look.

Lucia reached as far up the trunk as she could and spun the plank on its nail, flipping it upside down and revealing the hollow. Her fingers trembled as she carefully explored it. At first, she felt nothing, so she grabbed the edge of the hole with her free hand and hoisted herself up farther so she could reach deeper.

Her fingers brushed against something plastic, and she recoiled instinctively at first, then plunged her hand back in. She pinched the edge of the plastic between her fingertips and pulled it out of the hole. She stumbled, then quickly regained her balance and examined her find.

A yellow padded shipping envelope was enclosed in a double-zipped plastic freezer bag. She gave it a test squeeze to guess the contents and her fingers pressed the edges of several hard objects. Although it was impossible to tell without opening it, she guessed there were possibly more thumb drives or even an external hard drive. Whatever they were, they would have to wait until she got back to Sam's.

Discovering the final cache that Rich had left would be Lucia's proof to Sam that she was truly done watching from the sidelines. She would no longer sit back and stay quiet when she could take action and speak up. It wasn't just her own life that she had to worry about. Besides, if she wasn't willing to step up, then she couldn't count on other people to do the right thing either.

Lucia felt her internal fire, her defiance and integrity, spark and catch as she walked back to Tess with the package in hand. The horse had shifted its weight to one side and rested sleepily near the sapling she'd been tied to. She barely lifted her head when Lucia opened the saddlebag and secured the package inside. It would be too bulky to carry in hand as she rode back.

She also didn't want Liam or anyone else to see it and ask about it.

With one last glance, Lucia tried to admire the awe-inspiring beauty of the elder oak, convinced this was the last time she would ever see it, but her pulse raced, and her mind buzzed. The excitement kept her from fully experiencing the moment and seeing what she'd hoped to see.

The ride back was spent mostly at a walk as Lucia tested Tess's obedience and ensured the steady mare wouldn't dare to bolt for the barn. It also provided much-needed time for her to enjoy the silence of the forest and the surrounding fields. The quiet introspection further cemented her new resolve in her heart.

As Lucia rounded the last corner of the trail and the farm came back into sight, she noticed there was another car parked next to hers in front of the main barn. The thought of saying goodbye to the mare pained her, but Lucia knew it was for the best. It wasn't her horse, she couldn't afford to buy her, and she couldn't afford to keep her anywhere either. It was foolish to hold on to such a loyal creature out of selfishness rather than its own best interest.

With a few mournful pats to Tess's neck and whispered endearments over her dark mane, Lucia relished the last two hundred feet of riding back to the barn. The sunny morning and cloudless sky meant she could leave Tess at the tie post outside the second, older barn and brush her down before introducing her to the buyers. The older barn was empty, save for older tack and extra hay in the loft. She untied the saddlebags and slung them over one shoulder before heading toward the barn door. She hoped she'd have time to set the saddlebags out of sight from Liam or anyone else.

When Lucia pushed open the side door to the horse barn, she found Liam waiting for her with two visitors. Her stomach dropped when her vision adjusted to the dim light in the barn.

Standing next to Liam was none other than Phil, who grinned from ear to ear as he locked eyes with her.

Chapter 45

S am turned his truck onto the main highway and headed for the Pine River Equestrian Center. Although he'd never been to Liam Thompson's farm before, Lucia had spoken of it at great length. He felt he had a fairly good idea of where she would be riding and training, and where she'd go afterward. Waiting in the main barn until she finished would probably be best.

Getting to know her over the past ten months, he had become painfully familiar with her flighty personality. He understood that her relationship with Rich had deeply scarred her, and she was wary of being hurt again—of being trapped, tricked, and betrayed. It was something he would always have to contend with. But he also knew with the utmost certainty that he loved her, and only trust and time could overcome the pain of her past.

He had his own demons to deal with, aside from his jealousy and the way he withdrew in times of conflict. His nightmares, his memories, and the impenetrable guilt he carried were the largest of his baggage that Lucia had to deal with. In their time together, she had proven more than capable of standing beside him through it all. She'd been surprisingly helpful along his road to healing.

Now, he needed to reassure her that he was in it for the long haul, shootouts and ambushes be damned. He wasn't going to leave her, and he wouldn't blame her for the things that had happened. Even if he had almost been killed, it wasn't Lucia's fault. It was the work of criminals who were trying to silence her for their belief that she had evidence that could identify them and put them behind bars.

Since she'd been active in helping find and share information and run down the clues left to her, Sam had complete confidence she really was everything he ever wanted and needed in a partner for life. He never believed in love at first sight, learning early on that a woman's character didn't necessarily match a pretty exterior, but it was damn close with Lucia.

Hers was a character of resilience and, given the right support, bravery. Sam loved almost everything about Lucia, except her tendency to run and hide, but he had an inkling it was something she was growing out of rather than a permanent trait. Everything else about her was about as balanced as a real person could be, and he now believed she was the only woman for him.

He turned his pickup down the long dirt driveway into Liam's farm and parked next to a blue Audi in front of the main barn. Lucia had mentioned a buyer was coming to check out the horse today, which, if it resulted in a sale, would mean she'd have enough money coming her way to start over again. As he put the truck in park and turned off the engine, he could only hope that her new start would include him.

Stepping out of the truck and shutting the door, he paused to plunge his hand into his pocket. He thumbed the rounded edges of the object one more time before setting off for the side of the main barn. If the buyer and Liam were talking over the sale, he didn't want to interrupt. He would patiently wait until he could be alone with Lucia.

As he rounded the corner of the building, he spotted the grulla mare standing half-asleep at the tie post. Listening closely, he heard a man's voice from inside the barn. He hoped that Lucia would receive everything she hoped for today.

Sam took a deep breath, grabbed the handle of the side door, and swung it open.

Chapter 46

Lucia wanted to shake her head, unwilling to believe what she was seeing, but she was frozen in place. Liam was there with what she had hoped were buyers, but as soon as she recognized Phil, all her hope was swiftly extinguished. She didn't recognize the other man with him, but she didn't need to. Her stomach clenched, and her throat tightened. She had stopped only steps away from the door, but her eyes darted frantically around the barn to assess her situation and search for an escape route.

"I'm sorry, Lucia." Liam's voice was weak and tired, and his words confirmed her worst fears. Tears glinted in his bloodshot eyes.

"Nothing to be sorry for, old man." Phil grinned. The sight of the paradoxically happy expression on the killer's face made Lucia's skin prickle. "I just need to clear some things up with her." There was a razor-sharp edge to his deep voice. "Can we talk for a minute, Lucia?"

Her tongue stuck to the roof of her dry mouth, and she couldn't find the words to respond. Every muscle screamed at her to run. A sick feeling twisted her stomach as the adrenaline began pulsing through her veins. She was mindful of the saddlebags she carried on her shoulder. They held not only another package with possibly more damning evidence but also the Sig Sauer she had finally agreed to carry. Grateful as she was that Sam had insisted she carry her gun for safety, she could only hope now that she would live to thank him.

"I think you know why we need to talk. Didn't I tell you to keep your sweet little mouth shut? Now it's time to pay the piper," he growled as though he struggled to control his temper. He stepped forward, and Lucia tensed briefly before plunging her right hand into one pocket of the saddlebags. In a flash, she pulled out the Sig, switching off the safety before it cleared the pocket.

"Back the hell up," Lucia snapped as she raised the barrel of the Sig and pointed it at Phil's face. He was less than fifteen feet away, and she knew if she wasn't ready to squeeze the trigger, he could quickly close the gap and disarm her. If that happened, it would all be over.

Phil put up his hands and took a few slow steps backward. He frowned at first, but then a thin smile parted his lips. There was a darkness in his icy blue eyes that sent chills down Lucia's spine. She could feel the sickening peril of the moment permeating the air of the barn. Her trembling arms held the Sig up, still pointing directly at Phil's sharp-angled nose.

"Lucia." He tipped his head slightly and broadened his grin to a smile as Liam and the other man backed up behind him. "Nobody wants to hurt you. I just want whatever you have left. I want to make sure that what you think you know isn't what you tell the cops. Like any other man out there, I have a business to run. I'm trying to protect my livelihood. You know, I have a family to provide for, too." His voice was calm and reassuring, but the sentiment didn't reach his eyes. Lucia's stomach clenched painfully as cortisol and adrenaline mixed in her system.

"If you just wanted to talk, why did you threaten me at the funeral?" Lucia asked. She could barely hear her own voice over the sound of her blood pounding in her ears. "Why did you send those assholes in the Jeep after me? Why in the hell did you lure us into an ambush at the Tavern? Where the hell is Jordan, and why did you send Cassie to try to kill me?"

Phil's hands turned upward and chuckled as if there wasn't a loaded weapon pointed at him. "Really?" He shook his head. "Black Jeep? An ambush? I don't know anything about all that. And I know Cassie, but I didn't know she was back in town. You need to calm down and be rational."

Lucia hesitated, questioning her instincts.

If I'm wrong... The thought conjured up images in her mind of being arrested, embarrassing Sam, and being sent to Oak Rest, an in-patient mental health facility. She quickly shook it off and got her head back in the game. Her instincts weren't wrong on this.

"Nope. We are not doing this," Lucia said, shifting her weight to her left foot and sliding her right back toward the door. Phil sighed before drawing his own pistol from a side holster that his loose shirt had covered.

"I don't have to kill you," he said, his gun hand hanging at his side. "But I will if you don't give up that gun now and take a ride with me. If you don't start behaving, I swear I'll paint this barn's walls with your gray matter. Liam will take the fall for it and spend the few remaining years of his miserable old life in prison." He shrugged. "I'll also make Natalie's life a living hell until she draws her very last breath."

"Natalie?" Lucia asked in a whisper, afraid she would cry out if she tried to speak any louder. "No. Natalie's in Marquette."

Phil shook his head and laughed. "Natalie is my special 'guest.' I'll send her back to her dad when you agree to come with me."

Lucia broke her gaze from Phil to look at Liam as the truth struck her. He'd been working with Phil to get Lucia alone so he could save his daughter, the only living child he had left now.

"Do you know what we do with beautiful girls like her?" Phil said.

Lucia felt the bile rise in her throat as she returned her attention to Phil. The pictures from the thumb drive forced themselves to the front of her mind. She didn't respond, blinking back the stinging in her eyes.

"Where is she?"

"Natalie?"

"Yes, Natalie, you asshole!"

"Calm down," he growled through clenched teeth. His gun hand shook slightly. "There's no need for that kind of language. Keep acting like gutter trash, and I'll strangle you with your own intestines. I dare you to keep testing my patience!"

Lucia felt a single, hot tear slide down her cheek as she considered the situation. Liam was staring at the ground, his hands in his pockets. He couldn't and wouldn't help her. The other man, apparently one of Phil's thugs, slid a pistol from his waistband and held it to his side. With one word from Phil, she knew he wouldn't hesitate to draw down on her and fire.

She was cornered. Every bone in her body ached with the urge to run, but she could only imagine her own death. They would probably dump her lifeless body in the river like they had done to so many others. Like the man she'd found beneath the riverbank.

"What do you need from me to let me go?"

Phil shrugged. "What do you have?"

"Another package." She let the muzzle of her pistol fall a little, her muscles burning from the strain of pointing it at him for so long.

Phil's smirk vanished, and his blue eyes grew dark. "Where?"

"First, tell me what it's worth?"

"I don't know what's in it."

"Listen, I could give it to you and walk away from all this, or I can take my chances and try to flee, but I will shoot at least two of you." She forced a smile of her own. "I will take it straight to the cops. Oh, and there's more they'll get if I don't make it back."

"All right," Phil replied, his voice low as he raised his weapon toward her. "You've wasted enough of my time."

Lucia sucked in a breath and began to squeeze the trigger, but light and movement from behind startled her. She tried to glance left over her shoulder while dodging right. She pulled the trigger as she lost her balance and fell hard onto her side. At the same time, the sound of another gun firing thundered through the barn.

She didn't see who her bullet had struck, but she heard a man howl in pain from Phil's direction and fall with a thud to the dirt floor. Lucia rolled sideways into an empty stall nearby and sprung up into a crouch. She fired blindly around the corner once as a harassment shot. Then she glanced toward the door to see who had fallen behind her when the shots were fired.

The sight stilled her heart.

Chapter 47

Lucia's blood ran cold as she realized the person who'd opened the door behind her was Sam. He was now lying curled up on his side in the dirt. She wanted to see his face, but he'd fallen looking away from her.

"Lucia," Phil's voice cut through the ringing in her ears from the gunshots. "Who do we have here? Isn't this your new man?"

She fumbled in her pocket for her phone, struggling to swipe the screen one-handed.

"You wanna get him to a hospital? Or should we put him out of his misery like any other broken animal?"

"Shut the hell up!" she screamed. "I'll blow your fuckin' head off if you hurt him!"

"If you don't come out now, I'm going to finish him off," he said in an eerie cooing voice. The sick bastard loved every second of this.

Holding her phone in her left hand and the Sig in her right, Lucia raised the barrel over the stall door and positioned it between the bars before firing another shot in Phil's general direction. "If you kill him, I'll send all my online drives to the lead detective. It's ready to send right now, and I will fucking send it!"

"Listen, bitch," Phil said, the confidence and nonchalance gone from his voice. Her skin crawled as she dialed 911 and dropped it face-up on the dirt floor of the stall. "You give up that gun and come without any more fight, and we'll save your man."

"You shot him!" she shrieked, praying the operator had picked up already, and the call was being recorded.

"Yes," Phil responded, raising his voice, his anger vibrating through the space now. "And he's going to die soon if you don't cooperate. Throw your phone and your gun to me, now!"

"Fuck, fuck, FUCK!" Lucia hissed to herself, anxious to keep her fear and her bluff about online drives to herself.

She was trapped, and time was running out. It hadn't been long since Sam had been shot, but he wasn't screaming in pain like he should have been. He hadn't made a single noise she could hear since he fell. The man she managed to shoot, Phil's thug, was still moaning in pain. She couldn't hear Liam, and that terrified her. She was torn, hoping he hadn't been hurt and feeling betrayed that he'd been helping Phil.

Lucia peeked around the door at Sam. He was still on his side, and he wasn't moving. There was so much blood. She glanced at her phone and saw the emergency call was active. How long would it take them to arrive? The sound of shuffling steps interrupted her thoughts, and she fired another shot over the stall door again.

"Don't move!" she yelled before shouting toward the phone, "11395 South River Road."

"You stupid bitch! I'm going to skin you alive!"

Two shots resounded through the barn, and bullets ricocheted above Lucia's head as they hit the aluminum bars of the stall door.

She remained crouched, unsure of how she could fire back without exposing herself. He would be familiar now with her spray-and-pray method, though she had done it sparsely to conserve the ammo in her ten-round magazine. She had paused to count her spent ammo when she was struck by a white-hot pain that flared through her head.

Her vision went white as she crumpled to the dirt floor. She breathed the stale dirt into her mouth and nose, and it caused her to cough. When she tried to push herself up, something hard slammed against her ribs, and she rolled onto her side from the force. Her eyes adjusted just in time to watch a black boot smash into her abdomen. The sharp edges of the heel cut into her skin, and she cried out in pain, her hands flying to cover her stomach as the boot pulled away.

When Lucia opened her eyes again, she saw the boot swinging toward her face. Another white-hot flare of disorienting pain blinded her as the heel of the black western-style boot dug into her cheek.

"Look at me, bitch," he screamed as he straddled her, dropping onto her chest. "I was going to add you to my private collection, but no, you have to be the stuck-up little bitch you've always been. If you hadn't cost me so much already, I'd be nicer, but no! I'm going to torture the fuck out of you and then let every truck driver running I-90 have a turn at you. If you survive, your last miserable days will be spent learning how to be an obedient whore."

"I'm gonna kill you," Lucia wheezed, barely able to catch her breath. "You're evil, you sick son of a bitch!" She tried to spit at his face, but it landed on his shirt.

Phil laughed softly before hauling one hand back and slapping her across the face. Lucia screamed. He grabbed her hands, pinning them over her head with one hand, and grasped at her chest with the other. Lucia cried out again as he raked his fingers over her shirt.

"Evil? I'm worse than evil, you dumb bitch." He ran his hand up the side of her body and leaned down to bite her neck, causing her to scream again. "If there was a devil, he'd be scared of me." Phil ripped open her shirt before pulling down her bra and scratching his fingernails over her right breast.

"I would drink from the cup of his terror," he said, emphasizing the last word as he wrapped the fingers of his free hand around her neck. "I would desecrate the darkness of hell. Satan himself would kneel before me and beg for mercy."

He released her hands and loosened his fingers from her neck as her vision started to go dark. He slammed his fist into her right cheek, sending a wave of pain rattling through her head. She felt her limbs flail for a second before she regained control and struck at his face, missing. She clawed his arms but couldn't reach his neck.

Phil laughed as she struggled beneath him, her vision and strength returning as the oxygen flowed to her brain again. "You're going to kneel before me. I'm going to make you my good little bitch before I rent you for fifty cents an hour to every dirty schmuck who wants a piece."

Lucia felt the slam of his fist against her head again, and her world went white. Unable to see and dizzy from the hits, she now fought simply to maintain consciousness.

"Like your little college friend. Such a sweet thing. Oh, and since you didn't want to come with me like a good girl, I'm keeping Natalie. She'll take your spot in my private collection. It's time to go now so we can start your training."

Her vision started to clear, and she continued to scratch at his arms. The darkness in his eyes frightened her. She struggled in vain as he grabbed a handful of her hair and yanked on it.

"Let's go start your new life," he said as he started to rise, dragging her by the hair and causing her to cry out in pain. A click broke through the fuzz in Lucia's brain, and Phil froze.

Chapter 48

A gunshot thundered through the barn. Lucia screamed as hot blood sprayed her face. Phil grunted, his grip on her hair tightening before releasing. He fell to his knees before dropping to his side. She scrambled away until she'd pressed her back against the far side of the stall.

As Lucia struggled for breath, she realized she couldn't see anything until she wiped the blood from her eyes. When her vision cleared, she found Liam standing in the stall's doorway, the pistol in his shaking hand still pointed at Phil.

"You have to save my little girl, Lucia," he sobbed as he locked eyes with her, tears streaming down his cheeks. He lifted the pistol to his head.

"Liam!" Lucia croaked, her throat sore from being choked by Phil. She scrambled to her feet and rushed him. "No!"

She tackled him at the waist, and when the pistol fired, the shot missed his head. Splinters showered them as the bullet lodged in the rafters above. Lucia wrestled the gun from his hand and flicked the safety on before sitting him up and pushing him against the wall.

"Stay," she commanded, her voice hoarse. His glistening eyes were hollow and cold as he stared at some distant point behind her.

She took the gun with her as she crawled to Sam's side.

"Sam?" she whispered, gently stroking his cheek as she fought the lump in her throat.

His eyes fluttered open, and he looked up at her, but she could see their light was fading fast. "Lucia," he wheezed, then paused, his words broken by a sputtering cough. "I came for you. I'm here, Luce."

"I know, babe. Thank you." Tears rolled freely down her dust-covered cheeks. "I'm here for you, too. Please hold on."

He opened his mouth to speak, but no words came.

"Don't talk, sweetie," she sobbed as she stroked his cheek. "You've gotta hold on for just a few more minutes." She grabbed one of his hands and interlaced her fingers with his before squeezing gently. He didn't squeeze back.

"I got it... for you," he said before something changed in his eyes. He looked through her now.

"What? No!" she cried. "They're going to be here soon, I promise." She scrambled to the stall to grab her phone. Phil, crumpled in the dirt, blew shuddering breaths through the dirt on the stall floor.

Lucia pressed the phone to her ear and ran back to Sam, grabbing his hand again. "Hello?"

"I came for you," he repeated in a whisper, his eyes still focused on something beyond her.

"Ma'am," a voice answered on the other end of the line. "Officers are on the way. They should be there—"

Shouts cut off the dispatcher's voice as officers kicked open the front and side doors. The barn was quickly flooded with uniformed officers.

"Please help him," Lucia cried out to the nearest officer, her vision too blurred by tears to recognize faces she may have otherwise recognized. The phone slipped from her fingers as she let them pull her away from Sam. She watched, terrified, as two officers bent over Sam and pressed something against his chest wound.

The other officers swarmed the barn, searching every crevice and shouting when they found Liam sitting near Phil's motionless body. Paramedics came next and took over the efforts to save Sam. They lifted him onto a stretcher before fitting him with an oxygen mask and rolling him out the door.

The world went numb as she stared at the blood-soaked dirt where he'd been laying only moments earlier. Her muscles throbbed, and her vision blurred as she sat motionless in the dirt, frozen with shock. Although she was sure she had a concussion and other injuries, she just didn't care anymore.

A sharp, burning ache radiated through her chest with every breath she took. Gritting her teeth against the pain, she focused her attention on an officer who knelt to speak to her, but she couldn't make any sense of his words.

The horror that filled Lucia in that moment was all-encompassing, and she could no longer hold back the sorrow that overcame her now. There was no more pretending she was better off alone or that she could stand to be without Sam. He was the best man to ever love her, showing her the utmost kindness and patience, and yet she had held him at a distance. Without merit, she'd refused to fully trust him with her heart and her life.

Despair engulfed her as paramedics settled her onto a stretcher and rolled her out of the barn. She'd watched the light fade from Sam's eyes, and she didn't know if she would see him again in this life. That thought crushed her, destroying her will to fight on.

Overwhelmed by the pain and her all-consuming guilt over Sam, Lucia succumbed to the oblivion of unconsciousness as the paramedics loaded her into the ambulance.

Chapter 49

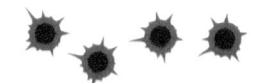

Thursday, September 6th

Visions of the slate-white interior of a hospital and a host of people dressed in medical scrubs filled Lucia's waking and sleeping moments. The line between consciousness and unconsciousness blurred. In between, she wondered if she was really alive or if she'd died in the barn and was now forsaken to wander through a bizarre purgatory.

It wasn't until her eyes opened to find Dan sitting in a chair beside her bed that she believed she might yet remain in the world of the living. He was leaning back in a chair and scrolling through something on his phone. When she groaned, unable to speak, his head jerked up, and he looked at her.

She tried to say Sam's name, but her throat was parched and her lips cracked painfully.

"Thirsty?" he asked.

She closed her eyes and nodded.

Grabbing a styrofoam cup from a small table beside her bed, he brought the straw to her lips so she could drink. The ice-cold water shocked her hot, cottony mouth, but she took a long drink despite the headache it caused.

"Hold on." Dan stood up and walked to the doorway. He asked someone Lucia couldn't see to tell a nurse that she was awake now. As he returned to her bedside, her memories slowly crept to the front of her mind.

"How are you feeling?" he asked as he sat down again.

"I guess I'm alive," she croaked. It was the barest of observations. As she studied the white blanket that covered her body, she was surprised by the hot tears that fell onto it.

Had it really happened, or was it all just a terrible nightmare?

Dan nodded. "The doctors say you'll be alright. You have a nasty concussion, some lacerations on your face, and a few broken ribs. Oh, and you took a bullet to the sternum."

Her fingers absently touched at her sternum, and she cringed at the tenderness. As shocked as she was to hear she'd been shot, there was only one thing she cared about.

"Sam?" she barely choked out his name, trembling as she waited for Dan's answer.

Dan shook his head. "I need a few more details first. Do you remember what happened? I need you to tell me everything, starting from why you were at the farm that morning."

Her head hurt as she tried to recall the morning in a linear manner. "Liam..." she started, but the lump in her throat kept the words trapped in her head, her compartmentalized trauma finally releasing in a wave. "Please..." Lucia met Dan's eyes. "Where's Sam?"

Dan shook his head again and pulled a scrap of paper from a pocket in his jacket. "A doctor should be in here soon to explain your injuries and everything you've gone through medically."

"How long has it been?" she whispered through her tears, no longer bothering to wipe them away.

"Two days ago."

"Two days?" She lifted a quivering hand to her mouth. How had days passed before she could regain full consciousness?

"As soon as the doctor clears you for it, we'll need to get your witness statement. I need to interview you about everything that happened."

"No!" Lucia objected, watching as he stood and walked toward the door. "Where is he?"

Dan stopped in his tracks and turned his hard eyes on her. "Everything that happened to him is because of you!" Dan snapped. Another officer poked his head through the door.

"You good, Guzman?"

"No," Dan glared at Lucia before storming out of the room.

His words jabbed at her heart. A renewed flood of tears streamed from her eyes, stinging as they saturated the cuts on her face.

She needed the pain now. She needed the punishment to drown her grief. The shadows of her guilt threatened to devour her soul.

A doctor arrived almost an hour later to explain her condition and fill in the gaps regarding her injuries. When Liam had shot Phil from behind, he'd been so close that the bullet had passed through Phil's chest and embedded in her sternum. Thankfully, the velocity and force of the bullet had been slowed significantly by its passage through Phil, but doctors still needed to extract fragments of it and Phil's flesh and bone from her chest.

She learned they'd keep on moderate pain killers until her body had more time to heal. She wanted to ask if she could refuse the meds but worried she'd be transferred to the psychiatric department. Although she was tempted to escape the emotional agony through physical pain or stronger doses, her desire to fully indulge her guilt over Sam kept her from pursuing either route.

Lucia believed she deserved to feel every ounce of suffering that she endured.

Between the recovery from the procedures to remove the bone and bullet fragments, suturing the lacerations on her head and face from Phil's attack, and monitoring her severe concussion, the doctor recommended that she stay in the hospital for at least three more days. Besides, she wouldn't be able to take care of herself with broken ribs.

Lucia didn't fight his recommendation as she would have before. She was finished fighting. No matter how much she asked about Sam, no one would tell her anything. Between Dan's silence and HIPAA, she couldn't learn anything.

Will I at least get to say goodbye? she wondered, feeling hopeless as a fresh wave of grief washed through her. All she could imagine was how she had watched Rich's casket lowered into the earth. Would she get to be there for Sam?

When Lucia could cry no more, she limped to the window and drew back the curtain. There was a sunny blue sky smiling through the clean glass.

She hated it.

She wanted rain and storms, the kind of weather that reflected the torment she felt inside. But life was already moving on around her as if nothing had happened.

Lucia felt so minuscule. Like a turtle crawling along a busy highway, taking hours to reach her destination while cars flew by in seconds, oblivious to her toil.

Wrapped in a suffocating blanket of grief, she spent the rest of the afternoon thinking about Sam, remembering his face and how it felt to touch him and to be touched by him. She hoped that if she burned it into her memory now, he would stay with her until the day she died.

It was now, in the desolate depths of her sorrow, that Lucia mourned the loss of the closeness she'd shared with him. Why had she always been running? Why couldn't she have slowed down and enjoyed life with her best friend and lover?

There were too many questions that she couldn't answer. It would take a lot of money and a damn good therapist to unravel the mess that brewed in her head now.

She couldn't even say his name without breaking down.

Lucia sometimes wondered why he'd showed up at the barn at all, but he had told her before the officers and paramedics took him away.

He had come for *her*.

Sam was the type to take quiet action to support her. She was sure he'd come to the barn to celebrate with her if Tess had found a new home.

Lucia would give anything to go back in time to that morning. She'd tell Liam she couldn't help that day and just stay home, watching movies and cuddling on the couch with Sam. Or she'd tell him that he didn't have to worry; she'd move in with him.

And she would have told him how much she loved him.

There was no time-travel scenario left unimagined in her mind when Dan reappeared. Lucia looked up briefly to acknowledge his presence, saying nothing. She let her tired eyes drift back to the window and the beautiful day she couldn't enjoy. A nurse came in and began unhooking her from the IV and monitors.

Chapter 50

"You need to walk around," the nurse said encouragingly. "The detective is going to help you."

Sure he is. Lucia could see the woman's kind smile from the corner of her eye, but she refused to look directly at her. She let the woman help her out of bed, then leaned against it until Dan took her gingerly by the elbow.

There was life in the corridors, though it was mostly quiet in this part of the hospital. People walked silently past them in both directions as Lucia limped forward, taking tiny steps that sent pain arcing through her ribs and chest. She'd never been to the hospital in Alma, having been lucky all these years to stay in fairly good health. She'd avoided it even in times of need since she never had the money to afford medical bills.

Soon she would be sent home, but she didn't have anywhere to go home to. While she was sure her landlord would give her a few more days to get her stuff out, she'd still need to leave, and she couldn't go back to Sam's. Another thought occurred to her, and she froze mid-step before staring at Dan, wide-eyed.

"Penny?" she asked, hope and fear intermingling in her chest.

"She's been staying with me. She's actually pretty sweet."

"Thank you," she whispered, then started walking again. She was sincerely grateful that the poor dog hadn't been left alone for days on end.

Her pride long gone, Lucia resigned herself to calling her parents for help. She couldn't move her stuff out of the rental house on her own, or get her things from Sam's house without a complete mental breakdown.

No matter how she'd tried to avoid it, she would need support to get back on her feet.

Besides, it was well past time that she apologized to her parents for being so stubborn and absent from their lives, despite the sorrow-filled pleas that filled the carefully written messages inside holiday and birthday cards.

Lucia thought of her brother and wondered what he would say. What would he think? He would never blame her, of course. He would call her foolish for wallowing in guilt, and she wouldn't expect anything less from him.

Everything that had happened to Sam was because of her, even if someone else had pulled the trigger. He never should have been there, and he wouldn't have been in the wrong place at the wrong time if it weren't for her.

"Lucia? Lucia!" Dan snapped his fingers in front of her face, and she realized he'd been speaking.

"Sorry." She stopped, leaned against a wall, and stared up at the ceiling. Although the doctors had warned her that difficulty concentrating was a side effect of her severe concussion, she also knew it was partly a result of being so deeply mired in her thoughts.

"Did you know he was coming?" His voice was gentler this time. She also thought she heard a hint of compassion. Not that she believed she deserved it.

"Sam?"

He nodded, and Lucia shook her head, fighting the stinging in her eyes.

"I'm sorry about earlier," he said, resting a hand on her shoulder. "I just... You know he's my best friend. We've been through hell together. All of us at the post like you, but sometimes we wondered how he got involved with a dealer's ex-girl."

Lucia clenched her jaw as the heat rose to her cheeks, undeniably offended that they'd characterized her in such a way. She started walking again, holding onto the wall as she took tentative steps, and holding her tongue against the words that could burn bridges. It didn't matter what anyone said or thought anymore. It wouldn't bring him back, and their fears about her had been proven right. She really had been bad for him.

"I mean, we realized you weren't into all that once we got to know you. But it was strange, you know? A good girl like you with someone like your ex. We can't get caught up with people like that." Dan paused and took her by the elbow to steady her before continuing. "Now we know you aren't like those people." He shrugged. "You just fell for the wrong guy back then."

Lucia couldn't resist nodding in agreement. She never realized how much it would screw up her life to fall for Rich. It seemed like she'd be paying for that mistake for the rest of her life.

Dan fell silent as he stopped once more and held her arm, gesturing for her to stop too. It was a long corridor, and Lucia hoped he might take her to the cafeteria for coffee. She couldn't remember the last time she'd had any. Although she wouldn't be able to eat much and didn't want to be around people, coffee was worth the discomfort. The rest of the world barely existed to her anyway. Every time she thought of Sam, her chest tightened, and she felt as if her insides were being ripped out.

A stinging sensation on her left cheek warned that she was crying again. Lucia sniffled and used the palms of her hands to wipe away her tears.

Dan passed her a handful of tissues.

"It's gonna be alright, Lucia."

A half-laugh, half-sob erupted from her throat. It was an alien sound, edged with cynicism and lost faith. She covered her eyes with the tissues and cried into them, leaning against the wall for support as her weak body trembled.

She heard the metallic click of a door latch and opened her eyes. Tired and miserable, she now hoped their long walk had circled them back to her room. Lucia could forego the coffee if she could simply be alone again. The sameness of all the corridors blended together, and she'd been too lost in her thoughts to keep track of where they'd walked.

"Hey." Dan's voice was low as he pulled her into the room.

She pulled the tissues away from her face and rubbed her eyes with her palms. As her vision cleared, she realized they were in a different patient room. An occupied patient room. There was someone in the bed.

Lucia blinked rapidly, then her breath caught in her throat. She launched herself forward on her weak legs, stumbling like a newborn fawn. She caught herself on the edge of the bed and dragged herself up with her arms before pausing in front of him.

Slowly, she reached a hand forward and touched his face, her fingertips trembling. Sam opened his eyes and smiled, catching her hand in his own and kissing her palm. Tears streamed down her cheeks, but this time, she didn't mind the way they stung her cuts.

"You know," he said through a cough, his voice raspy. "Because I love you, I've gotten multiple concussions, been involved in a car chase and a shootout, and now I've been shot."

Lucia didn't fight the sobs that broke from her throat. Her relief that he was alive mingled with the fierce guilt that stabbed at her despite his humor.

"But none of that matters," he said, his bloodshot eyes glistening. "I've always been yours, Lucia, and I always will be. Just no more shootouts. Deal?"

Lucia laughed, nodding through her tears. "Deal."

"I was going to," he paused to cough again, "bring you something." His eyes darted to the table beside his bed. Lucia followed his gaze. When she saw it, her heart skipped a beat.

Sitting on the bedside table, sealed inside a ziplock bag and covered in dried blood and clumps of dirt from the barn, was a little blue velvet box.

"I'd open it for you, but..." He let his words trail off before breaking into a coughing fit.

Lucia gingerly picked up the box, hands trembling, and clumsily fought to open the blood-splashed blue velvet lid. It revealed what she had guessed was inside. The gold band was topped with a glittering princess-cut diamond flanked by two smaller diamonds sparkling in the bright light.

"So?" He laughed nervously. She heard the hint of uncertainty in his voice.

Lucia held it to her chest, then pressed her face into his neck and hugged him.

"Ow!" he cried out, and she pulled back only a little as she cried into his cheek.

"Yes," she said, joy present in her voice once more. Happy tears made new trails down her face before falling onto his.

Epilogue

In a few days, Lucia's parents arrived to move her things into Sam's house. She learned that Dan hadn't told her Sam was alive because he had to wait until Sam gave his statement to be sure Lucia hadn't been the one to shoot or purposely endanger him. After everything that had happened, he had his doubts about her level of involvement. He only relented when Sam regained consciousness and could give his statement, reassuring Dan that Lucia hadn't shot him.

Liam confessed to his involvement, admitting to tipping off Phil to Lucia's presence because he was trying to get his daughter back safely. For his suicide attempt and having aided in an attempted murder, Liam would be held in custody and kept on suicide watch for his own protection–at least until his court date. Some big-time lawyer was apparently on his way to confer with Liam and work as his defense counsel.

Phil's family and their money showed up quickly, as evidenced by the retinue of lawyers that swarmed the hospital. He had survived the shooting. Although he'd been formally arrested, he remained in the ICU. The damage to his back, lungs, and chest from the gunshot wound had nearly killed him. Unfortunately for him, the final package Lucia retrieved contained clear video and photographic evidence of his involvement and orchestration in organized criminal activities across the state. Dan had warned her to avoid his family and their lawyers at all costs.

She also learned that the young woman who'd shown up barefoot and injured at the Pine River state police post had escaped from being held captive by the men in the black Jeep. After she was medically cleared, she led the police back to the farm, the same place Sam had suggested they search after the chase from the campground, but it was empty. She learned the girl's name was Shelby, and she was inconsolable when they told her the farm was empty, swearing that the other girls had been held there with her.

Once Lucia and Sam were discharged and allowed to go home, Dan and a few other officers from the post helped Lucia's parents organize a barbecue "recovery party." Thankfully, everyone else was happy to do all the cooking and setup since Lucia and Sam were still recovering.

Lucia's father, William, took a liking to Sam immediately, and she knew her dad was more pleased than he'd admit that she was dating a LEO. Her mother, Mayra, loved Sam right away too, promising to make him any number of delicious traditional Puerto Rican dishes before chiding Lucia for not having made them all for him already.

Sam and Lucia decided to keep their engagement quiet until they could have a proper party and make plans for the wedding. There was a lot to coordinate and organize, but this time Lucia wouldn't be running away from commitment, even if it seemed overwhelming right now.

Although she secretly couldn't wait to say "I do,' there were other things that still weighed heavily on her heart and mind.

After badgering him relentlessly during the barbecue, Dan finally took Lucia aside. They walked Penny together, moving as slowly as Lucia needed until they reached the edge of the woods behind Sam's house. It was far enough away from the party that the others wouldn't be able to hear them.

"You didn't hear this from me, okay?" Dan glanced suspiciously back at the house. "Read the news or something before you say anything to anyone."

"Agreed." Lucia nodded.

"Natalie and Jordan are both officially missing."

Her chest tightened, and a bolt of pain raced through her chest. "Missing?"

"Phones and wallets are in their residences. The last known location for Natalie was her dorm room in Marquette. Jordan was last seen at her dad's house in Muskegon."

Her heart raced. "What's being done to find them?"

"State and county police are doing everything they can," he said.

It sounded like something that was probably said to every missing person's family and friends. The words were hollow, meaningless.

"What can I do, Dan?"

"You aren't supposed to be doing anything but healing. People who do this for a living are handling it."

"I don't want them to disappear," she mumbled, feeling helpless once again. "I don't want them to be forgotten."

"They won't be forgotten. If you hear anything or have any information that can help, just tell me, and I'll get it to the right people. The search for them is being handled way above my paygrade."

Lucia nodded, and they turned together to walk back to the house. She breathed deeply, but calm wouldn't come. She couldn't be helpless this time.

Not again.

She kept her thoughts to herself for Dan's sake but swore she wouldn't rest until they'd been found.

When they returned to the party, a new face was waiting for Lucia at a picnic table. Deep brown eyes greeted her from a thin face framed by shoulder-length black hair. Her tawny brown skin was smooth, but deep worry lines were already forming between her eyebrows.

"Lucia, this is Shelby," Dan introduced them. "Shelby, Lucia."

The woman stood. "Good to meet you," she said, failing to hide her nervousness.

"And you."

"Can we talk?"

Lucia glanced at Dan, and he nodded before walking over to Mayra and Sam hovering near the *pastelillos*. Shelby rose and walked away from the group with Lucia.

"I heard your friends are missing," she said, keeping her voice low.

Lucia nodded, clenching her teeth. It was a painful reality to accept.

"So are mine. I need your help."

Lucia had already spent far too much time sitting back and doing nothing while the world spun out of control around her, and she wouldn't do it anymore. Natalie and Jordan needed her, and so did Shelby's friends. If they didn't do something, those women would simply be a few more names and faces added to the list of 3,888 missing persons in Michigan.

No wedding, no parties, no vacations.

No break until she found them.

She would not let them be forgotten.

Author's Note

There are many reasons for writers to want to publish a book, fiction or nonfiction, in any genre and about any topic. I am personally an eclectic reader. I love just about every genre out there. Compelling stories are what draw me and keep me coming back to my favorite authors. I hope that you found DESECRATE THE DARKNESS to be that kind of compelling story.

My goal for this book and this series is not only to tell Lucia and Sam's story, but also to raise awareness to the issues of human trafficking and missing persons. While human trafficking is an issue all over the world, I find it especially surreal that it is happening right here in our communities, in big cities and small towns all over the United States.

It is tragic everywhere and it needs to be extinguished everywhere. There isn't any form of modern slavery that is okay, and the deliberate trafficking of human beings in its many shapes and forms is a despicable evil that must be actively fought wherever it is found.

So, what is the difference between trafficking in the U.S. and elsewhere in the world? In the U.S., the U.K., and much of Western Europe, we don't have rampaging warlords or entire police forces that are actually under the direct control of criminal elements. Even though the U.S. boasts among the highest standards of living in the world, we still have this barbaric and despicable evil creeping just beneath the surface of our quiet communities, often hidden in the picturesque suburbs and ignored in economically depressed areas.

Without action from citizens to call out and alert the police to suspicious activity and to socially stigmatize sexual deviance (sex with children, rape, incest, violence, etc.), this evil will continue to fester and grow.

Every time we turn our heads to evil, it becomes more powerful.

Every day we pretend it doesn't happen in our communities is another day we encourage it.

Every moment that we believe it could never happen to our family is another moment that someone's daughter, son, sister, brother, or wife continues to suffer in the hands of evil.

Don't turn your head.

Don't pretend it doesn't happen.

Don't believe that it can't happen to you and your family.

Speak out against evil and speak up for the missing, those whose voices have been stolen and silenced.

What can you do?

- Share posts on social media about missing persons in your area. When you do, you increase the chances that someone will see and help identify that person.

- Use Google to search "human trafficking awareness events" and Google will deliver information about events happening in your area from multiple organizations (there are many different organizations dedicated to raising awareness about human trafficking)

- Learn what sex trafficking looks like in the US (and often other developed countries): https://ourrescue.org/blog/trafficking-looks-like-america

- Read about why victims are often trapped or can't speak up for themselves: http://ourrescue.org/blog/dont-victims-trafficking -just-run-away

- Review the signs of trafficking and the places where you might encounter someone who is being trafficked: http://ourrescue.o rg/blog/3-places-might-see-trafficking/

- Read trafficking survivor stories so you have a fuller understanding of what victims endure and what other signs are presented in these situations: http://ourrescue.org/blog/category/aftercare/

- Donate to organizations that fight human trafficking in your community and around the world. Here are some of my favorites:

  - Operation Underground Railroad: http://ourrescue.org/

  - The Polaris Project: https://polarisproject.org/

  - Unseen: https://www.unseenuk.org/

  - A21: https://www.a21.org/

  - Stop the Traffik: https://www.stopthetraffik.org/

  - Shared Hope International: https://sharedhope.org/

  - There are many more!

- Raise awareness. Share survivor stories and information about the signs of human trafficking on your social media or host a local awareness event with an organization near you.

Here's the Michigan State Police report I used for the number of missing persons presented at the end of the epilogue: https://www.michigan.gov /documents/msp/MisingPersonsCountsInMichigan_494225_7.pdf

Thank you so much for reading Desecrate the Darkness, and thank you in advance for being part of the solution.

Wishing you strength and bravery,

A.K. Hughey

Acknowledgments

I would like to thank the members of the Author Transformation Alliance for actively providing feedback and support; R.K. Fultz and Nan Sampson for being amazing beta and advance readers; P.A. Duncan and Nan Sampson for providing editing support; Mary Knapp for being my emotional and professional support throughout my writing journey and providing an excellent example of what it means to be a published author; K. McCoy for being my accountability partner and encouraging me and keeping me motivated throughout the writing process; my husband for encouraging me to focus on my writing; and my parents, for inspiring me and instilling within me the belief that I could do anything.

I must also express my gratitude for my incredible cover designer, Kristen Lee Design. Visit her at Kristen Lee Designs on Facebook and Instagram.

Read More

In chronological order:

- Desecrate the Darkness - Book 1

- Walking in Darkness - Standalone short story available on Amazon.

- Stand Against Darkness - Standalone short story.

  - Would you like to read it for FREE? Head to www.akhughey.com/freestand

- Hunting Darkness - Short story originally featured in the Make Them Pay thriller anthology.

  - Would you like to read it for FREE? Head to www.akhughey.com/freehunt

- Together Against Darkness - Short story featured in the March For Justice anthology.

- Falling Into Darkness - Book 2

- Rising From Darkness - Book 3

Would you like updates about upcoming releases, live events, giveaways, and reader parties?

- Join my Dark Angels Reader Bulletin at akhughey.com.

- Get access to Bonus Content like flash fiction, more short stories, books, audio, and more when you join me on Ream: https://re amstories.com/shadowsandscreams

About the Author

A.K. Hughey writes psychological thrillers and gritty vigilante stories from her home in the northern Shenandoah Valley, where the mountain-ringed landscape remembers more than it reveals. With a B.A. in English and an M.A. in Ancient and Classical History, her work reflects a sharp eye for patterns and a deep reverence for consequences. Her perspective is shaped by more than sixteen years in the military and defense, and by the years that followed, building stories, raising a family, and learning all the ways in which the silence can hold more than just secrets.

In her stories, the right to survive is earned, justice is a quest, and no one escapes unscathed. Her characters bleed, bend, and break as they battle the darkness. Sometimes, they are even forced to fight the ones they trusted the most.

A.K. HUGHEY

Connect with A.K. Hughey

Website: www.akhughey.com
Ream: https://reamstories.com/shadowsandscreams
Facebook: www.facebook.com/audreyiswriting
Instagram: www.instagram.com/audreyiswriting
Twitter: www.twitter.com/audreyiswriting
TikTok: www.tiktok.com/@audreyiswriting